SISTERGIRLS.COM

WILLIAM FREDRICK COOPER

EARL SEWELL

V. ANTHONY RIVERS

RIQUE JOHNSON

MICHAEL PRESLEY

SISTERGIRLS.COM

WILLIAM FREDRICK COOPER

EARL SEWELL

V. ANTHONY RIVERS

RIQUE JOHNSON

MICHAEL PRESLEY

A STREBOR BOOKS INTERNATIONAL LLC PUBLICATION
DISTRIBUTED BY SIMON & SCHUSTER, INC.

Published by

Strebor Books International LLC
P.O. Box 1370
Bowie, MD 20718
http://www.streborbooks.com

ISBN 0-7394-3944-8

Distributed by Simon & Schuster, Inc.
1230 Avenue of the Americas
New York, NY 10020
1-800-223-2336

Cover art: André Harris

Manufactured and Printed in the United States

Table of Contents

LEGAL DAYS, LONELY NIGHTS

WILLIAM FREDRICK COOPER

~

CHAPTER ONE

When Kyle entered the office of Stephen Cohen, principal partner of the firm Cohen, Schindler and Brody, he spied a gangly figure pacing the plush carpet, staring down on Manhattan through the window. Cohen was seated on an adjacent sofa, along with a bald man whose eyes sagged at the corners.

"I'm sure we can have this resolved by the time the season starts," he heard his boss finish.

Rising from his seat as he turned his attention to Kyle, Cohen gestured toward the pacing figure. One who needed no introduction. "Kyle, I want you to meet Stanton Curry of the Orlando Magic and his agent, Mark Rabinowitz." To the balding figure who remained seated, he said, "Kyle Watson is one of my brightest senior associates. I'm going to let him take the lead on this case."

Kyle received a dead fish handshake from Rabinowitz, who eyed him with skepticism. "No offense, Kyle, but…" The agent turned back to Cohen and continued. "Are you sure we…Do you think this is the best way to go?"

Cohen nodded and then responded, "I know what you're getting at. But Kyle's the best trial lawyer we have. Stan is your go-to-guy, Kyle is ours. Isn't that right, Watson?"

"I wouldn't be too concerned with appearances," Kyle retorted, eyeing Rabinowitz without a blink. "You might want to focus some of your concern on repelling the media attention this thing is receiving, unless you want Stan to get tried on the front page of every periodical in the city."Rabinowitz, slightly rattled by Kyle's confident tone, downplayed his own aggression. "Look," he stated, "I just want what's best for my client."

"*Our* client," Cohen corrected. "And Kyle is the best."

Kyle didn't let on that he and Stanton were former rivals on the court...Keeping his greeting strictly professional, he offered his hand and said, "How are you, Stanton? I've been following your progress since your career started."

Cueing on Kyle's lead, Stanton was cordial... "Nice to see you, man... Hope I haven't disappointed you."

With a sly smile, Kyle stated, "No way, man...You've been holding your own."

Rabinowitz squirmed in his seat. Kyle could sense his level of discomfort at their familiar tones and casual speech.

"Kyle, why don't you take Stanton to your office where he can give you all the particulars so we can get started on his defense as soon as possible," Cohen stated.

"Sure thing. Stanton, why don't you follow me." As they moved from Cohen's office into the brightly lit hallway, the sight and strides of two handsome African-American brothers dressed for business commanded everyone's attention. Each step from the statuesque duo seemed like a synchronized lesson in self-confidence to the Black clerks pushing mail carts; the message without words powerfully stating, "Go to school, get your degree and do something with your life." Secretaries in search of Black super men—those drop dead gorgeous hunks only found in *Ebony*— were peeking up from piles of work, whispering and batting eyelashes, seemingly under an alluring spell...

Before entering his office, Kyle introduced his well-known client to Trudy, his administrative assistant. His demeanor never wavered from corporate protocol as he requested a six-pack of Perrier with lemon from the employee lounge. Only after escorting Stanton into his office and closing his door did the veneer come down. And it did so with a process bred in the joy of knowing someone from around the way: a brotherly hug, a soulful handshake complete with a finger-popping finish and an inquiry, "Stan the man. What up, dawg?!"

"Man, nothin' but drama," Stanton announced, admiring Kyle's place of business. The old rivals spent a few moments getting caught up. Kyle knew Stan's story; Lincoln High, St. John's University, Orlando's first pick in the draft and seven first-team All-NBA selections in as many years. They discussed the whereabouts of a few mutual friends and acquaintances shared from their days as arch-rival basketball players in high school. Noticing the undergraduate and juris doctorate degrees from Georgetown University, the MVP plaques Kyle had accrued from intramural and lawyers' basketball leagues left Stanton shaking his head. "I see you still got game."

Kyle smiled. "Brooklyn point guards never lose their skills. You know that."

"You could've been breakin' ankles in the 'L', like I am."

"Different people take different roads in life, Stan. Though B-ball is still in my blood, I was born to be a trial attorney." They seated themselves in unison; Kyle behind his desk, Stan in his guest chair equipped with an ottoman. "Speaking of which, why didn't you play in the Rucker Tournament this year? Kobe Bryant came down, so did Stephon Marbury, Tracy McGrady and some of the old school players like Clyde Frazier and Tiny Archibald for a legends game. What's up with that?"

"Superstars improve their game in solitude. Got no time to showboat in the summer leagues. I want a ring next year."

Kyle nodded in agreement. "Tell me about it. I'm tryin' to be the first black partner here. With all the racist bullshit weakly disguised as politics,

I often work alone on my cases." Sensing the opportunity to segue to the matter at hand, he wasted no time in capitalizing. "What's going on with you, man?"

Lowering his head with the query and then raising it suddenly in defiance, Stanton stated his case. "Man, some cat is goin' for a shakedown. I was at Perk's in Harlem about three weeks ago, and this guy, who appeared to have had one too many, was clownin' me over the fact that we got bumped by the Charlotte Hornets in the first round this year."

"I would've too, the way Jamal Mashburn ate y'all up," Kyle quipped.

"Counselor's got jokes, I see."

"Just kidding, Stan. Go on."

"So anyway, I could tell this guy was drunk. His speech was slurred, he was staggering and struggling to keep his balance and he's razzing me something bad. The taunting didn't bother me. But then he spilled beer on me. Swinging wildly in my direction, the mug of beer he held tipped over, and the froth of it sloshed on my shirt and lapel. I sidestepped his clumsiness 'cause I didn't want him all over me. Before I could blink he lost his balance, fell on his face, and grabbed his nose. Then the bouncer intervened and they escorted me outside.

"I never saw him again after that, so I figured it was just one of those things. Two weeks later he pressed battery charges against me. So I turned myself in, made bail, and now I need a good trial lawyer to clear my name of this madness."

Kyle scribbled on a blank legal pad in the ensuing silence. "Is that all that happened?"

"That's it."

"So you never hit him?"

Stan sucked his teeth. "Look man, I ain't into throwin' cats through windows and shit. I was just trying to have some dinner and a good time."

Kyle sighed and then raised his hand to indicate his understanding. "I have to ask you these things, man, because this guy and his ambulance chaser are going to do everything in their power to prove that you assaulted him. They're creating an image; he'll be an unwitting, undeserving victim. So I need to know if you're leaving anything out, otherwise we'll be going to the theatre of the unexpected."

"You know everything." Stan nodded as he leaned back in his seat, brooding...

"Stan, personally, I'd be honored to clear your name. But know this, I'm a professional, and from this point forward I must treat you like a client. You might not agree with some of my actions, and you may even dislike my suggestions, but trust me, they're in your best interest. Because this is such a high profile case, until it's over, I want you to keep a low profile, meaning..."

"Stay away from the women, the bars, and the club scene," Stan finished, sighing.

"Exactly. Your visibility in these places can go a long way in the judge's final ruling." With those words, Kyle came from behind his desk, and in a moment of spiritual weakness, gave his brother in the struggle a loving embrace. "I got your back, dawg. Believe that."

I got your back, dawg... Those five words were a motivating tool for Kyle Watson as he labored from dusk to dawn preparing Stanton's defense. Additional incentive came in knowing that in October, some eight weeks away, Cohen, Schindler and Brody's fiscal cycle would end with the announcement of the firm's new partners. Having already established his brilliance by defending clients with the tenacity of a pitbull, emerging victorious in a case of this magnitude would go a long way in proving he merited strong consideration.

Winning a case of such importance entailed great sacrifice as well. Heeding Cohen's orders to concentrate solely on Curry's exoneration, every case that had been worked on prior to his assignment to Stanton was either compartmentalized or delegated to junior associates.

"Grunt work," Kyle mumbled from his home office a week into his prep work. Inundated with the task of preparing interrogatories, finding credible witnesses and conversing and consulting with his defense team via e-mail, his social and romantic life had taken a turn for the worse ever since his goal of partnership by thirty-three became an obsession. Recalling the words of his former fiancée, Anita Browne, had said to him when she broke off the engagement two years ago by moving out of their Riverdale condo, "Being with you is like being alone," Kyle was briefly saddened once again. The devastation that rose through him upon hearing those words compelled him to numb his pain with work. Assuaging his hurt with an inordinately large case load served as therapy.

Not on this night, however. Finally taking a break from the task at hand, Kyle the Recluse succumbed to his loneliness. Sipping white zinfandel after a hot shower, he tried to ignore the stiff feeling at his groin telling him it had been too long since he'd had sex, but his efforts were futile. Too wound up to go to sleep, yet too tired to step out and mingle at a local watering hole, too late for jumpers at a nearby gym, and too far removed from the dating scene to consider a booty call, the Internet would be a catharsis that evening...

Dimming the lights to his work study, Kyle refilled his glass of wine, placed a CD in the PC drive and instantly the case-related tension gave way to physical longing. Keith Washington and Chanté Moore serenaded him with "Candlelight and You" as he lit a match to the wick of a lavender-scented votive. After searching the usual websites devoted to sports and leisure, he came across a rectangular icon flashing in white letters amidst a red background advertising Sistergirls.com, a bachelorette website.

As the music drifted to R. Kelly's "Strip for You," Kyle let his mind wander a bit while contemplating his next move. Growing weary of cooking dinner for one and of the sleepless seasons passing him by in a lonely bed, the blend of wine and melody heightened masculine cravings and lowered his inhibitions. Desires now running rampant, he wished some seductive siren would knock three times at his door, drop her coat to the floor and help him release pent-up sexual tension. *Masturbation can only do so much*, he mused.

Clicking onto the link, the artistic portrait of three attractive ladies was a precursor to the numerous images of desirable, available women, each accompanied by biographical profiles, personality narratives and ideal match descriptions for potential suitors. There was something for every man: hotties and hoochies wearing daisy dukes and large earrings for thugs who coveted the around-the-way type; the conservative, debutante sort for professional men in search of eye candy; a couple even arched Kyle's eyebrows with brazen sexual demands and enticing photos.

Sifting though the diverse, yet delectable assortment of Nubian queens with cute and clever profiles, he was about to exit the site when he noticed the title, **CHOCOLATE KITTY IS DREAMING ABOUT YOU**, next to a pictureless bio. That she was faceless intrigued him. *Her bio had better be something*, Kyle thought as he scanned the page.

Dear Lover,

Though I could write a lot of starry-eyed platitudes regarding love and the quest thereof, I do not covet that at this point in my life.

Then what in the hell is she looking for? Kyle pondered. **I want lust before love. Are you man enough to play this game of on-line foreplay with me? Mmmm, I sure hope so...I love the chemistry between male and female, and what we can create in our sensuous, seductive cyber world of two...I love exploring the world of erotic fantasy and thoroughly enjoy the differences between the sexes; your thoughts, my thoughts and our dreams and desires in the throes of passion...**

I have a hunger to meet you on-line in a string bikini and be folded into your arms on a moonlit night along a foreign beach, sipping a cool Merlot and listening to hot jazz. I want to dance forbidden dances with you as we travel the world together in fantasy: Brazil, Argentina, Barcelona and Cancun all await our long walks and steamy nights in cyberland...Can we try every position imaginable, both in your place and mine? Can I satisfy your every desire and craving, your every need, in our virtual land of ecstasy? I sure hope so. This Chocolate Kitty wants to purr. I'll be waiting.

Chocolate Kitty – ChocKitty@sg.com

Upon completing his perusal of her profile, a mysterious mixture of heat and intrigue passed through Kyle as her flavor preference piqued his curiosity. *Is she as fond of chocolate as I am?* Collapsing back in his chair as he read her invitation once more, the throbbing at his lower body matched the intensity of his strong pumping heart. Drifting into fantasy, the thought of running a lively tongue along her bronze skin...But *is her skin bronze, caramel, or some other earthly shade?* Envisioning their full lips melding to one...*Are her petals full, or small and sweet?* he asked himself. *Are her kisses tender and teasing, or plundering and passionate?* Was her kitty in need of the warm milk that threatened to spurt from his pulsing masculinity? *Only one way to find out,* Kyle thought as he removed his hand from his protruding member. He would play her game of seduction.

The woman is witty and intelligent, he thought while reaching for a quart of chocolate milk in his portable refrigerator, *so my nickname and title must be catchy.* As he drank from the plastic carton he pondered this, but when he pulled the spout from his mouth and his eyes landed on the container's labeling, it came to him. Placing the milk on top of the fridge, Kyle's gaze moved from the quart to his groin, then back to the quart. A mischievous smile crossed his face as he clicked on the reply button and began to type. **CHOC-A-LOT WILL MAKE YOUR KITTY PURR...**

Taking his time as the sounds of Kenny Lattimore filled both mood and soul, Kyle wrote and rewrote the message he would send to this tempting tart.

Breathing heavily as he finished his response to his hopeful kitten, the eight inches between Kyle's legs stood as solid as an oak. Sighing with regret, oh, how he wished this mystery lady were there to relieve his aching sensation. *Another night with Miss Palmer and her five fingers,* he thought as he shut his workstation down.

~

CHAPTER TWO

"Counselors, approach the bench now!" barked Supreme Court Justice Amanda Powell.

The two attorneys glared at one another as they rounded their tables and started toward her. As different in appearance as night and day, Dale

Gordon was a portly, balding man in his early-fifties who seemingly took not a moment's care in his personal grooming as flecks of dandruff sprinkled the shoulders of his wrinkled and stained jacket. If not for his brilliant legal mind, Amanda was sure the District Attorney would have removed him from his roll years ago. On the other hand was the tall, impeccably groomed and undeniably handsome Kyle Watson. A bit too cocky for her liking, she could not, however, deny his keen legal prowess. As he strolled toward her, their eyes met and held. *Is he challenging me?* she wondered. *Well, if he is, I've got a surprise in store for him.*

Covering the microphone on her bench while giving the stenographer a sign that indicated an off-the-record conversation was about to take place, she spoke to the adversaries in a heated whisper. "If you two are finished with your war of egos, I'd like to proceed with this hearing. I will not...I repeat, will not have this petty bickering in my courtroom. If you two can't get your acts together and behave like the professionals you're supposed to be, I'll give you both a night in lock-up to think about the proper way to behave when you're in *my* house." Noticing the look of derision oozing from Kyle Watson's eyes, she added, "And Counselor Watson, if you've got a problem with what I'm saying, too bad!"

"Your Honor, I didn't say anything."

"I don't like your look."

"But..."

"Step back," she commanded.

~

The nerve of Watson, Judge Powell muttered while slipping out of her black judicial robe that evening. Ever since her early afternoon halt to the attorney haggle, her mind maddeningly drifted between conflicting matters: soaking up as much pretrial information in the Stanton Curry case as possible, and trying to overlook and ignore the annoying look of arrogance on the face of his representation. *Hmmph, he better come with his shit correct. I certainly hope this young brother doesn't underestimate me,* she mused. *I'm not your ordinary, run-of-the-mill judge.*

Amanda Powell was not this by a long shot. A graduate of Duke Law School and former congressional staffer, she, Amanda Powell, was well-received in many legal circles across the country, hence as she was her assignment to the bench seat at forty-one years of age.

In two short years after her appointment, she had been lauded by the American Bar Association for her brilliant, articulate yet direct, shoot-from-the-hip personality style that was well respected by peers and counsel alike. Even the law-breakers who came before her daily made comments which suggested she always "kept it real," as she occasionally spoke to the offenders in the latest street vernacular. It seemed only fitting that the judicial wheel would once again stop on her name when it came to presiding over a case involving a prominent sports personality.

⌒

Upon entering her Striver's Row brownstone that evening, the only thing Amanda wanted to do was light some scented candles, pour herself a glass of her favorite Johannesburg Riesling wine and soak in her Jacuzzi with the sweet sounds of Will Downing playing in the background. Dropping her keys and briefcase in the foyer, she climbed the carpeted staircase off the entryway and immediately set herself to the task.

Bone weary from her exhaustive day, the warm water was a soothing respite. As she lounged in her tub and sipped from her stemmed glass, the handsome visage of Kyle Watson pervaded her thoughts, causing an involuntary tingle to course through her lower region. Dreaming that he traced her body with the skillful, yet sensitive touch of his fingertips, unconsciously, Amanda's hand slid down her soapy frame until her fingers were perched at the entrance to her private garden. Slowly slipping a finger inside, she leaned her head back and let the combination of the tub's jets and her fingers dancing to the rhythm of the tune emanating from her stereo speakers take her on a trip to euphoria. Shocked by the sensation, intensity and inspiration for her explosive release, she quickly sat up, splashing the wine as she did. *Where the hell did that come from? This wine must be affecting me more than I thought.*

Quickly draining the water from her soothing haven, Amanda dried her body, replenished the liquid sedative and moved to her den. Turning on her computer, she hoped there would be correspondence in her mailbox on the Sistergirls.com website to rid her mind of her unprovoked fantasy. Bored with the daily rhetoric administered by battling attorneys, she came home one June evening and surfed the site out of curiosity. Deliberating for weeks before placing her on-line personal, tonight she hoped to discover a stimulating reply to her advertisement and maybe, just maybe, start something naughty. Sifting through the messages, she found the initial response to her post ridiculous.

Hear Kitty, Kitty, Kitty…
I would love to take you to Arooba and would caress the breast and lick you from head two to getting you wedda than you can ever get. I would slide my big black thik kat all da way up in ya, fillin ya up sumthin real nice. This goes on for a fue hours and then we lay and go to sleep then start all over again in Burmooda. If you are interested in a brotha 6'5" tall and ways 275 solid slightly bowleggd with dough eyes right me at Bigguy9@sg.com and let's make it happen.
Bigguy9@sg.com

Idiot, Amanda fumed while deleting the reply. *His dumb ass can't even spell.* Hopefully, the next one would be enticing, she thought.

A Chocolate Kitty is what I need to complete my recipe: Take one fine ass woman that wants to travel. Add one tall, caramel, handsome man. Add a pinch of affluence, a dash of arrogance, and many types of baby kisses. On your neck. Your spine. Your belly. Your hips. Add a slithering tongue on your silky legs and mouth on that sweet little pussy I know you have. Sprinkle in the fact that I would handle my business, that being to make you scream. Fuck the neighbors; they need to know I'm your daddy. Stir my semen into your oven and sauté until tender. We don't need to travel; my appetite has been whet by your kitty, and I want to baste it and taste it, girl!!! Holla back if you wanna be the entrée.

JuicyJay@sg.com

Shaking her head at this correspondence, Amanda was flustered. *Am I being seduced here, or am I being cooked?* She wanted confident, not cocky; assured, not asinine; simple and selfless as opposed to selfish and stupid.

Tempted to ignore the third posting, her curiosity outweighed her better judgment. She placed the pointer on the screen on the message's caption, **CHOC-A-LOT WILL MAKE YOUR KITTY PURR...**, then clicked her mouse to open it.

Chocolate Kitty,

I sit at my desk, lonely and longing to share a night of passion with someone, even if in the world of e-mails and instant messages. Reading your dreams and desires jolted my senses and seared my skin with a heated sensation. This agile king would love to meet the queen of your fantasy world.

Cool Merlot and hot jazz, you say? Have you ever tangoed in Madrid? Would you like to tangle in Morocco? Can our teeth and tongues clash in Monte Carlo? Can I inflict titillating torture while our bodies become one in cyberspace? Dreaming of dancing with you in an exotic wonderland, it would truly be an honor to take your hand and join you in this virtual world of ecstasy. Trust me, I will make your Chocolate Kitty purr.

Mr. Choc-A-Lot – ChocAlot@sg.com

"Now that's more like it," Amanda voiced with a smile. Reentering the world of fantasy, the blank-faced vision of this ebony knight appeared before her, causing shortness of breath. Longing to have the cavern of her wetness filled with something rich, thick and chocolate, a drizzle of her moistness trickled down her left thigh. Hoping that it would mingle with the saliva of this faceless prince's tongue trail, the mere thought of his oral lizard invading and arousing her feminine pasture had her fingers running over her clit once more. Soon, drizzles and droplets turned to ecstatic, orgasmic torrents of pleasure as a river of warm juices flowed from her.

Sighing with relief from the release brought on by self-gratification,

Amanda Powell knew the expressions of this man were real. Wanting to quench an inquisitive thirst for the person behind the words, she began tapping an answer.

Mr. Choc-A-Lot,
I must admit your response to my ad made quite an impression with me. (*If only he knew*, Amanda mused.)You seem well-traveled in the parallel virtual worlds of travel and passion, not to mentioned well-versed in the art of seduction. Your invitation to dance enticed me so much that I'm wondering Mr. Lot—Can I call you that?—are you real, or an apparition? Can you make me mutter *ooohs* and *aahs* in the throes of cybersex? Can you make me throb and ache, dizzy and wanting all of you, in all of me? Can we make the sands in the hourglass of cyber love stand still as our bodies become entwined after hours in our mutual world of fantasy? The wetness of my kitty tells me that you can. If so, meet me tomorrow night, at nine o'clock in the Sistergirls chat room so we can privately explore the Bahamas, as well as each other.
See you there – Chocolate Kitty.

"Mmmm, I can't wait," Amanda said aloud while turning off her computer. The chocolate vision she hoped would still the motion of her hips with his own movements in fantasy would be tomorrow night's treat. For now, a pillow between her legs would do the trick.

CHAPTER THREE

Frustration filled the face of Kyle Watson as he followed Stephen Cohen into his corner office. Feeling as if he'd squandered another day in the defense of Stanton Curry, he began venting.

"I can't believe Judge Powell didn't approve of my witness list. Is she trying to make an example of Stanton Curry?"

Gazing at the midtown summer twilight before taking his seat, Cohen lit a cigar, then replied. "Perhaps she's trying to set you straight, Watson."

"What are you talking about?"

"Maybe her actions are an indication of the seriousness of this matter. She's trying to show you that the litigation proceedings will not result in a cakewalk dismissal, like many of the 'Joe Fan versus the Popular Athlete' cases."

"I'm cognizant of that," Kyle responded. "But, Steve, our client wasn't accused of murder, you know."

"I'm aware of that, Watson. But given the notoriety of the defendant and the magnitude of this action, Judge Powell is leaving nothing to chance in terms of showing favoritism. I would do the same if I wore her shoes."

"You would wear heels, boss?" Kyle cracked.

Cohen grinned at his star pupil as he took a haughty puff on his cigar. "Another one like that and I'll take you off this case."

"Seriously, Steve, how do I handle this judge?"

Whenever Kyle said his first name with an inquiry, Stephen Cohen lightened this partner hopeful's befuddlement with a dead-on impersonation of Yoda the Jedi Master. "Use The Force, Luke."

"C'mon, Steve. Seriously."

"We'll figure her out in the morning," Cohen announced after another puff. "I'm giving you the night off. You know what that means, Watson?"

"Seven in the morning start. Right, boss?"

"See you at seven, Kyle. You have some work to do before going off to court tomorrow afternoon. Don't be late, Watson." As Kyle moved to the office door, Cohen stopped him in his tracks with a parting thought. "You have to admit, Judge Powell's quite the sight for sore eyes. Don't you agree?"

Startled by his boss' forwardness, he faced him once more and spoke like he'd been programmed by Bill Gates himself. "Steve, I haven't paid any attention to that detail. I'm attempting to win a high profile case for the firm, so the beauty of Amanda Powell is irrelevant at this juncture."

"Good answer, Watson. Good answer."

Heading homeward on the uptown "1" train, Kyle was still mystified by Cohen's final comment. Although undeniably handsome and naturally flirtatious, he had never, and would never, make a pass at a presiding judge. That is not to say any of those women of power would not make a play for him. Once, at the conclusion of a trial, he was passed a note from a court clerk, which read "you can put your shoes under my bed any time you like." Reviewing the note, he saw the judicial letterhead, Her Honor's signature, and quickly discarded it. He assumed that word had spread like wildfire since he'd been left alone.

Truth be told, he had been so engrossed in his recent quest for partnership that he hadn't paid attention to the beauty or advances of any woman. *Maybe Anita took more than my heart away when she left*, he mused.

Looking at his watch as the metal transit horse crossed the 220th Street Bridge adjoining Manhattan and the Bronx, Kyle noted the time. *Seventhirty and it's still daylight*. Zipping by the preceding stations, the train pulled into its final stop at 242nd Street and Van Cortlandt Park. Finding the thought of a stroll enticing, instant notions were dashed, however, when he saw the magenta-violet rays of light illuminating the skies above. Longing to share the beauty of a sunset with someone special—not to mention a turkey and Swiss hero from the local deli—his condo up the Riverdale hills went from obvious alternative to only option in the blink of an eye.

Inside, that choice proved satisfying to Kyle, for the midnight blue Brooks Brothers suit and shirt he wore magically became an athletically bare chest, white sweat pants and slippers as he consumed his meal. Hunger slaked, the combination of long hours and lethargy set in as he sipped from his wine glass in front of his PC.

Yawning while opening his Netscape Explorer address, Kyle's eyes were barely open as he wandered from site to site aimlessly. First, it was to ESPN to see how Barry Bonds and the San Francisco Giants were doing in the pennant race; then to Amazon.com to order *Gettin' Buck Wild: The Sex Chronicles 2*, the latest Zane collection for his secretary as a birthday present; and finally, to the Sistergirls.com site to what he thought would be an empty mailbox for MR. CHOC-A-LOT.

That one letter in his in-box was an injection of caffeine to his system. His pulse now alert as a familiar stiffening at his groin captured his attention, just seeing the CHOCOLATE KITTY address awakened Kyle as his eyes bulged with excitement and curiosity. After a mouse click, quick scan and time check, initial anticipation and inquisitiveness quickly turned to panic. *Shit, I'm ten minutes late!!!*

～

Five minutes. I'm giving him five more minutes, Amanda fumed as she waited in an empty chat room. Having downloaded the message from MR. CHOC-A-LOT, Judge Powell found it intoxicatingly arousing as she read it repeatedly while on the bench during lulls in the Stanton Curry pre-trial conference. Daydreaming about this cyber suitor's sensuous touch, Her Honor wondered if her thoughts of fantasy were obsessive, or was she simply horny and scared to do anything about it. At day's end, she decided that the chat would do it for her. *It's either that, or a cucumber from the local D'Agostino supermarket*, she thought.

The ensuing cab ride home refused to curb the anticipation of a tension release. Dreaming that CHOC-A-LOT had licked her from cleavage to cunt, her pointed, brown nipples threatened to come through her white blouse as her libido was on the brink of ignition. Trying to ignore a well-known throb of desire between her legs, her efforts were futile as her body ached with need. She hoped a conversation with a potential cyber mate would supply the perfect antidote for these passionate pangs.

So there Amanda sat. Having logged on the Sistergirls.com site at eight-fifty, she thought this Nubian knight of wondrous words would feel her excitement and log on early. Such was not the case. Assuming he would be on time for their chat, nine o'clock came and went, taking with it promptness and punctuality. *Assumption is the mother of all fuck-ups*, she railed. Ten minutes later, she was resigned that MR. CHOC-A-LOT was a pretender to the throne of erotic passion; she would give him five more minutes before sending a tactless response to his no-show.

Suddenly, an entry eased her loneliness and caused her loins to clench.

CHOC-A-LOT: Chocolate Kitty, are you there?

KITTY: You know, if this were a flight, it would have left you in the waiting area.

CHOC-A-LOT: My apologies for the late arrival. I just checked my messages a couple of minutes ago.

KITTY: I thought that you were backing out on me, Mr. Choc-A-Latte.

CHOC-A-LOT: That's Choc-A-Lot, Ms. Kitty.

KITTY: OK, Mr. Choc-A-Lot. Look, let's get a few things straight from the start. If you're going to be a part of my cyber fantasy world, you must follow one simple rule. Don't ever keep me waiting. If we have an appointment, I'm expecting you to keep it. And if you keep it, you must be punctual. I'm not looking for someone who wants to toy around when it's convenient for him. I covet a real man who can fulfill my every virtual world need on my time. Can you hang with that???

Kyle did a double-take as he paused before responding. *Who the fuck does she think she is, my mother?* Recalling the abuse he endured daily with the Judge's demands, he sure didn't need this. The response to her arrogance filled the screen quickly.

CHOC-A-LOT: Chocolate Kitty, I've already apologized. Things happen. And considering that we didn't have an appointment, your insinuation is not appreciated. But while you're at it, I have my own set of rules. If I'm to work that chocolate kitty of yours like the candy that it is, I will do it on my terms. This is *my* specialty. And I refuse to be dictated as to how and when it should be done. So yes, I'm hanging and for your information, I'm hanging pretty heavy. Can *you* handle that?

A wicked smile appeared on Amanda's face as she read his reply. Had she finally met someone who wasn't intimidated by her? Someone who would stand up to her and not squirm at her every demand? *He passed the first test*, she thought. *This could prove to be very interesting.*

KITTY: Hmm, assertive. I like that.

CHOC-A-LOT: Oh, is this a game to you, because I don't have time for games.

KITTY: Now, now, Mr. Lot. There's no need to get touchy. I'm not playing games, for my time is valuable as well. You're right, we didn't have an appointment and it was pretty darned presumptuous of me to assume you would be available at a time that was convenient for me when I don't know anything about you. (After a pause with no response from him, she continued.) Look, why don't we start from scratch. Tell me a little about yourself, so we can start this trip on the same page, at the same time, and from the same port of call. Truce? Mr. Lot, are you still there?

Kyle was still there, contemplating. Brooding, yet still contemplating. *Who in the hell is this woman? Well, she did apologize, sort of. Ah, what the hell.*

CHOC-A-LOT: Truce. What is it you'd like to know about me?

KITTY: Well, for starters, what do you look like?

CHOC-A-LOT: Whatever you want me to look like.

KITTY: Like Denzel or Morris Chestnut—LOL. Just kidding. Or am I?

Laughing out loud, *She sounds like a humdinger,* Kyle thought.

CHOC-A-LOT: Well, for the record, I've been told I'm quite the catch.

KITTY: Oh, so you must be pretty handsome. Did you just get in from work?

CHOC-A-LOT: As a matter of fact, I did.

KITTY: What line of business are you in?

CHOC-A-LOT: Don't go there.

KITTY: OK. Your wish is my command, your majesty.

CHOC-A-LOT: You can actually be submissive, Ms. Kitty?

KITTY: When I need to be.

CHOC-A-LOT: You don't strike me as that. You seem to be the authoritative type; a woman who likes control.

KITTY: Funny you should say that. I often hear that description at work.

CHOC-A-LOT: And where might that be?

KITTY: You don't tell, so I won't either.

CHOC-A-LOT: Touché. LOL.

KITTY: Turn-a-bout is fair play, Mr. Lot.

CHOC-A-LOT: That is so true. I'll go on the record and say that I'm in the legal profession. That's all I care to volunteer at the moment.

KITTY: Small world. I have ties to the legal community as well.

CHOC-A-LOT: I see our flight to the Bahamas has been postponed tonight.—Smile.

KITTY: You're right. Should we make an "appointment" to meet here tomorrow? I know when I get in from work, I usually like to take off my clothes, run a warm bath, put on some soft music and just relax before I do anything else.

CHOC-A-LOT: Mmmm, can I come over?

KITTY: Heel, Rover. What makes you think this kitty likes dogs?—LOL.

Kyle's imagination began to run rampant as he envisioned her lounging in a big, claw-foot bathtub, sipping from a glass of wine dangling from a lazy hand flung over the side of it.

CHOC-A-LOT: What kind of bathtub do you have?

KITTY: Excuse me?

CHOC-A-LOT: Your tub, is it set into the floor or is it on feet?

KITTY: It's a claw-foot tub, why?

CHOC-A-LOT: Just curious.

KITTY: Curiosity killed the cat.

CHOC-A-LOT: It also elicited a response from me to your message.

KITTY: Touché. However, you didn't answer my question about our "appointment."

CHOC-A-LOT: Are you free tomorrow night around ten o' clock, or is that too late?

KITTY: Well, ten's okay, but why so late?

CHOC-A-LOT: I'm expecting to have a long day tomorrow. A chat with you will be the perfect nightcap.

KITTY: Ten's doable for me.

CHOC-A-LOT: Cool, so until then, keep that kitty warm for me.

KITTY: Only if you promise to pet it.

CHOC-A-LOT: (smile) I promise to stroke it like it's never been stroked before. Until tomorrow, Queen.

KITTY: I'm looking forward to it, Sir Choc-A-Lot.

Pet it? I'll do more than just pet that kitty, Kyle thought as he clicked off his computer. Hungry for some sexual action, any type of stimulant would do as anxiousness enveloped him. Warm blood raced through his mind and chest, then headed south to harden the length of him once more. Rubbing his tool in anticipation and wondering what vision would invade the dreams of Chocolate Kitty that night, he would ask her to reveal them tomorrow.

CHAPTER FOUR

I want to be naughty and nasty tonight. Amanda Powell reached this conclusion long before she stepped into the cool Manhattan air that evening; her decision to do so cemented by the courtroom performance of Kyle Watson during the afternoon session of the Stanton Curry trial. Today marked the commencement of witness depositions, and she found herself in silent appreciation of the cross-examination techniques displayed by the defendant's lead counsel.

Judge Powell, while impartial to the actual proceeding, quietly admired the way Kyle Watson presented his questioning. Watching him gauge the aura of each witness, she noted his intuition, his immensely sensitive feel for each individual taking the stand. Utilizing this innate sense with expert precision, Kyle knew the exact moment when to thunder away, when to pull back, when to badger, and when to give pause. To her amazement, the prosecution had little argument to his cross-grilling; that Dale Gordon only objected twice during the three-hour hearing indicated such.

Somehow, she transformed his courtroom proficiency into human fantasy. Wondering if this legal wizard were a natural between the sheets as well, she tried to ignore her impure fixation, yet couldn't. *His gentle, albeit aggressive style of questioning tells me counselor is exacting, yet versatile. Fluid, confident, semi-bowlegged strides means that he's athletic. Athleticism translates into energy. Mmmm, I like that. I wonder if he has good hip motion. Intercourse isn't about in-and-out. A man must move in circles, too. Only close to orgasm would I let him fuck me, although letting him fuck me all the way through wouldn't be bad at times. Mmm, he's gotta take me there.* Her vagina heated up during these thoughts, causing her canal walls to pulse as she perspired slightly. Through it all, Her Honor remained composed to the public eye, save an occasional cup of water from the pitcher adjacent to her gavel. Coming to as the session ended, that Judge Powell remembered the particulars of the day's events was a miracle in itself.

The cab ride home provided its own anxiety, however, as Amanda had to address what was now becoming a difficult crisis. *Why am I lusting after Kyle Watson so much?* While again recognizing his striking features, the unmistakable confidence and unflappable demeanor, the undeniable self-assurance that oozed from his pores was also an alluring magnet. Under normal circumstances, she might indicate an attraction to him with a simple bat of an eye, a seductive wink, or a sensuous smile. Judge Powell could be easily smitten by this man.

Smitten that is, if she failed to acknowledge the glaring truth: that she was a presiding judge over a case in which the object of her unexplainable ardor was defending his high-profile client. *My case. His client.* Those two thoughts alone splashed cold water on her fantasy. As if she had been hit over the head with flashing red lights, she dismissed those thoughts and decided that she would have to find solace in what she hoped lay ahead during her ten p.m. rendezvous with Mr. Choc-A-Lot.

"Kyle, you really put them on their asses today in that courtroom," Stephen Cohen announced proudly in his office that evening.

Even Stanton Curry had to agree. "I'm so glad you're representing me," he chimed in. Rabinowitz stood by with a sardonic look, unwilling to give Kyle credit for a job well done.

"I'm just doing my job," Kyle said.

"And a damn good job at that," Stephen continued. "Did you notice that our adversary raised only two objections this afternoon. *TWO.* Even Judge Powell seemed to be taken. She sat behind her bench with a look of pure satisfaction on her face. I've never seen her react like that before."

"Mmmm," Kyle agreed while checking the time on his David Yurman wristwatch. *Seven-thirty. I can't be late tonight,* he thought. After today's action in court, he felt pumped and ready to end a perfect day by taking a certain kitty to the ecstasy that she obviously craved. He was more than ready to show this arrogant, brazen little kitty who was in charge, who was definitely The Man.

"Why the smirk?" Stephen cut in, bringing Kyle back to reality.

Momentarily startled, Kyle looked and realized both men were watching him, awaiting an answer. "I was just thinking about something personal, that's all. Look, Stanton," he retorted, quickly changing the subject. "Why don't we meet an hour earlier tomorrow morning. There are a few things I'd like to review with you before we go back to court."

Sensing he was being dismissed, Stanton stood and extended a handshake to his representation. "No problem. At the same place?" Upon Kyle's nod, he tightened his grip in appreciation. "Again, I can't thank you enough. You're doing a great job. I feel very confident with you representing me."

"No thanks necessary, Stanton. Just remember me when I need courtside seats in Orlando," he joked, bringing laughter from the trio. As the office door closed with Curry's departure, Stephen Cohen turned toward his prize pupil with curiosity all over his face.

"So what were you thinking about, Watson? A certain judge, maybe?"

"Hey, Steve, I thought I was handling all the depositions," Kyle quipped.

"Her eyes seemed to be glued to your body as you presented your case today. She looked like she'd been mesmerized by you."

"Oh, please," Kyle replied as he gathered his case file and inserted it into his briefcase. Although he noticed her beauty, he would never reveal this incriminating evidence to Stephen; not with a potential partnership hanging in the balance. Besides, his current distraction, Chocolate Kitty, was a welcome intrusion that awaited his attention online. Her interest was mutually noted by an urgent tingling in his pants in need of satisfying.

"Listen, boss, I'd like to stay and chat, but I've got an appointment that

I have to keep."

"A date while in the midst of the most important trial of your legal career? Perhaps an increase of workload is in order here. Don't you agree, Watson?"

Kyle chuckled defensively. "Steve, I'll touch base with you by cell tomorrow, after meeting with Stanton and before Judge Powell takes the bench. How's that?"

"Sounds good." Puzzled by his abruptness, Stephen followed him through the door wondering where he was off to.

Alone on the subway, Kyle finally steered his mental direction to the object of his virtual world's desire; the deep moans of Toni Braxton's "Art Of Love" flowing through the headphones of his Discman aided his transformation. *The Bahamas tonight? Let's see, dinner at the Poop Deck seafood restaurant; snorkeling in Freeport; dancing at the Zoo, and making love along the sands of Cable Beach...*As Toni uttered "Grab Mommy" he flashed a smirk while envisioning two damp bodies fusing and disconnecting in rhythm. One of the masses, his own, slid a massive tool in and out of this imaginary vision. Changing the tempo from slow and steady to breakneck banging, the special milk that flowed from her kitty drenched the base of his manhood. His erotic train of thought reached an abrupt end with a hard shoulder tap.

"Excuse me. Excuse me," the conductor said. "This is the last stop! Two hundred Forty-second Street! Last Stop!"

"Oh yeah, man. My bad." Leaving the iron vehicle with an embarrassed look on his face, Kyle glanced at his watch and saw that it was eight forty-five. Arriving home, Kyle filled the time before his date with a quick sandwich and shower. Setting the mood in his den as if having company in the flesh, an insane need for erotic fulfillment captured him as the sensuous, harmonic sounds of Silk's "Freak Me" surrounded the moment. Excitement emanating from the pit of his stomach surfaced as he dimmed the lights, then sipped from his screwdriver. The tenor was perfect for a sexual foray via cyber world. *Nine fifty-eight*, Kyle announced, glancing at his computer clock. *It's time to make that kitty scream.* To his surprise, his delectable delight was already in the chat room.

KITTY: Hey there, slowpoke. How was your day?

CHOC-A-LOT: (smile) You're funny. My day was pretty good, if I say so myself. So, Kitty, did you pack some whip cream for our trip?

KITTY: My, aren't we in a hurry.

Damn, I hope he's not like that in real life, Amanda thought as she paused.

KITTY: What's the rush, Mr. Lot? I want to know who and what I'm going away with. What do you look like?

CHOC-A-LOT: Again, does it matter? I'll tell you what. Give me two features of yours, and I'll reveal two of mine.

KITTY: OK. My hair is short and auburn, like leaves turning colors in the fall. I also have a tiny mole just above my lips, like Marilyn Monroe. I've been told it's very sexy.

CHOC-A-LOT: Mmmm, it sounds sexy.

KITTY: Does it make you hard?

CHOC-A-LOT: Sure does.

Kyle hardened rapidly.

KITTY: Can I stroke it for you?

CHOC-A-LOT: In a minute, Kitty. Don't you want your two features?

KITTY: Oh, I forgot. Give them to me.

Amanda had to blush at her own aggression. *Good thing he's not right here in front of me. He'd probably think I was some hot, horny ho in a hurry.*

CHOC-A-LOT: I'm about 6'1" and nicely built. Fill in the blanks with your imagination.

KITTY: Mmmm, something I can climb.

CHOC-A-LOT: I have something for you to climb, all right.

KITTY: Ooh, hearing that makes my kitty wet.

CHOC-A-LOT: Look who's going fast now? I haven't even stroked her yet.

KITTY: But you're making her purr.

CHOC-A-LOT: Already? We haven't even got on the plane yet.

KITTY: I must correct you, Sir Choc-A-Lot. I'm in my thong bikini already, on Cable Beach, nursing a Sex-on-the-beach.

CHOC-A LOT: Well, can I join you? Though I must inform you that sex on the beach can be quite abrasive when a kitty is on her backside.

KITTY: (blushing) I have my blanket for us, Choc-A-Lot.

CHOC-A-LOT: (smile) And I brought the champagne.

KITTY: Mmmm. What kind?

CHOC-A LOT: Veuve Cliquot.

KITTY: Forget the Sex on the beach. Would you pour me a glass?

CHOC-A-LOT: Sure. Here you go.

KITTY: Thank you, sweetie. Can we make a toast?

CHOC-A-LOT: Sure thing. Here's to doing away with legal days and lonely nights.

KITTY: I'll drink to that, my dear. Clink.

CHOC-A-LOT: Clink.

During the pause, Kyle sipped on his screwdriver. On the other end, Amanda took in some Riesling.

KITTY: Mmmm, tasty.

CHOC-A-LOT: Very tasty. But champagne is not only for drinking, Kitty.

KITTY: Mmmm, sounds kinky. What do you have in mind, mister?

Kinky, huh? Kyle thought. The muscle between his legs was bulging, and its longing thoughts began thinking for the head upstairs. *It's time to turn up the furnace*, it directed.

CHOC-A-LOT: Who knows? A drip here, a drop there.

KITTY: Anything you spill you have to lick up.

CHOC-A-LOT: Who said anything about spilling? "Pouring" is the operative word at this moment.

KITTY: So, Sir Choc-A-Lot, does my glass need a refill, or will this treat be poured in a different kind of receptacle?"

CHOC-A-LOT: Why don't you lie back on that blanket and we'll find out. (pouring) You like that, Kitty?

"Shit," Amanda mumbled as a quiver traveled from her neck to the lips of her aching slit. Moaning softly, she actually felt the liquid fantasy poured over her, causing another aroused shiver. She had to let him know how good the champagne adorning her body felt.

KITTY: Ooh, it's cold.

CHOC-A-LOT: It's supposed to be, Kitty. But you seem to be handling it very well.

KITTY: I handle a lot of things well. As you can see, my navel has a deep well. It's perfect for sipping; Though, I must say, those bubbles tickle.

CHOC-A-LOT: Do you have any other deep wells?

KITTY: I sure do, baby. And *that* well holds a lot more than champagne.

CHOC-A-LOT: Can I see it?

KITTY: Sure.

It's getting hot down there. Amanda, needing to cool off, exposed herself to the computer. *She needs air.*

KITTY: You like?

CHOC-A-LOT: Yes, I sure do. But I'm surprised that it's so empty.

KITTY: My well needs filling up. You think you can do that for me?

Kyle's eyes widened. *This woman knows what she wants.* His privates thickening to unparalleled girth, he stroked his length slightly to numb the volcanic sensation on the precipice of eruption. That salty white lava release would come later. For now, he had a woman online to satisfy.

CHOC-A-LOT: Can I lick your Kitty first? I want to taste it before plunging my steel in.

KITTY: Please lick it, Baby.

CHAPTER FIVE

Sitting at the defense table in court that morning, Stanton Curry to his right and the paralegal who'd been assisting him on his left, Kyle Watson's mind was a thousand miles away, in a special place reserved for him and a certain kitty. His mind still fixated on the conversation he'd had with his sultry, seductive cyber date, last night's sleep had been elusive as his mind repeatedly replayed their naughty banter.

Their shared fantasy the night before was the pleasant antithesis of a normal, boring, solitary evening at home. Adding an unusual spark to his night with her coquettish exchange, the impact of his online lover was so great that Kyle had even gone so far as to save their communication onto his hard drive and had printed it off before leaving for work that morning. Instead of reading the *New York Times* as he usually did on his morning subway ride, he perused the transcript of their chat, causing him to be transported back in time to those ninety minutes of pure, unadulterated pleasure he'd shared with the lascivious vixen known as Chocolate Kitty.

Fondly recalling the fantasy of an animate object between his lips fluttering like a butterfly as it made its way to a soaked rain forest, a secretive smile crossed his lips as he mused, *I'd love to stroke her fur.* Testing and teasing, probing and pleasing, he then envisioned his active tongue moving upstairs, from her brim to flushed cheeks, leaving nary a stone unturned. Her hungry lips, her neck, earlobes, forehead and chin, all would be at the mercy of the lively lizard that his mouth held captive for so long.

The vision that held Kyle's mind that morning would move to an imaginary bedroom. Placing her on a king-sized bed, his manhood swelled in need of the moist feeling between his kitten's sugar walls. Dreaming that he examined every inch of her body, the heat from both in this wonder world usurped prudent thoughts. As he guided his manhood into a sea of passion, he lovingly stroked her vagina with his magic wand. Soon, ardent tremors from his lover became uncontrollable contractions, quivers and quakes, a series of violent shakes. Meeting her physical bliss with a loud groan, Kyle pumped deeper and deeper, then removed himself from her pleasure chest and released a warm flood of white satisfaction everywhere.

Suddenly, the bailiff called the court to order, interrupting Kyle's reminiscent train of thought as Judge Amanda Powell made her way to the bench. Without giving recognition to anyone in the packed courtroom, the stone-faced judiciary took her seat. For the first time really, Kyle noticed how truly beautiful she was. Tall—about five-eight he guessed—with light brown skin and illuminated brown eyes that seemed brighter as the courtroom lights beamed on them, though her anatomy was concealed by her black robe, her ample bosom was modestly visible. Never having paid any attention to her facial features, she had always reminded him of those women in power who felt they had to be bullies to prove they could hang with the "old boys." Suddenly, something Kitty had written came to the forefront of Kyle's mind. "*...I have short auburn hair...and a mole above* *my mouth...*" A chill ran up his spine as he spied her. *No. It couldn't be.* Studying the extremely attractive adjudicator, he wondered. *Kitty is warm, witty and winsome. Judge Powell is abrasive, autocratic, and antagonistic.* Granted, being in the position she was in, it had to be abundantly clear that she wasn't to be taken lightly, but he couldn't even imagine her being the playful coquette he'd been conversing with last night.

"Is everyone prepared to continue where we left off yesterday?" Judge Powell suddenly asked.

"Yes, Your Honor," the plaintiff's attorney, Dale Gordon, voiced.

When there was no response from the defense table, Judge Powell commented, "Mr. Watson, are you with us?"

He was staring straight at her but hadn't heard a word she'd said.

Stanton's elbow in his ribs was what brought him back to the present. Rising quickly, Kyle answered, "Excuse me, Judge. Yes, the defense is ready to proceed."

"Don't let us inconvenience you, Mr. Watson."

"No, Your Honor. There's no inconvenience."

As his defense of Stanton Curry proved, Kyle Watson relished the task of clearing his client's name. Continuing his flawless courtroom perform-ance, it became more and more evident that it was an open and shut case favoring the defense. Revealing inconsistencies in the detailed accounts of eyewitnesses, his dissection of truths and untruths found holes in the theoretically impenetrable stories, making the purportedly complete look brilliantly incomplete. No matter how vivid the so-called recollections of the complainant's witnesses appeared to many, he shredded the credibility of a variety of individuals who sought their "fifteen minutes" in aid of the prosecution. A couple of bystanders even admitted their glory-seeking, money-making exploits on the witness stand. "If this were a basketball game," Stanton Curry said during the lunch recess, "then the home crowd would tell its opposition to start the bus home at halftime." It seemed the verdict for the defense team—a blowout victory—and Kyle's potential partnership was now a certainty.

Kyle, leaving nothing to chance, was cautious and, at day's end, he expressed this to his client.

"Are you sure the people on your side are credible?"

"Of course," Curry responded with a half-grin.

Why is he smirking at me? Kyle wondered. "Listen, Stan. I can say, with total confidence, that this case is over. But you can never be too sure about these things, so I'm going to call your bodyguards to the stand as a safeguard. Do you have a problem with that?"

"No, I don't," Stanton Curry responded, barely able to suppress his laughter.

What does he find so amusing? "As usual, we'll convene at eight forty-five for some pre-trial conversation. Is that cool with you?"

"Sure thing, Sir Choc-A-Lot. I'll see you tomorrow." Kyle's mouth was agape as he watched his client walk away from him, laughing boisterously. *Oh Shit! How does he know?* After a few minutes of deliberation, the afternoon visual of Stanton Curry perusing through a manila folder as he cross-examined his witnesses came to him. Embarrassed, he chided himself for making his private information so easily accessible and wondered what would happen if he revealed his carelessness to his chocolate kitten later that evening. Quickly brushing that thought aside, he decided there was no need and instead began to look forward to their fantasy trip to Rio de Janeiro later that night.

~

Amanda was weary from the daylong testimony of the Stanton Curry case; weary yet craving what awaited her at home. By her own admission, Mr. Choc-A-Lot had performed a hostile takeover of her mind and libido. Unaccustomed to such intense nocturnal eroticism, *I'm definitely not in control at night,* she thought with a smile.

By day, however, Judge Powell's desire was entirely different; live and in color, it was Kyle Watson. Throughout the day's testimony, she kept watching this dynamic attorney strut back and forth before her bench. Like a magnet to metal, Kyle was unknowingly drawing her into his aura.

Admiring his handsomeness as well as his non-stop energy, she fantasized about this chocolate prince and what his vital statistics would be without his Armani power suit. Wondering what it would be like to lick his bald dome and kiss those pronounced cheekbones, the only other man who'd ever invaded her mind this way was on her computer. *That can only do so much*, she mused as her daytime vision moistened her intimate cavity. Torn between two separate, yet equal passions, Choc-A-Lot had her craving as well, but that was about to change. Tonight *she* would take control. *She* would leave him begging.

Immediately after entering her domicile, Amanda began her preparations for their ten o'clock rendezvous. After soaking in scented oils, she set the mood as if expecting to make love the minute her distant lover came through the front door. After lighting incense and candles and checking the time, she had just enough time to fix an apple martini and sit in front of her computer donned in the caramel suit she'd entered the world in.

CHOC-A-LOT: Are you there, Chocolate Kitty?

KITTY: I always keep my appointments, Mr. Lot. You should know that by now.

CHOC-A-LOT: My bad. So, are you ready for Rio?

Taking a sip from her drink, a devious smile appeared upon Amanda's face.

KITTY: There's been a change of plans.

Confusion flooded Kyle's mind. Having formulated different ways to stroke his kitty and make her purr in Brazil, he was eager to carry out his plans. He wanted to be in control tonight.

CHOC-A-LOT: What do you mean, no Brazil? What do you have in mind?

KITTY: Something much better than watching topless women passing us by in South America; that's for sure. Tonight… *purr*…I'm taking you to paradise. Do you have any objections, Mr. Lot?

Anticipation filled him as her words sank in. *What the hell*, he thought, *paradise is good.*

CHOC-A-LOT: No objections here, Ms. Kitty. Now tell me something: Exactly where is paradise?

In my wet center, Daddy, Amanda thought. She couldn't bring herself to say it online, though.

KITTY: No questions, Mr. Lot. But there are preparations you have to make.

CHOC-A-LOT: What type of preparations?

KITTY: You have to dress for the occasion. Take off your clothes, Mr. Lot. Everything.

CHOC-A-LOT: (gulp) Everything?

KITTY: Unh, unh, unh, Mr. Lot, no questions. Take off everything, and don't keep me waiting.

Quickly disrobing, Kyle sat back in front of his computer screen and began typing.

CHOC-A-LOT: Okay, Ms. Kitty, I'm ready.

KITTY: No, not yet. Now put on this blindfold. Metaphorically, of course.

What the fuck am I getting myself into? Kyle thought. Although his mind said this, his erection had ideas of its own. For now, he would follow the thoughts of his privates.

CHOC-A-LOT: Where in the world can this be leading? Okay, it's on.

KITTY: Good. Now, do you feel that thick warmth dripping down the top of your head, slowly rolling down your back? That's flavored hot oil I just poured on you.

CHOC-A-LOT: Mmm, it feels good.

KITTY: Not so fast, Daddy. Do you feel the hot warmth at the base of your spine?

CHOC-A-LOT: Yeah.

KITTY: That's my tongue. I'm slowly working my way up and I must say that I love the taste of chocolate. It melts in your mouth, you know.

CHOC-A-LOT:And not in your hands, my dear.

She's fucking with me big time, Kyle moaned. That elongated pulse between his legs was in dire need of release.

KITTY: (Smile) I'm now at your neck, Daddy. I'm planting hot kisses along the nape of it. But I can't spend too much time there, Mr. Lot. I haven't reached paradise yet. Is the top of your head paradise? Please tell me it is, baby. I'm now rolling my tongue all over the top of your clean-shaven head. It is clean-shaven, isn't it?

CHOC-A-LOT: It's anything you want it to be, baby.

KITTY: Call me Mommy. I'm a mother in bed, Mr. Lot. And I will take care of you there.

Shit I hope so, Kyle thought. *If she's anything like the way she is in cyber world, then I better bring my "A" game.*

CHOC-A-LOT: Okay, Mommy.

KITTY: Good. Now take off your blindfold and lean back. You need to use all of your senses, here: sight, taste, smell and sound to go to paradise with me, Mr. Lot. Are you leaning?

CHOC-A-LOT: What about touch?

KITTY: There'll be plenty of time for you to use your hands.

CHOC-A-LOT: (smile) Okay. I'm leaning.

KITTY: Good. I'm now coming down your forehead to your nose. Can I suck it, Daddy?

CHOC-A-LOT: By all means, yes.

KITTY: Mmm, it tastes good. I'm moving to your mouth now. Your lips, do they need attention?

CHOC-A-LOT: Yes, they do.

KITTY: Mommy will take care of them. I'm touching them with the tip of my tongue, tracing them, teasing them with my own. Oh, but that's not enough. I want to dive in. Now open up, and say 'ah.' "

CHOC-A-LOT: Ahhhhh.

KITTY: Mmm, that was good. Now lie all the way back, Mr. Lot. I want to work my way down that hairy chest of yours. Can you feel the softness of my skin??

CHOC-A-LOT: Yes. I can. It's soft as silk.

KITTY: You know, Mr. Lot, '69 was a very good year, don't you agree?

A drop of pre-cum surfaced from Kyle's throbbing head as he grunted in arousal. Feeling the sacs tighten around his swollen member, the words of this woman had him reeling. He wanted to insert himself into the slick depths of her canyon, yet he couldn't. Yearning for that physical connection, the chat would have to do for now; that is, if he survived it.

CHOC-A-LOT: Yes, Mommy. It was.

KITTY: Can we have dinner for two, then? I want you to lick my wet triangle. Mommy needs it.

CHOC-A-LOT: Daddy's been waiting all day to lick your sweet kitten.

KITTY: That's good to know. Now, get to licking.

CHOC-A-LOT: Like that, baby?

KITTY: Ooh yes, just like that.

Tremors that were dormant in Amanda's body for what seemed like an eternity surfaced as she imagined his tongue slithering in and out of her drenched channel. Her swollen clitoris was jumping and bouncing as she bit her bottom lip to suppress the erotic storm moving through her.

KITTY: Mmm, shit, Daddy. I didn't know you could do that so well.

CHOC-A-LOT: Your Kitty tastes so good, baby.

KITTY: Please make me cum.

Shit, I really want to, Amanda thought as her imagination had her on the brink.

KITTY: Stick a finger in it while you lick me.

CHOC-A-LOT: Your wish is my command. Can you feel it?

Yes, I can, Daddy, Amanda panted as her index finger found a special place between her feminine lips.

KITTY: Yes, Daddy. Ooh, you've got some pretty long fingers.

CHOC-A-LOT: You know what that means, right?

KITTY: Mmm, I sure do. Big hands mean you wear big gloves.

CHOC-A-LOT: Yeah, fortunately "gloves" come in various sizes.

KITTY: But I need two more in me, sugar. Mommy's kind of hungry.

CHOC-A-LOT: And kind of deep, too. Just the way I like it.

Slowly stroking his length, seconds ticked by as Kyle awaited her reply. After a minute or more passed…

CHOC-A-LOT: Kitty, are you still there?

Amanda was still there, but barely. As her mental image fused with unconscious actions, she dreamed that she was Sir Choc-A-Lot's captive prisoner, bound to a king-sized bed by red scarves. Trembling with passion as her accommodating tunnel contracted and retracted around the digits swirling inside of her, her mind, body and soul ached for her cyber mate, but he wasn't there. Wishing her own probing fingers were something stiff, solid, soothing and attached to her dream lover, she felt his tongue in fantasy caress her spine, the small of her back, and, in a seductive, circular motion, her anus. Ecstatically exploding as she pushed her digits deeper into her cavern, erotic juices drenched her hand as a deep moan escaped her. Still feeling the vibrations of her orgasm, Amanda shivered as she licked her fingers clean and touched the keyboard once more.

KITTY: Shit, Daddy. That felt so good.

CHOC-A-LOT: Where did you go, Kitty? For a second there, I thought I lost you.

KITTY: Do you really want me to answer that?

Somehow, Kyle already knew his answer. She'd returned from a place he longed to go; that being the island one ventures to when crossing the dizzying threshold of pleasure and passion. And judging from the building tension between his legs, Kyle needed a ticket there as well.

CHOC-A-LOT: No, you don't have to answer that for me. I do, however, need a favor from you.

KITTY: I'm afraid to ask what it is.(smile).

CHOC-A-LOT: You don't have to ask. I'll tell you what to do.

KITTY: Ooh, I'm good at taking orders, Daddy.

CHOC-A-LOT: We'll see. Kitty, please stroke it.

KITTY: Mmm, I must say, Mr. Lot, you're quite the healthy one down there.

CHOC-A-LOT: I'm glad it meets with your approval.

KITTY: It feels so good in my hands.

CHOC-A-LOT: Would you like to taste it?

KITTY: I couldn't wait for you to ask me to. Mmm, baby, it's so hard now. You like the way my mouth feels, Daddy?

CHOC-A-LOT: Yes. I do. It feels so warm.

KITTY: Can I make it nice and sloppy?

CHOC-A-LOT: Mmm...Hell yeah.

KITTY: Like that, baby?

Yeah, Kitty, just like that. Gripping his solid muscle tighter, Kyle envisioned the oral cavity of his dreams, first licking the underside of his staff with an active tongue, then easily taking every millimeter of his flesh to the back of her throat. Slowly bobbing her head up and down on him while applying ample lubrication, he felt pressure building up in him as he cradled her head in his large hands. *Yeah Kitty, just like that.* Speeding up his self-manipulative strokes in reality, in dreamland his private passion increased the pace of her sucking as he came closer and closer to his completion. Panting heavily now, Kyle pecked out his reply with his left index finger.

CHOC-A-LOT: Mmm, I'm about to cum.

KITTY: Ooh, can I taste it?

Oh shit! She shouldn't have said that. Envisioning his temptress gulping frantically, he unleashed an ecstatic moan as his semen splattered in all directions. As any ideal fantasy woman would, his chocolate kitty caught some of it in her mouth, cleaned up his mess like a vacuum cleaner, then smiled contentedly.

CHOC-A-LOT: Mmm, that felt so good.

KITTY: Tasted good, too. (giggle)

CHOC-A-LOT: You're too much. Hold on a sec.

Trembling with post-orgasm aftershocks, Kyle wiped himself down— and then his monitor and keyboard.

CHAPTER SIX

"All rise," the Court Officer bellowed as Judge Powell took her seat.

"Please be seated," the judicial arbiter responded. The entire courtroom followed suit. "Can the witness approach the bench?" At that request, a burly, bald black gentleman dressed in a pinstriped, double-breasted suit approached the witness stand, amidst the glare of tabloid-feeding flashbulbs.

"Do you promise to tell the truth, the whole truth, and nothing but the truth, so help you God?" the officer asked the man twice his size.

His answer came loud and firm. "Yes. I do."

"Plaintiff's counsel, please begin the cross-examination of this witness,"

Judge Powell ordered, bringing Dale Gordon waddling from behind his table.

"Witness, can you state your name?" he asked.

"Orenthal Hill," he said, and Kyle couldn't help but notice the twelve smirks coming from the jury box. *Good thing he's not O.J.*, he mused.

"What is your occupation?" the plaintiff's attorney asked.

"Professional bodyguard."

"For many athletes?"

He shook his head, thumbing the gray tie that was suffocating his thick, tree trunk of a neck. "Only one."

"Is he in this courtroom?"

"Yes."

"Can you point to the party in question?"

"Yes, I can." As Orenthal pointed right to the defense table, Kyle's thoughts were mired in sarcasm as he wondered why his opposition felt the need to illustrate the obvious. *Duh, this guy Gordon is a winner. Where's he going with this?*

Dale Gordon continued. "Were you with him the night of the alleged incident?"

"Yes."

"Mr. Curry was in a venue of extreme revelry. Was he conscious and aware of his surroundings?"

As soon as the question left his lips, Kyle rose from the defendant's table. "I object, Your Honor, to the plaintiff's line of questioning. The inference of inebriation is being made in a last-ditch effort to smear the credibility of my client."

Judge Powell agreed. "Sustained. Please rephrase the question, Mr. Gordon."

Plaintiff's representation nodded while motioning to the court steno-grapher. "Strike that question. Mr. Hill, do you have knowledge of the drinking habits of Stanton Curry?"

Drinking habits? Drinking habits? Kyle seethed. "Objection again, Your Honor. What my client drinks socially is totally irrelevant to this proceeding. That my adversary has the audacity to imply alcoholism is ludicrous."

"Ludicrous? I didn't know Mike Tyson was in the courtroom today," Gordon cracked.

"Excuse me?" Kyle asked.

"Should I repeat it?"

Livid, Kyle moved quickly from behind the defense table and approached his opposition. His shimmering rage made him oblivious to the rhythmic pounding of Judge Powell's gavel and her command for order in the court. "Counselor, do you see Mr. Tyson in this courtroom? Are you making this case personal? Explain yourself, Gordon! You're supposed to be an intelligent man, so explain yourself! Because if you would like..." He raised his finger in a trigger-like fashion in the direction of Gordon's temple "...after the proceeding is over, I'd be more than willing to show you what Brownsville, Brooklyn is like."

"Yo man, then bring it on," Gordon mocked.

"I will! You better believe that!"

Quizzically, yet calmly, Gordon turned to the judge. Shaking his head incredulously, he continued his antagonistic ploy. "Your Honor, I'd like to move for an order removing defendant's counsel on the grounds of his inarticulacy and misrepresentation of his client."

"Plaintiff, your claims are baseless, and a mockery of the legal system!" Kyle railed as he returned to his table.

As the courtroom buzzed, Stanton Curry leaned over to his counsel. "What the fuck are you doing?" he strained through his teeth, barely above a whisper. "This is my life you're fucking with! Calm the fuck down, and do what you gotta do!" Kyle, heeding the voice of reason in his client's expletive-laden plea, buttoned his suit and regained his composure.

Judge Powell, stunned by the escalation of the outburst, stood up and said, "Officers, clear the courtroom, *NOW!* Recess until tomorrow morning, nine-thirty! Counselors, in my chambers, *NOW!*"

Pacing the floor inside her private confines, after throwing her robe on a nearby sofa, Judge Powell's scale was tipped toward anger as she sat down in the chair behind her desk. Reigning in her emotions slowly, she stood up once more as the bickering attorneys entered her chambers. Closing the door to her office softly, she issued a stern command. "Sit down." Like two obedient kids suspected of wrongdoing, they sat in the wooden chairs in front of her desk. Before doing this, Kyle tapped his seat to make sure it wasn't electric.

"It seems we have a problem in professionalism here," the judge intoned in a measured, yet stern voice. "In my seven years on the bench I have never witnessed such aberrant behavior in my courtroom. Ever! And while I…" She paused to gauge the tenor of her wrath as she moved to her seat. "And while the court cannot rationally explain the conflict between highly regarded professionals as you men are, much less resolve the apparent personal bitterness that stems from your differences, you cannot lose sight of the fact that this is my courtroom, and the inane absurdities witnessed today, in a case of this magnitude, could have you both spending time in jail!

"Your conduct today was inexcusable as well as intolerable. Any attempt at repeating today's actions will result in a mistrial! Mr. Gordon, your motion to remove defendant's lead counsel is denied on the grounds of insufficient evidence. Your claims of misrepresentation have no merit, and I am holding you in contempt, which carries a fine of five thousand dollars!"

Like a kid that had been slapped on his wrist, Gordon extended a hand to Kyle Watson.

"My actions were indecent today, and I owe you an apology."

Grudgingly, Kyle took the peace offering. "Yeah, man. Apology accepted." The reluctant truce was interrupted by the stern tone of an authoritarian with a job to do.

"Mr. Watson, do you have any explanation for your loss of control today?"

Planted squarely in front of the firing squad, Kyle paused as his eyes searched the floor for a prudent explanation for his loss of control. Then he spoke.

"No. I don't, Your Honor. I offer my sincerest apologies, not only to you, but to those present in the courtroom who witnessed the disgraceful scene, as well as the court system and the profession of which I serve."

His words now flowing smoothly, Kyle continued in the hopes that his eloquent take on the matter would lessen his punishment. "How do you manifest the acceptance of responsibility? Initially, by admitting your culpability, and then, by showing a sense of responsibility for your actions. I hope I have done this with my admission of guilt, for I do not wish to bring further or greater disgrace to the hallowed institution of which I revere dearly."

Throughout his hokey but heartfelt plea, Kyle explored the eyes of this adjudicator with the hopes of detecting any indication of what she was thinking, where she stood. That her face remained stoic was a bad sign.

His vibes were on target. Rising from her maple-colored chair, Judge Powell then positioned herself directly in front of Kyle, propping herself on her desk. Then, in a sharp, caustic manner, she laid down the law. "Kyle Watson, your menacing behavior today in the State Court of New York defied logical explanation, and we cannot lose sight of that. We also cannot lose sight that it is your duty as a professional to set an exemplary standard for others to follow. It is up to you to uphold the moralistic protocol of our legal forefathers. Your imprudent antics today showed that you have difficulty in doing so.

"Kyle Watson, you will be held in contempt. And while the verbal confrontation with Mr. Gordon will be treated as off-the-record communication and stricken from the minutes as you are allowed to continue in your representation of Stanton Curry, you will be fined ten thousand dollars for your threats of harm directed at Mr. Gordon. You are free to go."

Though defeat raced through him, Kyle took his reprimand with the controlled poise he wished he had exhibited earlier. "Your Honor, you have done the right thing, and again I apologize for putting you in an unenviable position," he said while watching Dale Gordon leave the chambers.

"I know I did the right thing, counselor." This is what Judge Powell's lips said. As she watched the shell-shocked attorney make his way to the exit barrier, Amanda replaced the hard judge for a second, trying to lighten the mood considerably. "So, you're from Brownsville, huh?"

Stopping in his tracks, Kyle was startled by the small talk. "Yes. The Tilden Projects, off Lavonia Avenue."

"I grew up there as well, Mr. Watson. On Riverdale Avenue, in a beige house between Bristol and Hopkinson. It's a small world, counselor."

"A real small world, Your Honor. A real small world."

He had lost, Kyle knew. Passing the media in an attempt to get a taxi uptown was an insult to his wounded pride; knowing he was the front-page news on every newspaper come sunrise tortured him even more. Curling his lips in an effort to conceal his obvious pain, the reality of Judge Powell's penalty had his head hunched between his shoulders as the vehicle sped off amidst flashing cameras.

Returning to his office at Cohen, Schindler and Brody looking forlorn, that Kyle Watson had to face his mentor after the events at court was an even worse fate. He had been hand-picked to defend Stanton Curry, and with one slip in judgment, he lost money for the firm and may have lost not only this high-profile case, but his job as well.

Another burden weighed heavily on his brain, causing him to wince. He had invested all his energies in being a role model for African-Americans and hoped that his ascension to partnership would deliver a message back to his Brooklyn roots. Feeling he had relinquished the mantle he felt honored to carry for those brothers pushing mail carts aspiring to "Be Like Kyle," the reality of his actions seemed unbearable. He had made it that much harder for the next brother trying to make partner.

All of these fears were amplified when he heard the "Please come to my office immediately" message left on his voicemail from Stephen Cohen. *Having one reprieve from the electric chair is agonizing enough,* Kyle thought, slowly making his way to the closed brown door down the hall. *No matter what, everything will be fine. Have faith, Kyle.* With that, he opened the entrance to his unknown.

"You wanted to see me, Steve?"

Stephen Cohen was looking out the long pane, watching the city's twilight from above. Turning to face his disgraced pupil, his ruddy face was emotionless as he took a puff from his cigar. "Please, Kyle, sit down."

Complying, Kyle felt that executioner feeling all over again. *Blindfold and cigarette please, or am I being strapped in?* he thought. "Listen, I just wanted you to know, Steve, that whatever you decide of my fate, I know it will be for the best interests of the firm."

"I know, Kyle. I know." Stephen Cohen, in spite of his aggressive nature, was a genial, compassionate man, especially toward his pupil. Veering from the subject of reprimand, the senior partner struck a comfortable rapport with his worried counselor, their topics ranging from fishing to the actual trial. As was the case earlier, Kyle was given no clue as to what the outcome of the conversation would be. Then suddenly, it came. "Mr. Watson, in trying to perform the impossible task of understanding your outburst, the fact remains that an associate with designs on partnership cannot conduct himself in an unprofessional manner; especially during a trial of this nature. Not to mention that you may very well have justified the racist reservations of our good friend, Mr. Rabinowitz." Kyle bit his lip as he again faced the seriousness and peril of his actions. Cohen continued. "However, due to your outstanding effort in your attempt to exonerate Stanton Curry, you will be allowed to continue in his defense. I have convinced our client—with no small amount of cajoling— that this was the best thing to do."

Making no effort to conceal his relief, Kyle finally exhaled; the weight of the world removed from his shoulders at last. "Thank you, Steve. Thank you."

Cohen smiled. "I spoke to our client about twenty minutes after the incident and got the particulars. Between you, me, and these four walls, that you didn't haul off and deck Dale Gordon for his obvious smear tactic was a feat in itself. Did he get disbarred?"

"No. He and I were held in contempt."

"That carries a heavy fine that the firm has to pay, am I correct?"

Kyle nodded. "Ten thousand dollars."

Cohen's smile dimmed as he turned beet red. Somehow, he remained poised. "That's a hell of a fine, Watson."

"I know." Kyle paused, and in a moment of candor, continued. "I guess my bid for partnership went out the window today, huh?"

Lowering his head as he heard the inquiry, the slow nod of Cohen's head told it all. Out of his mouth, however, came words of encouragement that came from mentor/pupil privileges.

"Try again next year, after this incident blows over. Listen, Watson, why don't you go home and get some rest. You have to come back strong tomorrow."

"I agree, sir."

Thinking in hindsight upon his arrival home, Kyle wanted to give himself a swift kick in the hind parts for losing his cool earlier in court. Unaccustomed to his defensive response, that he did this with such an aggressive undertone perturbed him. Taking a sip from his drink as he sat at his computer, he realized that the Curry case, while winding down, had exacted a heavy toll. It was important for him to maintain his focus and keep a level head regardless of what idiocy he might hear from the prosecution. Sighing, he closed his eyes and thought of the ramifications of what could have happened today. Though reprimanded from all corners, the fact that he still represented Stanton Curry and maintained the trust of the senior partner after a day of turbulence eased his pain. Winning the case would go even further in reestablishing his dignity, he thought. Taking that thought into another world, before long his breathing became a soft snore.

Damn, Kyle! Why couldn't you have kept your cool? I didn't want to punish you, but I had to. In replaying the courtroom incident all the way home, Amanda was saddened by its aftermath. Tortured with guilt for handling a precarious situation, for the first time ever, Judge Powell felt remorseful for the responsibilities of her profession.

Peering deep into Kyle's eyes that afternoon, she saw only remnants of the confident swagger he displayed in defending Stanton Curry, and the vultures of vulnerability were picking away at the remains. In her presence was a professionally exposed Black man that was a survivor of mean streets; rugged hostile territory she herself had overcome. She saw a man who probably ate jam sandwiches (*two pieces of bread jammed together*, she joked) during hungry nights at college and law school and probably struggled every day against White attorneys conditioned to believe their skin color is of preferred status in the court of law. Distraught over the fact that she had to administer the appropriate penalty for his actions, that she couldn't uplift his spirits afterwards only intensified her pain.

Somehow, she maintained her feelings of desire for Kyle Watson, for she noticed, and loved his intellectual diversity. *Mmmph. An articulate brother with a ghetto streak. I like that*, she thought. Recalling the attorney's urban ultimatum to his counterpart, she felt a chill race up her spine as she continued to eagerly fill in details of her burgeoning fantasy. *He's about six-one. Definitely a basketball player. I love his coal-colored pupils and his bald head. And damn, that chocolate skin has me tingling. This man could get done in a hurry.* As a slumbering juror might respond to the pounding of the gavel, Amanda recovered from her lustful thoughts with a jolt. In spite of her longing passions, she was a professional with a job to do.

Though determined to steer the right course in court, as she stood on her doorstep, Amanda was unable to shake the vision of the sexy Kyle Watson. Warring with the visible fantasy and wanting to rid herself from the trying day made her even more fervent in her desire to shower Mr. Choc-A-Lot with uninhibited affections and temptations, and have him return them in kind. Oozing at the mere thought of all of this, she went about the usual routine of dinner, news and a bath. At nine-thirty, Amanda realized that she had thirty minutes before her Chocolate fantasy appeared in their private chat room. Closing her eyes, she leaned back in her chair and began to reflect upon the Stanton Curry trial and the reprimand she levied to Kyle after the courtroom fiasco. Before long, a wave of sleepiness fell upon her.

She woke up in her desk chair, at 3:20 a.m., holding an empty bottle of Riesling. The night was so still, and her sleep so fitful that even the inviting tingle of the incoming message was enough to awaken her. *Oh God, how long has he been trying to reach me? I can't believe I fell asleep*, she muttered.

CHOC-A-LOT: Are you awake, Kitty?

KITTY: Mmm, what time is it?

CHOC-A-LOT: It's pretty early in the morning, and I apologize for this intrusion, as well as missing our scheduled chat. It was a long day.

KITTY: No apologies necessary. I had a pretty rough one myself. So, Mr. Lot, is this a kitty call?

CHOC-A-LOT: (sigh) Not really. I need someone to talk to.

KITTY: Hmmm. It must have been a bad day if you're not in the mood for some nasty, you cyber stallion.

CHOC-A-LOT: (smile) Yeah, well. You may not think so, but there's a lot more to me than just erotic words on a screen.

KITTY: I didn't realize that you wanted to reveal so much to me.

CHOC-A-LOT: I didn't want to, but I realize that there's more than a sexual connection here. There's a mental one as well.

Eyebrows arched, Amanda's inner thoughts were confirmed by his statement. Online, however, she remained coy.

KITTY: Oh, really? That's good to know. So, what do you propose we do about it?

CHOC-A-LOT: Well, Ms. Kitty, let's talk about the day we come from behind these words.

Amanda's eyes, with sleep in the corners of them, grew wide.

KITTY: Okay. Let's rap about it. (pause) I'm not going in with any predetermined attitudes, but I will say this: The fact that we had cyber sex makes me comfortable.

CHOC-A-LOT: So, are you sure that I'm not some kind of a freak? LOL.

KITTY: LOL. Well, are you?

CHOC-A-LOT: You'll find out. (wink).

KITTY: I'm looking forward to it.

CHOC-A-LOT: I should warn you that sometimes I have problems doing more than one thing at a time…At least well.

KITTY: Mmm, well that hasn't been a problem so far.

Kyle had to reflect for a second before venturing into unchartered territory. Initially, the chat with his favorite feline was just a diversion. However visible contact was forthcoming, and as much as he anticipated her presence, the words from a not too distant past haunted him. *Being with you is like being alone.* Torn between his past and hopeful future, Kyle decided to roll the dice.

CHOC-A-LOT: So, when do we meet?

⌒

" CHAPTER SEVEN

Y o, man, you straight?" Stanton Curry asked Kyle before they entered the courthouse. "We're not gonna have any more of those around-the-way threats today, are we?"

"Nah, man. I'm cool."

"Watson, are you sure?" Stephen Cohen, who came to oversee the day's events added.

"Boss, I'll be fine."

"That's good to know," Curry announced with a game-face look. "Now, let's go finish these dudes."

Cohen concurred. "Kyle, close the deal today."

Watson nodded as the impeccably dressed trio entered the house of Powell stride for confident stride, their swagger fully restored as they seated themselves in unison at the defense table.

Refocusing his energy on the case, Kyle watched his adversary, perhaps rattled by the events of a day earlier, bungle his cross-examination, making it more and more apparent to Kyle that he was ill-prepared for the excellence of the defense team.

This point was reinforced during Kyle's closing argument. Reiterating the point that this was a simple shakedown on the plaintiff's attack, he even took a shot at Dale Gordon, calling the district attorney's case against his defendant "softer than ice cream." Drawing guffaws from the media in tow, even Judge Powell's effort to conceal a smirk was futile as she sustained Gordon's objection out of sympathy.

Charging that the plaintiff tried to hold his client up as the epitome for everything wrong with sports, a poster child of all bad things, Kyle placed emphasis on the countless hours Curry devoted to charitable causes, not to mention the many appearances at cancer centers in both New York and Orlando visiting with the terminally ill. He closed his stirring testimony by asking the jury for objectivity. "Sometimes, people have the tendency to decide how much we like a celebrity, sports figure or politician before deciding whether or not to throw the book at them. I truly hope that is not the case here," he announced in a booming tone.

Upon taking his seat, Stanton Curry made no effort to hide his emotions. With tears lurking from the corners of his eyes, he greeted Watson with the soul brother handshake. "Thanks, man. You did well."

Leaning over to his client, he said in a whisper, "When I told you, I got your back, dawg, I meant it. Let's hope that the jury has it, too."

"It's only a formality," Stephen Cohen added.

Coming with an unexpected swiftness, after less than two hours of deliberation, the jury returned to the courtroom. An anxious silence filled the venue as Judge Powell asked the obvious.

"Has the jury reached a verdict?"

"Yes, it has, Your Honor." With that, the foreman handed her a piece of paper. As she read the verdict and peered the courtroom through sightless, impassive eyes, Kyle thought she would give the moment a split second before the jury would. She hadn't. Then, came the ruling.

"We, the jury in the above entitled action, find the defendant, Stanton Curry, not guilty of the crime of battery..." With the verdict, an air of professional attachment evaporated from the courtroom, causing a mild whiplash of reactions. Soaking it all in as his client pounded his back in exoneration, Kyle couldn't help notice the blatant polarization in the media circles. White journalists seemed dismayed at the news that they couldn't bring another brother down, Black correspondents gleefully put pen to pad as they restored the credibility of one of its own.

The more things change, the more they stay the same, he thought.

The victory came as a small piece of redemption for Kyle Watson, for the positive verdict restored his aspirations for higher ground. *Being partner by thirty-four isn't bad*, he thought as Cohen, noticing his blandness to the moment, approached him amidst the hysteria.

"You were exceptional, Kyle. Yesterday's events were a setback. Don't lose any sleep over it," his mentor stated.

"I had a great teacher. Thanks, Steve."

"Listen, Watson. After your office wrap-up, take a couple of days off. I'll see you on Monday."

"Thanks, Boss. I'll see you bright and early."

"Hey Kyle, thanks a lot," said Curry over the swarm of hounding paparazzi that surrounded them as they made their way to the street. "I owe you big time."

"I was glad to help out, bro."

"So check it out...I wanna celebrate this victory tonight. Let's say we meet up at Perk's..."

Kyle interrupted his client with a dubious look. "Man, isn't that how we got here in the first place?"

Curry, noticing the concerned expression of his overbearing agent, had to agree. "True dat. Besides, champions toil in solitude. Right?"

Smiling at the suggestion, Kyle knew exactly how he would really celebrate his achievement. *It's time to meet Chocolate Kitty.*

Judge Powell ended the day by soaking in a hot scented bubble bath. Sipping from a glass of Stoli Madras as she laid her head back on the bath pillow, she closed her eyes and reflected on the day's events. Pleased that the high profile trial was over, she was also relieved that Stanton Curry was exonerated. Hoping that he would never appear before her again, she prayed he would monitor his behavior in an effort to be a positive role model for the younger generations who idolized him.

The thought of not enjoying the daily sight of Kyle Watson in her courtroom, however, saddened her. There was something about him: maybe his stature, his magnetic presence and confident ability as a defense attorney, his swaggering stride; something about him stirred her sexually. From a professional standpoint, she was resigned to admit it was probably better that she didn't know what it was.

Brushing those thoughts aside, Amanda focused her mind on her meeting with Choc-A-Lot. Accepting his invitation to dinner at Copeland's in Harlem during their last chat, Friday night could not arrive fast enough. Agreeing to don a sexy red dress, that her cyber mate agreed to wear a matching tie heightened her anticipation. Careful not to reveal so much as a trace of her excitement, she ended their last chat with a sexy "meow." *Mmmm, I can't wait to purr for him in person*, she thought.

As Michael Jackson's "Break of Dawn" had her hips swaying underwater, the thought of clinging bodies joined as one in an erotic game of touch and go flooded her mind with questions requiring answers that only physical copulation would resolve. Would he be as sexy in person as he was during their chats? Or would he disappoint her? Amanda's instincts assured her that he wouldn't.

In her mind's eye, Choc-A-Lot, the name he had given himself, created the vision of rich mahogany skin—skin she couldn't wait to feel against her own silken perfumed flesh. Imagining his hard, chiseled body positioned above, she dreamed that he lowered himself, wrapped his full lips around her slick, steamy tunnel and ate away. Envisioning him licking and sucking her and moving his tongue in and out of every place he could find, every muscle in her body was straining at the edge of an orgasm.

Damn, Amanda thought, *it must be the drink*. Touching herself, she envisioned his member. Dark, thick and hard, yet velvety to her touch. Wanting to taste it, eager to suck it, yearning to feel it and longing to savor it, would he be a gentle lover, or would he be a rough rider? *A little of both wouldn't be bad*, she smirked. Imagining herself climbing upon him and sliding down his engorged object, she squeezed her muscles tight as if the tip of his purple bulb touched her womb, then entered her with a fierce stroke. Would she ride him until the break of dawn? *If it were only Friday night*, she moaned as she reached her peak. Panting and groaning as she descended, she quickly finished her drink and convinced herself that she had to have Mr. Lot, if only for one night. Friday would be that night.

~

CHAPTER EIGHT

The moment of truth had arrived for Kyle Watson as he departed the southbound "1" train at 157th Street. Wiping the nervous beads of perspiration off his chocolate pate, the cool, collected confidence Kyle the attorney displayed during the Stanton Curry trial was nowhere to be found; some tightly wound impostor was a stand-in this particular evening. And rightfully so: This was his first date since Anita gave him his walking papers two years ago.

Looking at his wristwatch and noticing the time—*eight forty-five*—he envisioned Chocolate Kitty at a table in the trendy soul food restaurant, awaiting his entrance. *In reality, she's just arriving, if she's the punctual type*, he mused. Requesting that his temptress arrive there first, that she eagerly agreed made him that much more jittery.

Deciding on the twelve-block walk in an effort to gather his bearings, a myriad of anxious thoughts bombarded his mind as he asked a florist for a single red rose. *What if she's a bore? Nah, she couldn't be. She's so sexy online, so open-minded, so witty. What if I'm the bore? Nah, I'm too cool for that. Or am I? I hope she likes her rose. Better yet, I hope she likes me.* Courtroom magic was as smooth to Kyle as a Savion Glover dance step, matters of lust and passion were an entirely different story. With each step down Broadway, however, his initial anxiety was replaced by a peaceful calm. *Fuck it. Whatever happens, happens.* He was going to go with the flow, he decided. By the time he turned left onto 145th Street, the preliminary insecurities were gone, having been hammered away by positive energy. Reaching the entrance barrier of Copeland's, he decided to peek through the window before going in. Sitting alone at a table in the middle of the restaurant wearing a provocative red dress was Judge Powell. *OH SHIT!!!*

⌐

OH SHIT!!! Amanda hoped she didn't see who she thought she did staring at her from the outside of Copeland's. *What is Kyle Watson doing here?* she mused as the handsome attorney opened the entrance. Admiring his attire as he walked in the direction of her table, *Hmmm, he's wearing that black, double-breasted suit well. And I love the way that red tie complements his white shirt. Where's his date?* Then it hit her. *That red tie. That single red rose.* By the time the shock worked its way through her heated bloodstream, Kyle was handing her the flower of passion.

"Excuse me, Miss. Is this seat taken?"

Amanda had to be sure it was him. As a judge, she was not about to take the chance of assuming and making a complete ass out of herself. So she quickly responded, "Actually, it is. I'm meeting someone here tonight. Someone by the name of…"

"Choc-A-Lot," Kyle answered a little too easily. The knowing smirk on his face telling her all she needed to know, *Oh God, it is him,* she thought. Relieved by the revelation yet hesitant to let her guard down, the adjudicator in her motioned to the empty seat. "Sit down, counselor."

Once Kyle complied, an awkward silence hung over the table as the couple evaluated the situation they now found themselves in. Sensing their shared discomfort, Kyle broke the ice. "I guess no introductions are needed."

"I guess not, Mr. Lot." When the waiter appeared with a bottle of champagne and began pouring, Amanda explained, "I hope you don't mind. I took the liberty of ordering a bottle, in celebration of our meeting."

"Of course not," Kyle responded. As the waiter left, giving them the privacy they so desperately needed at this point, he continued, "So, Ms. Kitty. Now that we've come from behind the facades, I guess our little cat and mouse game is over, huh?"

Smiling through her numbness as they clinked glasses, Amanda responded, "Oh no, counselor. I think not. Mr. Lot made some rather enticing promises that I intend to hold him to. Of course," she continued as she took a sip from her flute and sat the glass back down, "I could always hold him in contempt."

Taking her abandoned glass, before Kyle moved to respond to her statement, he found the print of her red lipstick and sipped away. "Mmmm, you taste as good as you look." Pausing to capture her blush with wanting eyes, he next entertained her thoughts. "Contempt? Contempt of what?"

Leaning forward, Amanda smiled wickedly. "Contempt of kitty."

"Ohhhh. The *kitty*. We can't forget the kitty, now can we?"

"I think not, counselor. The kitty's been in heat ever since she came in contact with Mr. Lot. It looks like he's got some work to do. Do you think he's up for it?" As she took her glass back from him, Kyle felt a foot tugging, then climbing under his pants leg. Rubbing her wayward stem, that her calves were muscular and shapely set his groin afire with desire.

Leaning back toward her, Kyle retorted her challenge with a whisper. "For your information, Ms. Kitty, Mr. Lot has been up, *been standing at attention*, from day one. So the question is, is my kitty ready to purr? Can she handle it?"

"Oh, yes, Mr. Watson." Flushed with want, Amanda stood, anxious to go.

"Where are you off to, Ms. Kitty?" Kyle teased with a smirk.

"It's time to bring this charade to an end. Let's go." She threw enough money on the table to cover the champagne.

Kyle, after picking up her currency, returning it to her soft hands, and placing his own down, deliberately tormented her. "But what about dinner? I was a little hungry."

Cocking an eye that indicated only one thing, Amanda replied saucily, "You'll get your dinner. Now let's go, Mr. Lot. It seems to me you have a job to do."

~⁓⁓

"So, Mr. Lot," Amanda said as they reached her Striver's Row abode.

"Would you like to come up for an aperitif?" Having discussed the trial during their eight block stroll, as well as getting acquainted, Kyle felt as if his dreams were realized once he talked to Amanda. Though nine years older than he at forty-two, he was amazed at her bubbling youthfulness. Enamored with her passion for weight and cardio training, all her nervousness was gone when he revealed his passion for basketball, and the fact he regularly had his way with Stanton Curry during summer league games.

"Why aren't you in the "L" like he is?" she asked. Upon hearing the phrasing of her query, Kyle knew he had struck gold. Not only was Amanda Powell a well-respected intellect, but an around-the-way girl as well. *After all, she's from "The Ville,"* he thought. He could have the best of both worlds, if they got involved.

Not tonight, however. This chocolate kitten awakened hibernating passions in a soul longing to display the fruition of a mental, physical and carnal connection. And he wanted to act on those feelings.

"Yes. I would love to join you for a cordial," Kyle answered. It was on.

Inside, Amanda dimmed the lights and turned on her stereo. Instantly, the seductive sounds of Brian McKnight's "Lonely" invaded their shared zone. "Mmmm," she moaned in a deep, raspy tone. "Can you move your hips to the time of this song, Kyle?"

Eyebrows arched yet again, this time however in full view for his hopeful to see, Kyle moved to her, placed himself close, and felt her heat as their bodies became one in rhythm. Kissing the nape of her neck slowly and tenderly as his strong hands made their way up and down her frame, no answer was needed at this point. Feeling the contours that strained for its release from a form-fitting red dress, Kyle's masculine staff offered strong encouragement for an outfit change.

Grabbing his erect tent as she turned to face him, Amanda pecked his full, kissable lips and consented to his mind downstairs. "I won't be long," she said, scurrying away.

She returned about ten minutes later, to the sounds of Janet's "Oooh, Baby." Dressed in a silk red Asian robe while carrying body lotion, that she mouthed "When you're fucking me…" as Ms. Jackson sang those lyrics had Kyle hoping he packed his "A" game. Moving to her bar adjacent to the sofa he was on, Amanda fixed herself a milky beige drink appropriately called a "Screaming Orgasm." Watson got the message loud and clear.

In case he hadn't, she was sure to deliver it with what came next. "Can I sit on your lap, Mr. Lot?"

Slowly, Kyle nodded, and in a matter of seconds his kitten straddled him. Taking delight in the enlarged girth beneath her wide hips, she said, "I see you come as advertised, counselor."

"You look different without your makeup. Even more beautiful."

Amanda smiled seductively. "I'm not Judge Powell anymore, Kyle. I'm Amanda, your Chocolate Kitty." As if to emphasize her point, she purred like Eartha Kitt, then lapped from her drink like an aroused feline. "Mmm. Chocolate Kitty loves to drink milk."

Feeling an immediate rush of blood race through him, Kyle pecked the lips of his fantasy come true. "Would you like to taste my milk?"

His answer would come not from words, but from action. Submitting to the moment, Amanda's tongue began a dance with his, triggering a series of tremors throughout her body. Sharing this mutual mamba, Kyle inhaled her scent and breath as he joined this treasured torture. Venturing into this deeper place with his kitten, a place calmly wild in sensations and fantasies, the kiss between the couple deepened as they scaled the walls of ecstasy…together.

Feelings of color and passion escaped Amanda as Kyle removed her robe. Her stunning anatomy craving animalistic satisfaction, hues of turquoise, violets and magentas came to surface as her chocolate vision ferociously flicked at her nipples with an out-of-control snake between aroused lips.

Laying her down on the couch gently, Kyle quickly undressed himself, then returned to the passionate fire before him. Meeting her mouth once more while gazing into bubbly eyes, that he saw an equal hunger gave strong indication to the pleasure that lay ahead. Teeth and tongues clashing like a harmonious jazz note, a deep wave of ardor pounded his senses.

That same intense rush that was torrential in depth enveloped Amanda as well. Her body tingling from the sculpted wings encompassing her, she appreciated the form of his back as her hands ventured from his small to his buttocks. Kyle's response to her exploring shocked her.

"Stick a finger in. It's okay."

"Shit! You are a freak!" Hearing his request turned Amanda on to the ninth power. Reaching for her lotion and lubricating her index finger, she locked Kyle in a deep French kiss as she teased his rectum in a circular motion, then slowly inserted a finger. Slowly increasing the tempo, Chocolate Kitty wanted him to erupt.

By this time, Kyle had the feeling described in male circles as *The Knot*. Also known as *blue balls*, the aching, wanting sensation at his groin was akin to a Federal Express placement: its release of tension must absolutely, positively be delivered to its erotic destination. On time, tardy, whatever: it *must* be released in a timely fashion, somewhere.

Somehow willing his pending explosion to wane, she would have to wait for his creamy satisfaction. *Time to purr, Kitty*, he thought as he put a halt to his own gratification. Removing her from his anus and venturing south, Mr. Lot moved his tongue along her firm body affectionately. Fluttering like a butterfly as he teased her navel, then her inner thighs, he felt her body tense in preparation of pleasure as he went lower. Touching his lips to her entrance, he complied to Her Honor's next command.

"Don't give it to me yet, Kyle…Please don't…Not yet, baby…Not yet…"

Tracing his tongue across her vaginal lips, the fire of Amanda's libido was on the precipice of ignition as he made her clit jump with his nose. It felt like heaven to her when Kyle invaded her with a finger, then two.

"Please, baby, put one more in," she panted. Obliging, the steel at Kyle's groin throbbed in expectation of something juicy. He had to taste it first, so after licking her essence off his digits, his brim slithered into her salty sweet channel of lust.

From the minute his mouth pried open her nectar, it became *his pussy*. Weak from the turbulence of long suppressed desires, tremors that were dormant in Amanda's belly for what seemed like an eternity surfaced with Kyle's tongue bath. Caressing her tunnel, he matched the fluid motion of her hips as he went from labia, to its interior, then, to the swollen nodule that renders a woman weak.

Heating a burning ember and flaming coals of rapture as he performed an oral solo on her starved furnace, Kyle pleasured Amanda with an unrestrained abandon. His masterful performance caused his kitty to grit her teeth so vigorously she almost removed their enamel coating.

"Mmmm, you're making my kitty so happy," Amanda groaned. "Get that shit, Daddy...sssss...Oh...Shit...get it, Kyle..." Lost in a passionate zone of lust, Amanda was approaching another world, a pleasurable dimension where orgasms have substance, sight, texture and sound. Unable to hold back any longer, Amanda pressed his face to her hips as the muscles in her legs matched the wave of contractions going through her. Drinking the liquid that flowed from his kitty, the taste of her reminded Kyle of pineapple juice: tart, yet sweet.

Having survived these seizures, Amanda's body trembled uncontrollably as all she could do is look down at him with a mixture of amazement, disbelief and unending gratitude. "Kyle, that was better than I imagined online," she announced as her tremors trailed off.

"I'm glad you enjoyed it, Amanda."

"It's your turn, baby. Chocolate Kitty needs her milk."

Knowing what was next, the couple repositioned themselves so Amanda could quench her insatiable thirst. Stroking him in her hand, she could feel the pulse of his manhood as it thickened. Increasing the tempo as she slid her hand up and down his long, chocolate shaft as her mouth formed a wet, welcoming entrance. As she moved her tongue along its aching tip, a deep groan escaped Kyle as she took him in inch by inch.

"Yes, Kitty, just like that..." Her oral tunnel retreating and resubmitting his hardened tool in nice, sloppy pastures, Amanda relaxed her throat and accommodated his eight inches easily, taking him to the base of his pubic hairs with nary a gag.

"Mmmm, my Choc-A-Lot bar sure tastes good," she drooled. Stroking him with her hands as she sucked, she placed the right amount of pressure on his veined tool. Feeling him get harder and harder in her mouth as he whimpered, Amanda kept doing what she was doing as Kyle tried to swim from the waves of euphoric bliss flowing through him.

"Mmm, give it to Mommy," Amanda moaned as he released a warm stream of Choc-A-Lot milk. Wildly swallowing as much as she could, like the kitten she was, Amanda licked the salty excess from her caramel paws and nibbled on his still swollen head.

"You're one of those, I see." She smiled from his waist.

"Yes… I am," Kyle responded as he regained control of his body. He was one of those men who maintained a full erection after ejaculation.

"Let me ride it slowly while you catch your breath." Feeling the length at his groin throb once more as they moved to her plush bedroom, Kyle lowered his kitten onto the queen-sized bed.

"You don't have to ride it, Mommy. Daddy wants to take care of you." Hearing those words moistened Amanda with anticipation. Waiting so long to fill the wetness of her kitty with his hardness, she could hardly contain herself as she was desperate to bury him into her.

Feeling her sugar walls grip, then pulsate around his muscle, Amanda widened her caramel, stem-created "V" to accommodate Kyle as she trembled from his first stroke. Kissing her with a sweet tenderness as he started slowly, soon Amanda's soaked passage eagerly accepted his long staff, and the tempo quickened. Biting his lip to suppress this long-anticipated feeling of physical bliss, Kyle's pleasure was harder and harder to disguise.

"Shit, Kitty, you feel so good."

"Then show me, counselor. Show me how much you like it!" Amanda barked.

With that, Kyle began to pleasure her with the unchained ferocity of a tiger. Accelerating and accentuating each down stroke, this chocolate kitty would become his with each thorough thrust, each pace increasing plunge into her amorous abyss. Hitting it as if his life depended on her total satisfaction, the unbridled passion of the moment set both ablaze.

"C'mon Choc-A-Lot! Take this kitty from me! Take it! Take it!"

Gasping for breath below, gripping his shoulders as the intensity of her urgency increased, an urge to be as deep within his lover as humanly possible drove Kyle to uncontrollable heights. Sinking her nails deep into his back, the pleasure felt from titillating pump after tantalizing pump turned this kitty cat flush.

"Ooh, Dadddeeeeee...I'm goonnnaaaa cummm foooor yoooou reaalll haarrdd!" Amanda shouted as she went wild, tossing, twisting and screaming in joy. Shaking violently, she pursed her lips as her juices drenched the sheets.

Approaching his climax as well, Kyle's body stiffened, then shuddered as he experienced the light-headed rush whenever a man surrenders his seed. Taking a cue from his explosion as if she'd made love to him in a prior life, Amanda milked his chocolate steel with her muscles, pulling him deeper in as he pushed.

Breathless, the cybermates turned sex partners collapsed in total satisfaction as the sensuously simultaneous pounding of their hearts spoke volumes.

"So, Your Honor," Kyle said through labored breaths. "Let's talk about that ten-thousand dollar fine."

"Don't even try it, counselor!"

Finding just enough energy to shrug his shoulders, Kyle laughed. "Oh well. Can't fault a brother for trying."

You're making me wet

EARL SEWELL

~

CHAPTER ONE

"All right, come on, Dad," urged Ted as he hovered over his father at the rear of the bench press. "Give me ten good reps," he recapitulated as he prepared to spot his father. Samuel hoisted the bar up off its stand. "Come on, this is easy money." Samuel allowed the steel bar, which had two hundred pounds on it, to come completely down to his chest before he pressed it back up in the air. By the time Samuel reached the eighth repetition, his muscles were taxed and he could feel his strength diminishing. "Come on, Dad. Push it. Push it." Ted continued his squawking. "Come on. Two more." Ted watched as Samuel struggled a bit with the ninth repetition. "Come on. One more," he roared. Samuel released a grunt through clinched teeth as the last rep took its toll.

"Wooo!" Samuel exhaled as he placed the bar back on its rack and sat upright on the bench.

"That was all you, Dad," Ted commented as he waited for his father to give up the bench and give him a spot for his last set. Ted tussled with his set and was only able to squeeze out six reps before he had to put the bar back on the rack.

"That's it for me, man," uttered Ted. "It's time for my butt to hit the shower."

Samuel replied, "I can agree with you on that one because both of us are funkier than morning breath."

"That's not funk, Dad. That's just hard work," Ted explained as he grabbed his towel.

"Oh, is that what they're calling it nowadays?" Samuel laughed.

The two men made their way downstairs to the locker room where they both removed their clothes and walked into the shower area of the health club. Samuel turned the handle, stepped to the side, and waited for the water to warm up. When the temperature was just right he stood under the stream, closed his eyes and allowed the pressure of the water to relax him.

"Do they have hot water up in here today?" asked Ted, breaking Samuel's euphoric moment in the shower.

"Yeah, it feels good too." Samuel placed his hand under the soap dispenser, pressed the button, and lathered up his chest. He looked at his son as he turned on the water of another shower stall on the opposite wall. He paid close attention to his son as he lathered up his shoulders, arms, and long, brown shaft. Ted was an exact replica of him, only younger. Their skin was a rich hue of dark brown that sometimes appeared to have a mysterious purple glow to it. The old folks from down South would say that the sun had kissed their skin because of the glow. Samuel admired his son's defined calf and hamstring muscles as the white soapy water trailed down the back of his legs. Both of them had the same tight, narrow buttocks that had deep dimples on each cheek. Ted's back and shoulder muscles were broad and well-defined just like his own.

Ted had just returned home from college for the summer and next spring he'd be graduating. *My little man*, Samuel thought to himself as he remembered bathing him as a baby in the kitchen sink. His heart filled with pride as he recalled those moments of long ago. Back when Ted was six months old, he had a chubby body with fat creases every-where. Samuel enjoyed bathing him in his little blue bathtub. *He was so precious*, he thought as he recalled his baby boy being fascinated by the fact that he couldn't hold water in his hand.

"Where did the water go?" Samuel asked Ted, who was staring down at the water around his belly. Ted cooed as he slapped the water with the palms of his chubby hands.

"That water isn't too cold for him, is it Sam?" asked his wife Shawn, when she walked into the kitchen where they were.

"No, it's just right," Samuel answered while watching Ted clutch the face towel for inspection. Ted was also teething at the time and had allowed a line of drool to stretch from his bottom lip all the way down to his plump belly.

"You like the water, don't you?" Samuel spoke in baby language.

"Don't keep him in there too long, Sam. This house is drafty and I don't want him to catch a cold." Shawn placed a drying towel on the counter next to him and then checked the status of his bottle of milk, which was being warmed up in a small pot of water on the stove.

"Turn your wrist over," Shawn requested as she held the glass bottle upside down. Samuel did as she asked and exposed his wrist to her. Shawn squeezed a bit of the milk out through the bottle's nipple and allowed it to drip on his skin. "That's about how warm the milk should be when you give it to him," she said.

"Baby, I know that. I got this. I know what I'm doing," Samuel grumbled, a bit insulted by the fact that Shawn didn't feel comfortable about leaving Ted with him. "I know how to take care of him."

"I know that, baby. I'm just a little nervous, that's all. Just bear with me. This will be the first time that I'll be gone from him for more than a day." Shawn sat the bottle down on the counter and smiled at Ted.

"This isn't easy for me," she admitted. "Just look at him. I think he knows I'm leaving. Look at how sad he looks." Shawn was more emotional than she needed to be.

"Come on, little man. Up you go." Samuel lifted his son up and out of the water. Shawn then took the towel and wrapped it around his body.

"Look at that booty," Shawn spoke to Ted as she dried the water from his skin. "Look at that fat booty," Shawn continued to tease her son.

Samuel walked out of the kitchen and up the stairs into the master bedroom where he laid Ted down on the bed. He removed the towel and rubbed his chubby bubble belly with baby powder. Ted kicked and stretched his legs as he squealed with delight.

"You like that, aye?" Samuel spoke to him. "You're as naked as a jaybird and you don't even care, do you?" Ted squealed a bit more, enjoying his father's attention.

"You're my little man and I'll always love you. I'll always be there for you, no matter what." At that moment Shawn entered the bedroom with a fresh pamper and some clothes for him. She placed the miniature blue cotton-jogging suit on the bed.

"What are you two in here talking about?"

"We're just having a father and son conversation, that's all." Samuel chuckled as he moved out of the way and allowed Shawn to finish the process of dressing Ted.

"Now, you're going to eat your crushed peas, young man," she said to him. "I don't want you spitting it out all over your jogging suit." Ted stopped squealing and turned his gaze toward his father, who was hovering over him. Ted's eyes pleaded with Samuel. His eyes seemed to ask, "Do I really have to eat that mess, Dad?"

"What are you looking at your father for?" Shawn teased. "He can't help you."

"Dad, why are you looking at me like that?" Samuel snapped out of his daydream and focused on the present. Ted would be twenty-one in September and by all standards a grown man. "My, how time flies," Samuel muttered under his breath. "Do you like peas, Ted?"

"No, I hate peas," Ted answered.

"Humph, the more things change, the more they stay the same." Samuel laughed out loud.

"Dad, you're really not making any sense here." Ted gave him an odd look as he turned off the shower.

"Time, son," Samuel spoke as he stared directly into his son's beautiful clear brown eyes. "It's so strange how time slips by so quickly."

CHAPTER TWO

Samuel stood wet and naked in the bathroom mirror and took stock of himself. He gazed at his reflection but focused on his eyes, which had thin wrinkles on the outer edges. His wrinkles were most noticeable when he smiled. He tilted his head down and rubbed his fingers lightly across the top of his head, which had thin patches of hair. He was hoping that somehow, someway, his hair would regenerate and start to grow once again. He began going bald and getting gray hair shortly after Shawn passed away six years ago. He kept his salt and pepper haircut low around the sides and the back since the hair at the top of his head was almost completely nonexistent. He grew a beard, thinking that somehow it would blend in and make him look younger than he was. But now even his well-maintained beard, sprinkled with gray hair, didn't conceal his hair loss. *Well, at least my body is still in respectable shape*, he thought to himself. He studied the mixture of gray and black hair on his still broad and muscular chest. His abs didn't have the well-defined eight-pack that his son's had, but he wasn't carrying a huge belly either. Ted wasn't as tall as his father, nor was he as thick, but that would come with time. Samuel grabbed a drying towel off the bar, wrapped it around his waist, and headed down the hall past Ted's bedroom and into his own. After he got dressed, he descended the staircase and went into the kitchen where he could smell the scent of bacon burning as well as the sound of it sizzling.

"What's up, Dad?" Ted asked, standing in front of the skillet.

"Boy, you're burning up that bacon. Turn the fire down some," Samuel ordered as he wrinkled his nose at the scent of charred meat.

"Oh, my bad," Ted said as he readjusted the flame. "Do you want some of this?"

"No, you finish cooking your food, then I'll cook my own." Samuel shuffled over and sat down at the kitchen table.

"Here you go, Dad." Ted poured his father a glass of orange juice and grabbed the morning paper off the counter for him. "How have things been going at work?"

"It's the same ole' same ole'. Being a state trooper, I have my good days and I have my not so good days."

"I was checking out that Ford Mustang squad car they gave you. What happened to the Crown Victorias they used to issue?"

"Motorists could spot us a mile away in the Crown Vic. Now, with the Mustang, it's difficult for them to spot us," he answered as he flipped the paper open to the real estate section.

"So…" Ted paused searching for the right words. "You know that I'll be a senior this coming fall, right?"

"Yep," Samuel replied without glancing up at him.

"I'll also be twenty-one this December," he said, taking his bacon out of the skillet and placing it on a slice of white bread.

"Yes, and I can't wait. Then you can start buying your own meals and the law says that I don't have to take care of you anymore." Samuel didn't really mean what he'd said. The burned bacon annoyed him and he wanted Ted to know that without being direct.

Ted ignored his dad's comment. "I've done what you told me. For three years straight, my GPA has remained above 3.5. You said that if I do that, you'd buy me a car in my senior year."

Samuel suddenly stopped reading and looked at his son. He began thinking to himself. "Did I say that?"

"Yes, don't you remember? We were sitting right here at the table talking about it. You said that if I didn't get a chick pregnant, didn't get into any trouble and kept my grades above a 3.5, you'd buy me a car. And dad, let me tell you, a brother really could use some wheels."

"Is that a fact," Samuel replied as if Ted's situation was of no real concern to him. He knew that his indifference would make his son squirm. He remembered what he'd said but he was just waiting for Ted to bring it up. He'd already saved up four thousand dollars for the car.

"What's that supposed to mean?"

"It means that I remember." Samuel grinned at his son. "I've just been waiting for you to bring it up." Samuel paused for a moment as his heart began to feel warm. "I'm so proud of you and what you've done. I'm proud of the way you've gotten your act together. Because the good Lord knows that you were taking me through some changes. I know that your mother would be proud of you as well."

Ted felt his heart soar because he'd made his father proud.

⌒

Throughout the day they traveled from one dealership to another in search of a car that fit Samuel's budget as well as Ted's tastes. They'd narrowed their search down to two cars. Ted had his eyes set on a used red Eagle Talon but Samuel wanted him to get the used black Toyota Corolla.

"Dad! A Corolla? Come on, man. I'm not going to look cool in a Corolla."

"Ted, this isn't about looking cool. This is about getting you some reliable transportation," Samuel argued.

"The Talon is reliable," Ted fussed.

"Son, let me explain a few things to you. Number one, you never ever buy a used sports car. The chances are too high that the previous owner dogged it out. Number two, the Corolla comes with a one-year warranty and the sports car doesn't. Number three, if you choose the sports car and it breaks down on you, not only are you not going to look cool, but I'm not going to pay to get it fixed."

Ted thought for a moment about what his father said and how he was guiding him. Although Ted didn't want to admit it, what his father was saying did make practical sense.

"All right, hook me up with the Corolla. But we've got to put a better sound system in it, ok?"

"What's wrong with the one that's in it? I'm not about to buy one of those loud ass trunk amps."

"Dad, it only has an AM/FM radio. Can you and I at least install a CD player in it?"

"Yeah, we can do that," he agreed with a laugh. "We can go to Best Buy, pick out one, and install it tomorrow."

CHAPTER THREE

On Sunday morning, Samuel woke up and went through his routine of taking a shower and taking stock of himself. He then went downstairs into his office where Ted was eating a bowl of cereal while he was talking to someone in a chat room on the computer.

"Who's that you're talking to?" Samuel asked as he opened up the tall black metal file cabinet.

"Oh, this is my girl. I was just telling her about my new ride," Ted answered with a mouth full of cereal.

"Your girl or your girlfriend?"

"It's Kelly. Don't you remember me telling you about Kelly?"

"Sort of. Remind me again," Samuel uttered as he began searching for the file with his bank statements.

"Ok, a few months ago I met her through this website called Sistergirls.com. She had her picture, bio, goals and all of that on the site. I took a chance and shot her an email telling her who I was, my interests, and that sort of stuff. Well, one email led to another and the next thing I knew we hooked up, met each other, and now we've been dating for about six months."

"Was it really that simple?" Samuel replied, half-listening to his son as he opened up the file that he'd been searching for.

"Yeah, and Dad, let me tell you. I'm really feeling Kelly. I think she may be the one."

Samuel glanced over at Ted and chuckled out loud. "Well, before you go off the deep end, talking about she's the one, make sure you take a good look at her momma."

Puzzled by the statement, Ted asked, "Why?"

"Because she'll end up looking like her mother twenty years down the road."

Samuel found his comment amusing but Ted didn't because of his feelings toward Kelly.

"Dad, that's not nice," Ted said as he typed a message to Kelly telling her that he'd talk with her later on that evening when he picked her up to take a spin in his new ride.

"Hey, that's what your grandfather told me when I said that your mom was the one for me."

"Well, I think he was wrong for saying that."

"Hey, it's just something that men say. There's no need to get your feathers all ruffled up about it, lover boy."

"Speaking of girlfriends, how's Vera?"

"I put the axe on Vera."

Ted picked up on his father's mood switch right away. "You broke up with her?"

"Yeah, she had too much damn baggage." Samuel placed the file back in the drawer and slammed it shut.

"It sounds like you two had a major falling out," Ted said, shutting down the computer.

"Ted, I just don't understand these women and their sons. You know that she has a 24-year-old son, right?"

"Yeah, I remember you saying that."

"Well, the boy's a jailbird. He just got out and he's still doing the same crap that got him locked up. He's a thief and a liar and she doesn't have the strength to put his ass out and make him stand on his own two feet. He stole her debit card and used it to party and take out his girlfriend. Vera called me up crying about all of the bounced checks and overdraft fees that she was charged because of what he'd done. I felt bad for her so I helped her out. I told her that she needed to put that fool out and she agreed with me. But agreeing with me and following my advice are two different things. Two months later she's crying the blues again because he took the keys to her car and had an accident in it. He messed up her brand new Saturn. He claims that he was run off the road by an eighteen-wheeler and side-swiped a guardrail. When I looked at her white Saturn, it had blue paint on it."

"What?" Ted expressed his shock. "That sounds like he ran into someone."

"That's what I said, but she believed his story."

"You're kidding me?" Ted couldn't comprehend how Vera could be so gullible.

"You heard me. Then she had the nerve to fix her mouth and ask me if I could give her nine hundred dollars to help her get her car fixed."

"No she didn't?" Ted was both stunned and intrigued at the same time.

"Man, I'm telling you. The woman asked me for nine hundred big ones without hesitation."

"So what did you do?"

"I told her 'hell no,'" Samuel replied with an ugly expression on his face because he was reliving the moment. "Then she got all indignant with me and hung up the phone."

"I take it that you haven't heard from her since," Ted assumed.

"Wait a minute, son. It gets better. About three weeks passed by and I didn't hear a word from her. Then one evening she drops by, all unannounced, upset because her building's management company had been harassing her. Apparently, her neighbors complained to management about her son and his hoodlum friends hanging around the property drinking, loitering and littering. I knew that she was up to something because she came over full of apologies, which was unusual."

"What was she up to? Don't tell me she was trying to get you to give up a unit in the three-flat that you own."

"Yup."

"Aw, come on! Why is it that when you own a rental property everyone that you know suddenly has a desperate situation that requires you to allow them to move in?"

"I don't know. But I'd just finished remodeling a vacant two-bedroom apartment and that's the one she wanted."

"Did she at least want to pay full price for it?" Ted asked, disappointed that his father's relationship had gone sour.

"I didn't care if she was willing to pay full price. I wasn't going to allow her and her grown ass son to move into the building. I have stable working class tenants in the building. I wasn't about to let her son and his hoodlum cronies bring down my place."

"So you told her no?"

"You're damn right I did. You know me, son. I don't have time for bullshit. And Vera seemed to be full of it."

"So you two have broken up for good, right?" Ted said, knowing the answer before he asked the question.

"Yeah, I cut her loose, but she owes me a hundred dollars that she said she'd get back to me. I'm going into the kitchen," Samuel said as he turned to walk out of the room so that he could go and fix himself something to eat.

Ted got up from the computer and followed him. "You know, Dad, you can find a woman much better than her." Ted sat at the kitchen table.

"Who says that I'm looking for a woman?"

"Come on, Dad. You need somebody. After I graduate, I plan on getting a job and place of my own. You'll be here all by yourself."

Samuel was pouring a bowl of cereal and stopped pouring when he thought about what his son had said. He would miss him and he would feel alone.

"I'll be all right," he replied, tossing the thought from his mind.

"Dad, I'm serious. If I continue to do well this football season, I may have a shot at playing for the pros."

"Don't put all of your eggs in one basket, Ted. Going pro would be nice but finish your degree first."

"I know, Dad. The degree is my priority. But if I do go pro, Lord only knows what team I'll end up playing for. You really need to meet someone."

"I do know how to meet someone," Samuel said. "I was dating long before you came along."

"I know that you can meet someone. You're a nice looking man, you're financially stable, you don't have any health problems, plus you keep yourself in shape."

"You're right, but women nowadays don't even look my way," he admitted.

"Do you want to know why?" Ted asked, as his father brought the bowl of cereal and milk to the table where he was sitting.

"Yes, Mr. dating expert, why don't women look my way?"

"It's the comb-over dad. You'd look so much better as a bald man."

"Bald!" Samuel suddenly got sensitive and began touching the top of his head. He allowed his hands to glide down to the sides where there was hair.

"Yes, bald. Get rid of that Homie the Clown haircut. I'm telling you that women are into men with bald heads. You have a perfectly round head and going bald would look so cool on you."

"Naaaa, that's ok, it may grow back," Samuel said, not believing that his hair would. He just couldn't come to grips with cutting off the rest of his hair.

"Dad, let's keep it real, ok. If you shave your head bald, shave the beard down to a goatee, and get one of those tiny magnetic earrings along with some cool shades, dude, ladies will definitely notice you."

"Oh yeah," Samuel chimed, warming up to the idea. "Do you really think so?"

"Yes, I know so. Let me go and plug up the clippers and I'll show you what I'm talking about."

Samuel was quiet for a moment as he was making his decision.

"Come on, Dad, trust me on this one."

"I don't know. Let me think about it."

"What's there to think about? I'm telling you, it's going to look good on you."

"All right, I'll try it," he said, giving in to his son's request.

Samuel was sitting in a chair in front of the bathroom mirror with a towel draped over his shoulders. There was a distrustful look on his face as he noticed his hair floating softly to the floor. His insecurities began to get the best of him as he glanced down at a pile of hair.

Ted sensed his father's discomfort. "Don't worry about it. I'm going to hook you up nicely."

"You'd better because if you don't, that's your ass," Samuel threatened playfully.

"Just close your eyes and let me do my thing, ok?"

Samuel huffed, but did as his son suggested and closed his eyes. During the grooming process Samuel had gotten so comfortable that he dozed off to sleep and didn't realize it until Ted said, "Ok, you can open your eyes now."

Samuel opened his eyes and looked at Ted, who was standing in front of him.

"Now you look cool, Dad," Ted said, inspecting his work. Ted stepped out of the way so that Samuel could look at himself in the mirror.

"Oh, man!" He couldn't believe his eyes. "I look like a totally different person." Samuel ran the palm of his hand across his smooth chocolate bald head.

"Do you like the look?" Ted asked, looking for approval.

"Yeah." He brushed his hand up and down his smooth cheek in total amazement. "I like how you trimmed up the goatee. Hell, I actually look younger."

Ted smiled. "You look distinguished, Dad. The salt and pepper goatee really says a lot."

"Yeah, I agree with you." Samuel was smiling at the reflection of himself. "This was a good move, son. I like it better than I thought I would."

"Cool, now let's go get a new CD player to install in my car. I want to wash and wax it too, so that everything is perfect when I pick up Kelly for our date tonight."

"You're really serious about this girl, aren't you?"

"Dad, she's everything I've ever wanted in a woman."

"Tell me again how you met her?"

"On the Internet at this website called Sistergirls.com."

"Don't you think that's sort of dangerous?"

"Dad, get with the times. People are always meeting each other on the net. You should give it a try."

"Naa, I'm old school. I like to know a little bit more about a woman before I start dating her. I prefer to meet them in person at a gathering or something. Not in a club or a bar; I'm just too old for the scene."

"Dad, you just shoot the person an email. People communicate first by email and then, if things sound good, you exchange numbers and go from there. Look, I'm going to leave the website address by the computer. When you get a moment, just check it out."

"Ok, I'll think about it," Samuel said as he picked up the chair he was sitting in to take it back downstairs to the kitchen. "Sweep up that hair for me, son, okay?"

CHAPTER FOUR

L ater that afternoon, after Samuel and Ted installed a new CD player in Ted's Corolla, they drove both of their cars up to the do-it-your-self carwash. Samuel pulled his gold Pontiac Grand Prix GTP outside of the wash stall next to the vacuum cleaner. Ted pulled his Corolla in the stall next to his father. Samuel removed the floor mats from his car and went about the task of gathering trash to be tossed out. He popped open the trunk of the car to clean it out as well. While his head was tucked inside of the trunk, another car pulled up on the other side of him. A young attractive woman in her mid-twenties got out of a Chevy Cavalier and made her way over to the dollar bill changer. When the young woman returned to her car, she began placing the contents of her trunk on the ground so that she could vacuum it out.

"Hey there, handsome," the young woman said as she tossed an empty shoe box on the ground. Samuel didn't think that she was speaking to him so he didn't reply.

She was now looking directly at him. "What's the matter, sweetie? You don't know how to speak?"

"Oh, no, it's not that," Samuel said, smiling and a bit embarrassed by his rudeness. "I didn't think you were talking to me."

"You're the only one standing there," she responded with a smile that made her perfectly round cheeks rise up and meet her eyes.

"I'm sorry. I thought you were saying hello to my son who's in the stall washing his car," Samuel answered, giving her a friendly chuckle.

"No, I was talking to you, handsome," she said, making sure that he knew that he'd caught her eye.

Samuel was completely tickled by the entire situation. "You know, I'm old enough to be your father. Maybe my son is more your speed. The apple doesn't fall far from the tree."

"Why should I settle for the apple when the tree is right in front of me?"

Samuel was speechless and all giggles on the inside at the same time. A young tender thing was paying him some attention. "If I didn't know any better, I'd say that you were flirting with me."

"Well, I am, and I'm harmless. You're a handsome man, and I just wanted you to know that you caught my eye."

"Well, thank you," Samuel replied, scratching his head and not believing that he was actually getting a little play. He'd been coming to the same carwash for years and nothing like this had ever happened.

The woman went about the business of cleaning out her car. When she was done she said, "Nice talking to you." She wiggled her fingers goodbye. "I just stopped up here to get some quarters and toss some things out. Maybe I'll see you around."

"Yeah, maybe so," Samuel said, smiling so hard that his cheeks were aching. The woman got in her car and pulled off.

"Who was that?" Ted came out of the stall to talk with his father.

"Just some woman who thought I was handsome."

"It's your new look, Dad." Ted smacked the back of his hand against his dad's chest. "I told you, the ladies are really into bald men."

"Yeah." Samuel rubbed his bald head and smiled like a Cheshire cat. "I see that now. You know, I think I'm going to splurge a little bit. I'm going to go shopping and pick myself up some new clothes."

Ted replied, "Oh Lord, now I've created a monster." Both men laughed. "Dad, I grabbed the digital camera because I wanted to get a few shots of me standing next to my very first car."

"All right, when you get done cleaning it up, I'll snap a few shots. In fact, I want you to snap a few of me as well," Samuel said, feeling young and alive.

&

CHAPTER FIVE

Sandra stood in front of the microwave oven waiting for the rapidly popping popcorn to stop before she took it out and placed it in the glass bowl on the small nook table beside her. After a busy day of shopping with her daughter Kelly, who had a date with her boyfriend, the only things Sandra wanted to do were sit back, eat her popcorn, and watch a movie called *Two Can Play That Game*. She opened the door on the microwave oven and removed the hot bag of popcorn. She shook it up a few times and inhaled the buttery scented puffs of steam.

"Ok, Mom how does this look?" Kelly walked into the kitchen and stood in the center of the floor modeling a pair of tight blue jeans and a fitted black V-neck top that brought attention to her breasts.

"You look fine," Sandra said, tossing a few kernels into her mouth.

"What about the shoes? How do the pumps look?"

"You look good, honey. You make me wish that I was still your size." Sandra sighed. "You go out and have yourself a good time, okay?"

"I will," Kelly said.

Sandra took her bowl of popcorn into her bedroom where she had the movie paused. She rested her back against the bed's headboard, picked up the remote and was about to press play when Kelly entered her room.

"Mom, are you going to be okay?"

"Yeah, why are you asking?" Sandra knew something was on Kelly's mind by the tone of her voice.

"I'm worried about you? I mean, I want you to find yourself someone that makes you happy."

"Baby, I'm not interested in a man right now. After dealing with Ronnie and his lying, good for nothing ass, men are just not on my good list right now. Besides, men have a way of making me act crazy when they screw up with me. I don't feel like being pushed into getting all ignorant and ghetto the way I did when I cut Ronnie's trifling ass loose."

"Mom, that was over a year ago. Come on, now. You knew better when you hooked up with that fool." Kelly didn't want to discuss the issue of Ronnie and his lawsuit money from a discrimination case that he was supposed to share with her mother, so she got to her point. "Everybody needs love in their life," Kelly said as she sat on the side of the bed.

Sandra smiled at her daughter. "I have you, baby, and you give me all the love I need."

"What about when I leave home? I'll be graduating next year, Mom. I'll take a job and move out on my own. Then what?"

"Honey, you don't have to leave or move out when you graduate. I've told you that already. You can stay here for as long as you like."

"Mom, Ted and I are getting serious. We've made a commitment to each other and if things continue to go well this year, who knows, we might get married."

"When am I going to meet this boy that you met on the Internet?"

"Soon, Mom. Speaking of the Internet, have you gotten any responses from the Sistergirls.com website?"

"No," Sandra said, half-annoyed that no one had responded to her and half-annoyed that Kelly even mentioned it. She wasn't real keen on the idea of meeting someone through the Internet but she was giving it a try since Kelly insisted.

"Just give it more time. Someone will respond." Kelly rubbed her mother's hand as if she were dying.

"Like I said, honey, I'm doing just fine without a man. I don't have an issue with being celibate."

"Mom, you're in your forties and in your prime. You can't live the rest of your life without being loved. If you do, you'll end up being an old bitter and frustrated woman."

"Kelly, don't ruin my evening. You're getting on my nerves now."

"Mom, I'm not trying to make you mad. I just want you to be happy."

"I'm happy Kelly, see?" Sandra gritted her teeth and smiled. "Now get on out of here before you make me lose my temper."

"Okay, all right, but just promise me you'll keep checking." Sandra didn't say anything; she just clicked the remote and started her movie. "Mom!"

"Yes, I'll keep checking, all right?" Sandra wrinkled her facial muscles into an expression of anger.

"Good, love you," Kelly said and kissed her on the forehead before she left the room.

CHAPTER SIX

The house was empty when Samuel returned from shopping and picking up a movie called *Two Can Play That Game*. Ted had already left in his new car to take out his girlfriend. He opened the refrigerator and pulled out a large bag of green seedless grapes. He then got a small bowl from the shelf and placed a few grapevines in it. He rinsed the fruit off thoroughly and then headed toward the entertainment room where he placed the grapes on a small table next to his Lazy Boy chair. He placed the disk in the DVD Player, sat down, picked up the remote, and started his movie. When the movie ended, he was satisfied with the way it had entertained him. He turned the television off and then dozed off to sleep. He woke up around midnight because he thought he'd heard Ted come in. When he got up and went downstairs to see, he discovered that he was still the only one in the house. He was about to go lie down in his bed when he noticed a yellow post-it note stuck to the computer monitor in his office. He walked into his office and flipped on the light switch.

He removed the note and read it:

Dad, just log onto the website and check it out. www.sistergirls.com.

Samuel exhaled as he sat down and turned on the computer. He logged onto MSN and began reading the news updates. After he read the news headlines he typed in the website address and waited for the site to come up. The site had photos of attractive women from around the country who were looking for several types of relationships. Some were just looking to communicate with different people online, others were looking for their soul mate and still others were just looking to date and meet interesting people. Samuel got hooked on the site as he began clicking around looking at photos and reading their bios. He clicked on the link for women in his area and found a few interesting photos but the women were much too young for him. He wasn't trying to be anyone's sugar daddy. He was about to log off but decided to randomly click another link. He waited for the photograph to download and was stunned to see a very beautiful and attractive looking woman in her early-forties. He quickly scrolled down and read her bio.

My name is Island Paradise. I'm a full-figured woman who lives in the Chicago land area. I have a master's degree in business and I work for a well-known hospital. Men who are broke, jobless and still live at home with their mother, please don't bother contacting me. Arrogant men and men with unresolved emotional issues from childhood, please stay away. I don't have time to be your mother. If you're a confident, well-groomed man who has his act together, both mentally and financially, I may be the woman of your dreams. If you're secure with your manhood and can complement a strong woman with an independent mind, I may be the woman of your dreams. If you're my type of man, drop me an email.

Samuel was completely intrigued. He studied her photo again and became mesmerized by her beautiful smile, bright eyes and full face. *What the hell*, he thought, suddenly feeling playful. *I'll reply to her.* Samuel clicked her email address.

Dear Miss Paradise,

I saw your bio on Sistergirls.com. I'm a 43-year-old man who is an Illinois State Trooper stationed in the Chicago land area. I adore full-figured women, even moreso if they're tall. I think that I meet your strict requirements and would love to see if I can pass your inspection process. I imagine that it is a rigorous one, but I'm willing to bet that I'm the type of gentleman you're searching for. When you have a moment, I'd love to hear from you.

Yours truly,

Officer Friendly

Before Samuel could rethink his decision, he clicked the send button and the message was gone. Before he logged off, he decided to check the rest of the weekend forecast. As he was reading the forecast, the Microsoft Outlook bell dinged indicating that there was a new message in his mailbox. Samuel clicked over to his mailbox and was surprised to see a reply message from Island Paradise. He quickly looked at the computer's clock, which said that it was 1:30 a.m. *What in the world is she doing up so late?* he wondered. Samuel opened up the message.

Dear Officer Friendly,

You're correct in assuming that I have a rigorous inspection process. I've never done anything like this before and I have my reservations. In fact, the only reason I have a listing posted is because my 21-year-old daughter suggested that I try it. To be honest with you, you're the very first person to send me a message. I was starting to believe that my criteria were too strict for men.

Anyway, I'm pleased that you decided to send me a message and I must admit that I want to know a bit more about you. In other words, prepare yourself for an inspection, (smile). Tell me about yourself, I'm waiting.

Smooches,

Island Paradise

"Hot damn!" Samuel slapped his hands together and rubbed them as he prepared his fingers to respond back in a timely manner. He was about to type a response when he heard Ted come in.

"Hey, Dad. You weren't waiting up for me, were you?"

"Naw, boy. I've got better things to do other than wait up on you," Samuel said, not even turning around to look at Ted.

"Wait a minute. Who are you online talking to?"

"Son, you're dipping and dabbing in grown folks' business. Now go on to bed," Samuel said as he typed "Dear Island Paradise."

"Oh, well excuse me," Ted said. "I'll leave you alone then. Goodnight."

"You mean good morning," Samuel replied.

"Whatever, Dad," Ted said as he walked away.

"What did you say to me?" Samuel wasn't about to let his attitude slip by unnoticed.

"You're right, good morning," Ted shouted back to him.

⌒

CHAPTER SEVEN

S andra was smiling at the computer screen and didn't hear Kelly when she walked into her room.

"Hey, Mom," she spoke softly.

Sandra got so startled that she leapt up out of her seat. "Damn, you just scared the hell out of me," Sandra said with the palm of her right hand resting flat against her chest.

"I'm sorry, I didn't mean to do that," Kelly replied. "What are you in here doing?"

"Nothing," she said just as her computer chimed indicating that she had a new email message.

"Are you talking to someone online?" Kelly was looking at her mother suspiciously. "You know it's almost 2:00 a.m., don't you?"

"Um, excuse me," Sandra said, getting up to escort Kelly out of her room. "I raised you, remember? Now get out of here and go get some rest. I know that you must be tired."

"Okay, there's no need to push me out of the room," Kelly answered with an even more suspicious tone in her voice.

"Goodnight," Sandra said now that Kelly was outside of her door and standing in the hallway. Sandra grabbed the door, gently shut it, and locked it. She exhaled and closed her eyes for a moment and then rushed back over to the computer monitor. She saw that Officer Friendly had replied to her. She couldn't believe that the man was up at this time of night. She clicked the envelope icon and opened the message.

Dear Miss Paradise,

First let me say I enjoyed the smooches that you tossed my way. I love getting and giving smooches, hugs and similar types of affection. It would seem that you and I have something in common. I too have a child in his early-twenties who suggested that I give the website a try. My son seems to believe that I'm going to be some grubby old lonely man if I

don't find someone to share my life with. I had to remind him that I was dating long before he arrived on the scene, (smile). I'm widowed; I own my home and a rental property on the city's South Side. I followed in my father's footsteps and became a state trooper. I've been on the force now for eighteen years. I don't have any momma's boy issues and a woman with a strong mind who knows how to handle her business is a big turn-on to me. Now, tell me more about yourself. I'd love to know if there is an easy-going woman who enjoys having a good time underneath all of the seriousness.

I'm looking at your picture and touching the screen.

Officer Friendly

Sandra couldn't read the message fast enough. Officer Friendly certainly had her attention. She decided to take a chance and ask him if he had Instant Messenger so they could talk without the delay of email.

Dear Officer Friendly,

Do you have Microsoft Instant Messenger on your computer? If so, add Island Paradise to your buddy list so I can tell you just how easy-going and fun I am.

Before Sandra reconsidered rewording her flirtatious note she clicked the send button and logged onto Instant Messenger. A few moments later an Instant Message came through from Officer Friendly.

Officer Friendly: Miss Paradise, is that you?

Island Paradise: Only if you're the trooper that I have been talking to.

Officer Friendly: Yes, it's me.

Island Paradise: You have me at a disadvantage, officer.

Officer Friendly: Oh really, how so?

Island Paradise: You know exactly what I look like but I don't have any idea of how you look. Can you email me a photo of yourself?

Officer Friendly: Yes, actually, my son encouraged me to change my look yesterday. We took some pictures with a digital camera this afternoon. Give me a second to download them and I'll send you one.

Island Paradise: Don't keep me waiting a long time.

Officer Friendly: Don't worry, sugar, I wouldn't do you like that.

Samuel hastily plugged up the digital camera and downloaded the pictures that he and Ted had taken at the car wash. He sent a picture of himself and then informed his online buddy.

Officer Friendly: You've got mail.

Island Paradise: Ok, let me go check you out.

Sandra shrunk the Instant Message window and restored her email window, which had another email with an attachment from Officer Friendly. She opened up the message and closed her eyes. Please, Lord; please don't let this be a hideous-looking man. Sandra opened one eye and looked at the monitor. When she saw Samuel, she quickly popped open the other one.

"Oh, damn!" she shouted out loud.

She enlarged the photograph, which showed him smiling and leaning with his back against the car door with his large muscular arms folded and resting just below his chest. He was super chocolate and super fine and she couldn't take her eyes off him. She enlarged the photo again so that she could look into his eyes, which seemed to be staring right at her.

Officer Friendly: Hello? Are you still there?

Island Paradise: Yes, baby, I'm here.

Officer Friendly: Oh, now I've graduated to being called baby? I think I like that.

Island Paradise: Where have you been hiding yourself?

Officer Friendly: You're funny. I haven't been hiding anywhere. I take it you like my photo.

Island Paradise: Baby, how tall are you?

Officer Friendly: I'm about 6'2".

Sandra bit her bottom lip. "Lord, have mercy," she cooed to herself as she continued to glare at his photo. If he had a deep voice to go along with his height and chocolate skin, she was going to scream out loud. She hadn't been with a man in over a year and her imagination suddenly began to run wild. *I wonder how good he is,* she thought. *I wonder if he tastes as good as he looks. I wonder if he knows how to kiss a woman. I wonder if he knows how to caress breasts and lick my island paradise.* Her thoughts were causing twinges of excitement to rush through her. She suddenly began flapping her legs open and closed like the wings of a butterfly and she couldn't bring herself to stop. She had to restrain her vivid imagination. She had to be calm and think of a way to approach him without seeming like she was an anxious woman.

Island Paradise: I'm so glad that you're a tall man because I'm a tall woman.

Officer Friendly: Is that a fact? How tall are you?

Island Paradise: I'm about 5'10". I'm a full-figured woman. Just your size, I would think.

Officer Friendly: You're making me smile with all of your cute comments.

Island Paradise: I'm glad to know that I've given you something to smile about. What's your real name?

Officer Friendly: Samuel, what's yours?

Island Paradise: Sandra.

Officer Friendly: Well, Sandra, I'm glad that we've met. Although I must say that I'd like to meet you in person. Perhaps we can have a cup of coffee one day.

Island Paradise: I think I'd like that.

Officer Friendly: Good, I'm glad you feel the same way. Why don't we meet online tomorrow evening and make some plans? I just looked at my clock and I see that it's now 4:30 a.m. My eyes are tired and I'm sleepy.

Island Paradise: How about 6:00 p.m. tomorrow evening? Will you be online?

Officer Friendly: Yes, I'll be here. Just make sure you are. Don't disappoint me. Mmmmmauuuhhh, there's a goodnight kiss for you. You can put it any place you want.

Island Paradise: I know just the place, (smile). I'll talk with you tomorrow night. Smooches.

CHAPTER EIGHT

S andra damn near broke her neck trying to get in the door and get to her computer. She'd been out shopping most of the afternoon trying to find something to wear for when she met Samuel for coffee. It was 6:15 p.m. and she was fifteen minutes late. She prayed that the man hadn't gotten offline. She turned on her computer and waited for it to warm up.

"Come on," she hissed impatiently as she waited for her desktop to show up. She got online and logged onto Instant Messenger. She saw that Samuel was still online. She quickly double-clicked on his name so that she could send him a message before he disappeared.

Island Paradise: Hey there, Samuel, sorry I'm late. Can you find it in your heart to forgive me?

Officer Friendly: Wow, you caught me just in the nick of time. I was about to log off.

Island Paradise: Well, I'm glad you waited. How can I make my tardiness up to you?

Officer Friendly: Call me. My number is 777-9311. Give me a second to get offline before you call.

Island Paradise: Ok, I'll call you in about ten minutes. Talk to you soon.

Ten minutes later Sandra was lounging on her bed and holding the telephone up to her ear, listening to it ring.

"Hello?" a deep voice answered the phone.

"Samuel, is that you?" Sandra asked all excited by the sound of his voice.

"No, I'm his son. Hang on a second."

She heard the sound of the phone being set down. Then she heard another much deeper voice with more bass. "Ok, I have it. You can hang it up now." Sandra heard the sound of the phone being placed back on its cradle. "Hello, this is Samuel," the deep, rich, lazy-sounding voice said.

"Hi, this is Sandra."

"Hey, Sandra," Samuel said with excitement in his voice.

"What's that I hear in the background? Is that music?"

"Yes, I was playing my smooth jazz CDs. Are you hip to that new young white boy named Remy Shand?"

"Is he the one that sings that song "Take a Message from My Love"?"

"Yeah, that's him.," Samuel said, turning up the music a bit so she could hear it.

"I didn't know he was white."

"Yeah, he is. It's strange, the soul that some of these white boys have."

"Yeah, like Kenny G. I don't care what you say, that boy has got some black blood in him somewhere." Sandra laughed along with Samuel. "I'm also willing to bet that if they did a background check on our former president Bill Clinton, he has a black great-grandmother or-father somewhere."

Samuel laughed harder. "I'd have to agree with you on that one."

"So, what have you been doing all day, Mr. Officer Friendly?"

"I ran some errands today and then came in and cleaned up the house a bit. For the past hour or so, I've been playing my music and thinking about you."

"Oh, have you now?" Sandra was delighted to hear that.

"Yes, I have." Samuel moved back over to the stereo to turn the music back down.

"Wait-a-minute. Hold on. Is that the New Temptations that I hear?"

"Yeah, it's their song called 'Stay' they put out about a year or so ago."

"I love that song." Sandra began bopping her head to the music playing in her mind.

"Then perhaps one day I could interest you in an evening of listening to music and a glass of wine."

"Well, listen to you, trying to get all romantic on me."

"Well, when I see something I like, I don't like to let it get away from me."

"My, aren't you aggressive." Sandra was smiling so hard that people would've thought she was a relative of the Joker. She rolled over onto her back and wound the phone cord around her index finger. She couldn't believe that she was feeling this way about a man she'd just met online and had never met in person.

"No, I'm not being aggressive. I'm just a confident man," Samuel said as he bop danced around the room pretending that he was dancing with Sandra.

"Now you're going to use my words to your advantage, I see." Sandra giggled and Samuel loved hearing her laugh.

"So why don't we get together and meet each other in person?" Samuel asked.

"I like the sound of that. In fact, since you like smooth jazz so much, why don't we meet next weekend for Sunday brunch downtown? WNUA hosts a Sunday brunch every weekend down at the Swiss Hotel."

"Yes, I know. I listen to that station all the time."

"So, does it sound like something you'd like to do?" Sandra asked, tickled to death that their conversation was going so well.

"It sounds like a plan to me," Samuel responded likewise.

The two of them made their plans for the following weekend. Samuel made Sandra feel comfortable but she wasn't ready to give him her home phone number just yet so she gave him her cellular number. She wanted to see him in person first before she did that. After she hung up the phone, she kicked her feet and squealed out loud with delight. She got up and went downstairs to listen to some music of her own. She pulled out her Nina Simone and Etta James CDs. She popped in Etta James and listened to her sing "At Last."

"That's right, girl," she said as she sensually moved her body around the room and sang with Etta, "At last, my love has come along. My lonely days are over and life is like a song."

CHAPTER NINE

Although Samuel tried very hard not to show it, his nerves were on edge as he sat with one leg crossed over his knee in a straight-back chair in the lobby of the Swiss Hotel. He'd arrived forty-five minutes early to ensure that he wasn't late and wouldn't have her waiting on him. He was glad that he'd gone shopping for some new clothes to go along with his new look. He'd purchased several casual suits from Bachrach's Department Store. He was wearing a pair of brown windowpane trousers, along with a beige silk top that accentuated his brawny physique. He had on a pair of brown whip-stitched shoes that had a fresh coat of shoe polish on them along with a matching belt. He flipped his wrist and looked at his watch that read 9:55 a.m. Once he glanced up from his watch, that's when he saw her coming down the carpeted hallway toward him. His bottom jaw dropped open and he lost his breath for a moment. Lord, have mercy, he thought to himself as he studied the rhythmic and sensual sway of her hips. It's a damn shame the way her hips silently say that they'll rock me all night long.

He glanced down at the thickness of her calf muscles, which made him yearn for an opportunity to kiss them. Everything about the way she moved said classy, sensual, and sophisticated. He drew his attention back up to her beautiful round face and short haircut. Her eyes were much larger than they had appeared in her photo, but he didn't mind because they were catty, dreamy, sexy bedroom eyes.

Sandra had spent most of her Saturday at the beauty salon getting her hair fixed and eyebrows arched. She'd gotten up extra early and had taken extra time to make sure that she applied her Fashion Fair make-up just right. She was wearing a cream-colored Liz Claiborne skirt suit, which accentuated her mahogany legs. As she made her way down the hallway toward the elevators, she saw a man stand up, capture her gaze and smile at her. It was Samuel. Her heart began pounding so loudly, she thought for certain that anyone within a ten-mile radius could hear it. Samuel looked handsome, debonair and stylish. He began to approach her with a slightly bow-legged stride.

"Good morning, Sandra," he greeted her as he placed a moist kiss on her cheek.

She exhaled as she felt her womanhood tingling with anticipation. She knew right then that she wanted to sleep with him. She took a deep swallow before she spoke so that she could bring some type of composure to herself.

She stepped back a bit and extended her hand for a handshake. "It's nice to meet you."

"Yes, it is," Samuel said, moistening his chocolate lips. "You're even more stunning in person than in your photo."

"Why, thank you. You're quite a piece of eye candy yourself," she responded as she tried to restrain the electricity between her thighs that was trying to suggest that she get wild and outrageous with Samuel by suggesting they just get a room, so that she could get the monkey off her back.

"The brunch is on the 40th floor. The elevators are down this way."

Samuel extended his elbow so that Sandra could lock her arm inside of his. The two of them made their way to the elevator, both of them hoping that they could begin a solid meaningful relationship that was decent and loving.

CHAPTER TEN

Sandra pushed open the front door and tussled with her suitcase and a bundle of mail from her mailbox. She kicked off her shoes, walked over to her sofa and plopped down feeling weary. Five months had come to pass since Sandra first met Samuel online through Sistergirls.com. Although they hadn't made love yet or introduced each other to their children, they were enjoying the process of their courtship.

During the months of September and October, Sandra's job required her to do an extensive amount of traveling, which made it difficult for her to see her man the way that she had grown accustomed to during the summer months. Now that her last business trip was out of the way, her schedule would be less hectic. Sandra was looking forward to spending some much needed quality time with Samuel. She was also ready to take their relationship to the next level by being intimate with him, but she wanted their first time to be as natural as wet is to water.

She stood up in front of the sofa, reached around her back and unzipped her skirt. She took it off along with her pantyhose and tossed them toward the other end of the sofa. She picked up the mail that she'd tossed on the glass cocktail table and walked into the kitchen wearing nothing but her lavender panties and bra. She turned on the radio that was in the kitchen and sat down at the table to sift through her mail. She opened up a letter from a social club that she'd joined a while back. The organizers of the club were throwing a Halloween masquerade dance downtown at the Field Museum of Natural History. She read the details about the music and dinner arrangements along with the time, date, and RSVP deadline. She studied the flier in search of the price when her phone rang. She got up and picked up the phone that was on the wall near the light switch.

"Hello?"

"Hey, baby," Samuel said. "I'm glad to see that you've made it home safely."

"Well, aren't you sweet? How's my boo boo doing?"

"Your boo boo is doing just fine," Samuel answered, adding a bit of extra bass in his voice because he knew how much she loved hearing his deep voice.

"I like the way you said that." Sandra stretched the phone cord and took a seat at the kitchen table. "Aren't you supposed to be working?"

"Yes, but I couldn't go another minute without hearing your voice."

"Do you really mean that?" Sandra asked, turning to mush on the inside. Samuel chuckled playfully. "I called, didn't I?"

"Well, I can't wait to see you tomorrow. I'm going to shower you with hugs and kisses."

"I can't wait to see you, either. Well, I just wanted to make sure that you'd made it in all right. I've got to get back to work. I'll talk to you tomorrow, ok?"

"Ok, baby," Sandra said and hung up the phone.

The following afternoon Sandra came over to Samuel's home for the very first time and she was stunned to see how beautiful it was.

"Kick your shoes off," Samuel said. "I'll give you the grand tour of my home."

He started off in the living room, which had tan carpeting, plenty of windows and a gas fireplace that could be activated by flipping a wall switch. Near the fireplace, there was a tan chaise chair with matching pillows and a throw. Samuel had matching straight-back chairs and a sofa that was trimmed with dark brown wood. He had a dark brown, floor-model television that was positioned in front of the sofa. The glass cock-tail table in front of the fireplace had a beautiful and healthy fern plant surrounded by a few books and the latest issue of *Men's Health*. Samuel could tell that Sandra was impressed.

"Come on, let me show you my favorite room in the house." Samuel took her hand and led her around through the living room, around a corner and up the stairs. He opened a bedroom door, which he had converted into an entertainment room. There was track lighting on the ceiling, speakers positioned around the room, and a giant screen television. There were two brown Lazy Boy chairs positioned in front of the television. There was a wall unit that had a ton of music CDs, VHS videos and DVDs.

"Watch this," Samuel said as he picked up a remote control from the seat cushion of the Lazy Boy. He clicked a button and two panels in the wall began to open up like curtains being drawn.

"Oh my goodness," Sandra said as she stood with her hands on her hips. "I would've never guessed that the wall unit moved."

"Yeah, that's where all of the stereo equipment is. I installed the moving wall myself." Samuel clicked another button and Freddie Jackson singing "You Are My Lady" filled the room.

"Hey now." Sandra began sensually moving her body to the music and, at the same time, noticed a ton of tiny red lights bouncing up and down on the stereo. "That's my guy there."

"So, do you think a guy like me can get a dance with you?"

"Tuh, well I think that can be arranged Mister Slick."

"Slick? Why do I have to be called Mister Slick?"

"Because you planned that," Sandra said, wrapping her arms around his neck. "You don't fool me, mister."

"Well, do I at least get points for my effort?"

"Yes," Sandra said, giving him a quick kiss on the lips. Samuel was a good dancer and Sandra enjoyed the way that he dipped his knees and patted her on the butt in perfect unison with the music.

Since the temperature had gotten up to the upper-seventies, which was unusual for late October, Samuel suggested that they spend some time cuddling up on the hammock in his backyard.

"I'll take my portable CD player out there so that we can listen to some more music," Samuel said.

Sandra loved the idea. Samuel grabbed a light blanket in case the fall air became chilly along with two pillows. Before they climbed into the hammock, he got the music set and Freddie Jackson was now singing "Have You Ever Loved Somebody." Sandra felt loved as she rested in Samuel's strong arms, glancing up at the wonderful colors of autumn leaves while the hammock swayed slightly.

"Baby, have you ever been to a masquerade?" Sandra asked, snuggling her head against the pillow, which was resting against his chest while she looked up at a few fluffy white clouds in the sky.

"No, why do you ask?"

"Because I want to go to one; this social club that I joined is having one. The gala is going to take place at the Field Museum on Lake Shore Drive. The organizers have rented out the entire museum for the event. Tickets are limited though. If I asked you to go, would you?"

"Of course I would." Samuel tugged and pulled her sweater up so that he was able to place his hand on her soft stomach. He circled his index finger around her belly button. The stirring sensation was causing light butterflies to float between Sandra's thighs.

"Good, because I'm going to get us some tickets," she said, trying to ignore her desire. "We'll have to get some really nice costumes."

"Who do you want to go as?" Samuel asked, tickled by that fact that they were going to play dress-up and behave like children.

"I don't know. I mean, I've always wanted to go to one but never thought about who I wanted to go as. Who would you want to go as?"

"Hmmm…" Samuel pondered. "I'd want us to pick characters that fit together."

"What, like Batman and Robin?" Sandra asked.

"Yeah but not those two," Samuel said, still thinking.

"What about me going as a witch and you as a warlock," Sandra suggested.

"That one has possibilities," Samuel said, allowing his fingers to creep under her pants and rub the hair of her womanhood. Sandra was about to stop him but couldn't bring herself to resist his touch.

"I got it, baby," Samuel said. "We could go as Gomez and Morticia from the *Addams Family*."

"That's a wonderful choice." Sandra was now beaming with excitement. "We should go and rent the movie this afternoon so that we can get costume ideas."

"Do you really like my choice?" Samuel asked, removing his hand from under her pants.

"Yes, we can have so much fun being Gomez and Morticia. They were such a freaky, kinky and romantic couple. I think that you and I can live up to those standards," Sandra said with cheekiness in her tone of voice.

"It sounds as if you and I need to go out and get that movie."

"Let's do it now," Sandra said, all excited as she removed herself from his embrace and got down from the hammock.

CHAPTER ELEVEN

After watching the movies of the *Addams Family* and its sequel *Addams Family Values*, the simple plan of dressing up to go to a Halloween party had turned into a mission to make a fantasy reality. Sandra and Samuel loved the chemistry and sexual tension between Gomez and Morticia so much that they decided they would go the distance to ensure that their costumes and behavior looked and sounded authentic. They went to a costume shop that tailored costumes for local theater and movie production companies. Sandra had a sheer black dress made with a low-cut V-shaped scoop around the collar. There were ruffles around her wrists and ankles. When she held her arms out, fabric draped down for added effect. She went out to the store and purchased a black wig with hair long enough to rest gently on her shoulders. She purchased fire engine red lipstick with matching fingernail polish. She purchased rich black eyeliner to apply to her eyes and black pencil liner to darken up her eyebrows to create a more mysterious look.

Samuel had a three-piece gray and black pinstriped tuxedo with tails made. He also purchased spats, a top hat, a cane and a fake pocket watch for added effect. He went to a wig shop and purchased a black wig to wear since he was bald. Samuel also spent time learning how to speak like Gomez so that he could make Sandra feel as sexy and beautiful as Gomez made Morticia feel. Samuel had to admit to himself that he was just as crazy about Sandra as Gomez was about Morticia. He had that same type of unbridled desire and passion for her; even though they'd yet to be completely intimate with each other. It was the way the tension between the two of them had swelled up that was driving him over the edge with desire for her.

It was 6:30 p.m. on Halloween night when Samuel parked his car in front of Sandra's condo at the corner of Everett and 57th Street, in Chicago's Hyde Park neighborhood. He had his music system turned all the way up because a local radio station was playing "Thriller" by Michael Jackson. The song was about to end and he was waiting for the part when Vincent Price bellowed out his haunting laugh. Samuel, who was feeling grand about being dressed up as Gomez, laughed along with the song.

Once the song ended, Samuel got out of the car and noticed an adult accompanying a small group of children trick or treating. There was a ladybug, a Power Ranger, a cat, and a ninja. The children were cute and full of energy as they walked along chattering about how much candy they had. Samuel paused for a moment as he thought about one year when he'd taken Ted out trick or treating. Both he and Ted dressed up as army soldiers and had the time of their lives playing and pretending.

Samuel snapped out of his daydream and walked into the lobby of Sandra's building. He greeted the doorman who complimented him on his costume before he rang Sandra's bell. Sandra buzzed him into the building and he took the elevator up to the fourth floor where her unit was. It was the first time he'd ever been to her home.

Sandra opened the door slowly so that Samuel would get the full effect of the time and effort she'd put into making the fantasy as real as possible. She'd arched her eyebrows, applied her make-up, got her wig to fit just right, and sprayed a special scent on the area of her ample bosom that was exposed from the V-neck dress.

"Damn, baby!"

Sandra could see that Samuel was appreciative of her efforts.

"Gomez, darling," she said with a seductive tenor in her voice. "I was beginning to worry that you might not make it."

Samuel fell right into Sandra's role-playing game. "Nothing could keep me away from you, Morticia my love. Not even a violent mob anxious to behead me."

"Oh, Gomez my darling." Sandra was being overly dramatic as she embraced her man and ran one of her long, red painted fingernails down the side of his cheek as if it were a dangerously sharp knife.

"How many times has that mob beheaded you?" She didn't give him a chance to answer her. "It drives me wild when they arrive with their torches, machetes, pitchforks, and violent threats. Will they be at the party tonight?"

"They're already there, my darling, waiting for you to give them the signal to chop my head off, and do with it as you please."

They both split open with laughter at that moment.

"You're good at this," Sandra complimented Samuel.

"You're not so bad yourself, and my, I must say, that you look fabulous."

"You look rather dashing yourself," Sandra said, kissing him on the lips. "Give me a moment to grab my coat."

Samuel sat down on the sofa in front of the television, which was showing a clip from the *Rocky Horror Picture Show*. It was the scene where everyone was dancing to that weird song called "Let's do the Time Warp Again." A moment later, Sandra came out of the other room with her coat and purse.

"Are you ready, my darling?" she asked.

"Of course I am, my pet."

Samuel spotted the remote and clicked off the television. As Sandra made her way to the door, Samuel playfully smacked her on her thick and tight behind.

"Keep that thought in mind for later, my dear; when it's time to pull out the whips and chains." Sandra glanced over her shoulder at him with a wicked grin spread across her face.

"I will, but you know how anxious Thing can get; he just loves spanking that ass."

"Come on here, with your silly self." Sandra laughed some more as she closed her door and locked it.

Samuel turned off Chicago's Lake Shore Drive and into the parking lot of the Field Museum of Natural History. The organizers spared no expense to make the event look like a Halloween spectacle. There were two giant searchlights that shot bright white beams of light up into the night sky. There were small clusters of partygoers dressed up in outrageous costumes marching toward the steps of the museum. Samuel parked the car and he and Sandra blended in with the crowd. Sandra gathered her dress in her hand as she carefully walked up the steps of the museum, which had stone steps and pillars like that of an ancient Greek Palace. When they got to the entrance, someone wearing a Richard Nixon face mask greeted them.

"Welcome, Gomez," greeted Mr. Nixon. "Do you think that I can get a dance with your lovely wife Morticia later on?"

"I'm afraid not. She doesn't like Tricky Dick," Samuel answered. The people who were in line behind him split open with loud laughter at Samuel's quick wit.

"I'm not a crook," said Nixon. "I will not steal her away from you, I promise." Nixon shook Samuel's hand and allowed them access into the building.

"Here you go, baby. Here are the tickets," Sandra said, handing him the tickets as she took off her coat and approached the ticket counter. A woman dressed up as Olive Oyl was collecting all tickets.

"You guys look fabulous," Olive Oyl complimented. "Girl, you know that you're wearing the hell out of that dress," she said, which made Sandra glow on the inside. "Go toward the giant, stuffed elephant. There are drinks and food over there. The coat check is on your right, or if you want to place your things in a small locker, I believe that there are still a few available. Oh, and don't forget to check out the haunted section of the museum."

"Thanks, we won't," said Samuel.

The music was loud and the orange and black Halloween decorations, along with white cotton spider webs, made the spectacle look all the wackier. A ten-story high skeletal structure of a dinosaur had been decorated with spider webs, plastic body parts, and a welcome banner. There were tables that had candles on them, which added an interesting effect to the dim lighting of the main floor. The DJ made a few minor announcements about having a good time and then played "Family Affair" by Mary J. Blige. Sandra and Samuel made their way over to an empty table and claimed it. The dance floor was crowed with folks in all sorts of outrageous Halloween costumes, bouncing to the groove of Mary J. Blige.

"Look over there, baby." Sandra pointed out on the dance floor.

"Dracula is dancing with Xena the Warrior Princess," she said, laughing.

"Check out my man dressed up like Blade dancing with the woman dressed up like the chick from Tomb Raider."

"Well, I see why Blade is sticking with her. She looks like she's about to burst out of that little bitty ass outfit she's got on."

"Oh, look right over there to your left. Dorothy is backing that thang up against the Scarecrow. The music switched a bit and the DJ played the theme song from the movie *Ghostbusters*.

"Can I get you something to drink, my pet?" Samuel asked.

"Why yes," Sandra said, crossing her legs on the stool she was sitting on. She scratched the hair underneath Samuel's chin with her long red fingernail. "I'll have a glass of wine, please."

At that moment the DJ played "Rock the Boat" by Aaliyah and the pace of the dancing slowed down and got a bit more sensual.

"I'll be back in a moment, my darling," Samuel said as he rushed off to the bar.

"Don't get beheaded without me," Sandra joked as he stepped away.

By the time he returned Sandra was rocking in her seat to the groove of Rick James and Teena Marie singing their hit song "Fire and Desire." Sandra was spying on the couple dressed like Dorothy and the Scarecrow. The Scarecrow was singing along with Rick James about his fire and desire. Dorothy had all of her attention focused on the Scarecrow as Teena Marie bellowed out a high-pitched note that caused Dorothy to close her eyes and exhale. At the very same moment, Sandra gasped as goose bumps blanketed the side of her face and neck because of the triangular transference of emotions that was occurring between Teena Marie, Dorothy and herself.

"You know," Sandra said, tossing her hand in the air as if she were testifying to something. "When I first heard this song, I knew that Rick and Teena were messing around because they were singing with such passion." Sandra put her hand down and took a sip of her wine. "The call and response pattern that they perfected in this song is just too perfect for words."

"I could tell that, too," Samuel agreed with her as he sat and scooted his stool up close behind her. He wrapped his arms around her stomach and began rocking with her while he nibbled on her earlobe. Sandra felt a wonderful chill race down her neck every time he clinched his teeth on her lobe. Before she realized it, Sandra had finished her glass of wine and was in the mood to dance. Without waiting for Samuel to ask her, Sandra stood up, took him by the hand, and led him to the dance floor.

The moment they found a slice of real estate to dance on, a fog machine released its vapors in the air and added mystery to their surroundings. Eddie and Gerald Levert were harmonizing their hit song "Baby Hold onto Me." Sandra rested her arms on his shoulders and locked her fingers behind his neck. Samuel put one hand on each hip and drew her closer to him. Sandra gazed directly into his brown eyes and Samuel recognized her dreamy stare of desire for him immediately. The sight of her made his manhood grow stiff and tight with pressure. He drew Sandra closer, twined, and grinded their hips together so that she could feel him. The moment she felt Samuel's stiffness, the yearning between her legs made her feel lightheaded. She closed her eyes and exhaled as she felt a wave of pleasure whirl through her body, and made her island paradise ache for Samuel. Samuel tilted his neck downward and kissed her on the lips. He then began sucking on her bottom lip slightly as he pulled away. Sandra felt a light explosion erupt between her legs. She held on to Samuel even tighter as she reveled in yet another untamed wave of passion.

"You're making me wet," she whispered to him as she blinked her bedroom eyes at him. Samuel squeezed her tightly as he continued to twine and grind his manhood against her. His manhood was under a tremendous amount of strain, like the tension of water through a fire hose.

"You've gotten me so hard that I feel like I'm going to explode," Samuel whispered back and allowed his hands to leave her hips and caress her rump. Sandra exhaled again and bit him on the side of his neck like a vampire. The song ended and Sandra released herself from his embrace. The crowd of people shuffling off the dance floor provided the perfect cover for her next move, which was to reach back, grip, squeeze, and stroke Samuel's erection.

"Damn, baby, you're going to make me scream," Samuel said with short controlled spurts of breath.

"That's what you get for making me wet," Sandra responded, full of defiance and mischief. "Come on, follow me," she instructed him. "I have a surprise for you."

In the darkness of the museum, they snuck past the velvet rope and rushed off down a corridor toward the exhibits in the restricted area of the museum. They wandered pass the wax statues of cavemen and stuffed animals. As they went deeper into the halls of the museum, they came across the Egyptian Pyramid exhibit. Sandra led him inside of the pyramid to explore the inside. They looked at the writings on the wall, went down a narrow passageway, and stopped at a small bench inside of the pyramid.

"Baby, what are we doing back here?" Samuel laughed. "I'm supposed to uphold the rules, not break them."

"Oh, I'm positive you won't mind breaking the rules this one time." Sandra sat down on a small bench and had Samuel stand in front of her. "Let me show you what an uninhibited grown woman can do." She undid his belt buckle, unfastened his pants, and pulled out his rock-hard cock, which was as straight as an arrow. "Damn, you're chocolate all the way through. I've wanted to taste you for a long time," Sandra said, looking up at him with innocent eyes.

Samuel's eyes rolled up into his head when she slipped him past her soft juicy lips and inside of her warm wet mouth. She took long deep sucks as she stroked and squeezed his erection. He propped his hand against one of the tomb's walls to keep his knees from buckling. He felt a squirt of his own nectar erupt and Sandra eagerly slurped his juices up.

"Oh, damn, Sandra." Samuel glanced down at her working her neck and mouth on him. Sandra glanced up to meet his gaze with her seductive eyes and slowly blinked them at him. For Samuel, the sensual motion of her eyes blinking at him made him feel closer to her. He reached down and caressed the side of her face, wanting to seize that moment in time.

"You mean Morticia, Gomez," Sandra corrected him.

She removed him from her mouth, pulled his slacks and underwear all the way down to his ankles and raised his erect member up so that she could lick its length and kiss his balls.

"I bet you didn't know that I was a damn good ball player, did you?" she teased.

"Shit, you're right. I didn't know that you were a ball player," he whimpered as she opened her mouth wide, placed one in her mouth, and gently sucked on it.

"Oh, Lawd," Samuel moaned, feeling as if he'd died and gone to heaven. At that moment, they both heard the clicking sound of the night watchman's shoes approaching.

"Come on. We'd better take this back to my place before we get busted," Samuel whispered.

"Yeah, we better," Sandra agreed. "Because you're about to make me take my panties off and have you right here."

"Whew, let's hurry up then. I can't wait to show you how much I want you."

On the way home, Samuel stopped at a 24-hour Walgreen's Store and picked up a bottle of wine for them to enjoy. While Sandra was upstairs in the bedroom, Samuel was in the kitchen pulling down wine glasses and grabbing the corkscrew. Before he rushed upstairs, he made sure that he didn't forget to lock the front door. When he entered the bedroom he saw Sandra resting on her back positioned in a manner that was both naughty and seductive. Samuel ran his lustful tongue across his lips.

"Gomez," she cooed, willing and wanting to take the fantasy all the way to the edge. "Tonight when we were inside of the tomb, your moans reminded me of a wild animal about to howl out uncontrollably at the moon."

"I didn't mean to frighten you, my pet."

"It turned me on, baby. Would you please frighten me again? I want you to moan like that again."

Sandra circled her fingers around her nipples through the fabric of her clothes. The sensation she felt made her toes curl up into a tight fist.

"Morticia, my love." Samuel was into the fantasy. "You're my moon and whenever I'm near you, your beauty saturates my thoughts and causes me to behave like an untamed scoundrel."

"I love it when you talk dirty to me, Gomez," Sandra said, feeling herself getting wetter by the moment. She shifted her body on the bed and squeezed her legs together, enjoying a few light contractions.

"I'm going to enjoy every bit of you," Samuel muttered as he began to remove the cork from the wine bottle.

"Do you think you can handle all of me?" Sandra said, caressing her ample breasts once again through the fabric of her costume. Samuel handed her a glass of wine and she sipped it at first, but then just went ahead and gulped it down. She was hot and needed him to make love to her. It had been well over a year since she'd been with a man and her kitty-cat, or her island paradise as she liked to refer to her womanhood, was on fire.

Samuel sat down on the bed beside her and began removing his shoes. Before he could get the second one off, Sandra grabbed his shoulders, pulled him down onto his back, and began kissing him passionately. She circled her tongue around his and sucked on his tongue and bottom lip. Both she and Samuel were racing toward the edge of an escapade that had been long overdue.

Neither Samuel nor Sandra could contain their passion, desire and lust for each other, nor could they allow themselves to remain clothed. So, without further thought, they hurriedly removed their clothing as if they were on fire. Sandra knew that her eyes were telling everything that was on her mind as she studied Samuel's naked body. He had long strands of black and gray hair that covered his broad muscular chest. His hair ran all the way down his belly, which wasn't as defined as his arms and shoulders. That didn't matter to Sandra; a man with a love handle or two wasn't a turn-off to her. His manhood was like a big chocolate candy bar and she had one hell of a sweet tooth. It was deep dark chocolate, long, thick, erect and curved to the right. She stuck the tip of her thumb in her mouth and bit down on it as she felt her island paradise pulse with anticipation. Sandra still had on her black lace-trimmed thigh-high stockings and hot red panties. She wanted Samuel to be turned on by the sight of her hosiery and take pleasure in the removal of the remaining barrier that lead to her island paradise.

Samuel guided her down onto the bed, situated her on her back, and began kissing her neck and nibbling on her earlobe. He felt her hand caress his bald head, which caused butterflies of anticipation to rush through him like a raging river. He stopped for a moment, sat up, and studied her. He was mesmerized by the look of desire in her eyes and the euphoric expression of her face. He unclasped the front latch on her bra and studied her beautiful full breasts and her chocolate nipples, which were large, thick, and rigid. The sight of them made his cock throb and his mouth moisten. He tenderly caressed her breasts, and then ran his index finger down her brown stomach and played with her belly button.

Sandra laughed. "That tickles."

"Are you really ticklish?"

"Only in certain spots."

"Do you mind if I explore you so that I can locate all of your ticklish areas?"

"Be my guest," she answered.

"Hold still," Samuel requested. "I need to get a drink." He got up and poured himself a glass of wine.

"Baby, I'm on fire. What are you doing?" Sandra questioned him, a bit puzzled by his absence.

"I'm about to make you wetter than you've ever been before," he answered. "I want to drive you to the edge of desire with plenty of fore-play." Samuel removed the belt from his cloth robe, which was hanging on the back of the bedroom door. Just hearing those few words made Sandra's island paradise contract several times, causing her to close her eyes, rub it, and exhale.

Samuel sat the cloth belt on the side of her, next to her hips.

"Hold still," he requested as she was enjoying the moment of bliss her fingers were providing. Samuel tipped his wine glass just above her belly button. "This is going to feel a bit unique," he warned her as he poured a small puddle of wine into her belly button.

"Ahhhhhhh," Sandra cooed with a bizarre sense of delight.

Samuel stuck his tongue inside of her belly button and slurped up the wine. Sandra didn't know if it was the slurping sound or the sensation of having her belly button turned into a wine chalice that made her shiver uncontrollably. Whichever sensation it was, he'd made her so wet that she felt her own juices seeping through the fabric of her panties. She flopped her thighs open and began rotating her full hips, which were eager to receive him. Sensing that she would explode if he didn't deliver the goodies, Samuel teased her for a bit longer with the wine in her belly button, and then finally removed her panties. He rubbed his fingers through the pressed curly hair of her womanhood, enjoying the discovery of her wetness. Her hips were moving with purpose now and he paid attention to her every movement until he located the spot that she was discreetly directing him to.

"Ooooh," she began to pant as she clamped her thighs close to hold his fingers in the exact spot that she needed him to be in order to get her first gratifying release. Samuel watched her with delight as she grabbed the bed sheets. Her back arched and squalled.

"Do you want me now?" Samuel asked, already knowing the answer.

"Yes," she answered without hesitation.

"Then flip over, get on your hands and knees, and prop your ass high in the air. I want to enter you from behind."

Without waiting another moment, Sandra did as he requested. She grabbed a pillow to rest her head on as she bowed down and raised her behind to him.

Samuel began his journey of sexual exploration by kissing her ass softly and gradually making his way to her center, which was overflowing with her thick white juices.

"I'm going to drink every drop of your juice," Samuel said as he opened her up a bit wider with his fingers, exposed her hard clit, and let the tip of his tongue greet it with a French kiss. He began slurping up her sticky nectar and Sandra responded immediately by shivering with pleasure.

"Oh, baby," she said as she pushed her ass higher in the air so that he could drink all of her.

"Do you like that?" Samuel asked.

"Yes,"

"Do you like the way I'm licking it? Slowly and softly?"

"Yes, baby, I like it."

"Do you want me to suck your pearl tongue?"

"Please!" she begged, almost screaming it out.

Samuel traced the rim of her pussy lips before he finally puckered up and sucked her throbbing love bead.

"Oh, baby, I'm going to cum," she howled out. "Keep doing that," she pleaded as her movements became more passionate. "Suck it harder," she demanded and Samuel complied.

She finally reached her point of no return and fell forward onto the bed. Samuel enjoyed the sight of her ample ass flexing and grinding the bed. He took the palm of his hand and spanked her delicious coffee-brown rump.

The sound of her behind being slapped excited Sandra. "Smack it again, baby," she instructed him.

Samuel complied with a series of loud popping smacks that made Sandra suck in wind through her teeth. He grabbed her hips and pulled her back to him. He entered her love tunnel, which was wet, warm and slippery. She responded to his presence immediately by pushing her ass against his stomach. Samuel was in heaven. He held onto her hips and began to maneuver her ass in a fashion that he preferred, up and down instead of back and forth. The sight of her brown sugar ass, his long black cock saturated in her white juices and the sound of her rapid panting thrilled him.

"Do you like what I'm doing to you?"

"Yes, baby," she answered. "You're so deep," she cried out.

"Do you like me being deep inside of you?"

"Yes!" she yelled. "You're making me so wet."

"Then I'm not doing my job right," Samuel said as he grabbed his terrycloth robe belt. He threaded the belt under her stomach and around her hips. He coiled each end of the belt around his hands tightly. Now that he had her bridled he could ride her any way he wanted.

"Oh, God!" Sandra hollered out as she felt every inch of him inside her.

She felt an orgasm building so quickly that her body began to quake frenziedly.

"Damn, baby, you're hitting my spot," she informed him as the tip of his manhood kept touching the back wall of her island paradise. She exploded with pleasure and wanted to once again fall forward and enjoy the calming aftereffects of her orgasm but she couldn't.

"Where are you going?" Samuel bawled out. "I've got you."

He pulled on his makeshift bridle and reined her in. Sandra was racing to the edge of erotic madness. The sensations that she was feeling were attacking her so fast that her mind didn't have time to process every emotion that she was feeling. The only thing that she knew was that she had never in her life been manhandled the way that Samuel was manhandling her. She could feel all of his strength and energy with every move that he made. By no means was she a small woman but Samuel made her feel as if she were as light as a feather. In one breath, she wanted him to stop so that she could show some type of composure but then, in another breath, she wanted the wild sexual abandon to go on forever. Samuel kept pumping himself into her, and she felt as if they were bound to each other, like two savage barbarians unwilling to act tame. She grew delirious with every penetrating stroke that he pumped into her. The pleasure that she was experiencing was so wonderful that she shrieked at the top of her voice.

"Oh damn!" Sandra yelled out, feeling another scream stirring. "You're going to make me scream again, Samuel."

"Well, holler for me then. Howl out at the top of your voice. Make me hear how good it feels to you."

Sandra couldn't believe her ears when she heard her voice screaming out so loud. It was like she was listening to someone else and not herself. She felt Samuel's cock begin to pulsate.

"Oh, shit!" she screamed. "I can feel you, baby. I can feel you about to release."

Sandra immediately saw stars as she felt his hot liquid whiz inside of her like a wave crashing against the shoreline. She screamed out again, but into the pillow this time to muffle her sound. Samuel freed her from the bridle and she fell forward onto her stomach. She turned over to look at him. She wanted to see his face; she wanted to know if she'd pleased him the way that he'd pleased her. Samuel's body was slick with sweat but he looked both gratified and tranquil. Sandra removed her stockings and placed the soles of her feet against the hair on his chest. Samuel smiled as he grabbed her ankles and rubbed her feet up and down against his chest.

"That tickles," Sandra said.

"I guess I've just found another ticklish spot," Samuel answered as he brushed her feet up and down against his chest faster.

"Stop it!" she demanded and snatched her ankles away from him. "What are you trying to do to me? I lost count of how many times you made me cum."

"Just trying to prepare you for round two." He smiled and then winked at her.

Oh, damn! Sandra thought. *My ass is in trouble.*

CHAPTER TWELVE

The following morning Sandra crept out of bed before Samuel; eager to show him her gratitude for an evening of incredible lovemaking. She was about to exit the room when she caught a glimpse of one of Samuel's pressed uniform shirts and his state trooper's hat hanging in the closet. She giggled to herself as she slipped her arm into the sleeve of his shirt and put his hat on her head. She went into the bathroom where she surveyed herself in the mirror. The hat was too big for her head and slopped down on her forehead, hiding her eyes a bit, but she didn't care because it was saturated with the scent of Samuel's hair. Sandra snooped around the bathroom and was elated to find that there was a spare unopened toothbrush and fresh towels. As she brushed her teeth, she peered around for signs of another woman but couldn't find any. That's a huge relief, she thought to herself. Once Sandra finished, she bounced down the stairs and into the kitchen. She hoped that Samuel had some breakfast food because she wanted to demonstrate that not only was she good in bed; but she was first-rate in the kitchen as well. She searched his cabinets and pulled down a box of grits. She opened the deep freezer and found some turkey sausage. She opened the refrigerator and found a can of buttermilk biscuits along with some jumbo eggs.

"Now, if I can find some green peppers, cheese and mushrooms, I'll be all set," she remarked as she inspected the bottom of the refrigerator. To her surprise, she found all the vegetables that she needed to make the omelet she had in mind. She located the skillet for the sausage, a pan for the biscuits, and began preparing a hearty breakfast. Sitting on top of the refrigerator was a small white radio that she turned on. Missy Elliot was singing her hit "Get Your Freak On."

"Hey now!" Sandra shouted out as she scooted the brim of the hat back so that it didn't cover her eyes so much, and then began popping her fingers and bouncing around singing along with Missy.

"Get your freak on. Get your freak on. Get your freak on. Get your freak on." Sandra got caught up in the music and began dropping her ass like it was hot. "That's right, girl! Represent for the big women because we know how to get our freak on." Sandra laughed out loud to herself. "I got my freak on, damn it!" she said as she tossed a few sausage links into the hot skillet.

"Is that a fact?" Samuel chimed as he entered the kitchen with a smile.

"Hey, baby," Sandra answered him, feeling like a giddy schoolgirl. She skipped over to him, locked her fingers behind his neck, and began rocking her hips to Missy Elliot's music.

"Do you like the way I'm moving, baby?" she asked with her teeth nibbling her bottom lip.

Samuel put his hands on her hips and searched her eyes. "What are you down here doing?"

"Cooking for my man."

Samuel ran his hands over her behind. "I like the way you said that."

"You better," she said.

"Is that a threat or a warning?"

"It's both," Sandra said, getting a bit more serious with him. "I'm only giving my love to you and no one else," she said as she unlocked her fingers and took a firm grip on his manhood. "If I ever find out that my shit…" She squeezed his cock and kissed him lightly on the lips at the same time "…is someplace that it isn't supposed to be, I'll cut it off."

Samuel realized that she was dead serious. "No need to get violent, baby. I'm all yours."

"Good, I'm glad we understand each other," Sandra affirmed as she knelt down on her knees. "Because you can have me any way that you want me as long as you're loyal to me." She put him inside of her warm mouth. Samuel gasped. "Are you going to be loyal to me?"

"Yes," Samuel answered, feeling his knees beginning to buckle.

"That's a good boy," she said and sank her fingers into his tight butt cheeks and pushed him deeper into her mouth.

CHAPTER THIRTEEN

Sandra stood at the kitchen sink with a red scarf tied around her head, washing her greens for the Thanksgiving dinner that her daughter Kelly had pleaded with her to prepare. Kelly wanted her mother to meet her boyfriend, Ted, who she'd been with for almost a year.

"So I finally get to meet this mystery boy," Sandra commented with a bit of sarcasm. Her cycle had just started that morning and her stomach was very bloated, which was making her more irritable than normal. "Something must be wrong with him because you certainly weren't in a rush for me to meet him."

"There's nothing wrong with Ted, Mom." Kelly got defensive. "I just wanted to make sure that he'd last for a while before I started bringing him around."

"Ok, if you say so," Sandra said. "Where are his people from?"

"They're from Oak Park. His mother died a few years ago so it's just him and his dad now."

"Oh, really," Sandra said, thinking about Samuel's son Theodore. *Could*

Kelly be…Naa. She dismissed the thought, thinking that it would be too awkward if something like that were true.

"So, did you ever get any responses from the Sistergirls.com website?" Kelly inquired.

"Yeah," Sandra said, being intentionally vague.

"Really!" Kelly's voice rose about four octaves. "Why didn't you say something? What does the man look like? Where is he from? What did he say?" Kelly was firing off one question after another.

"That, my dear, is grown folks' business," Sandra answered being a bit coy.

"Oh, no you didn't go there with me?" Kelly was a bit surprised that her mother was suddenly treating her like she was nine again.

"I just did," Sandra shot back. "Are you almost done with those potatoes?"

"Mom!" Kelly began whining.

"What?" Sandra wanted to play dumb with her.

"I'm your best friend. You have to tell me."

"Says who?"

"So you're really going to be like that?" Kelly was pouting so Sandra decided to offer her a little scrap of information.

"Ok, I got a reply from a gentleman who lives nearby. We've talked through Instant Messenger a few times and we've even talked on the phone a couple of times."

"And?" Kelly was eager for more information.

"And what?"

"And what did you guys talk about? Come on, Mom. Don't make me pull this out of you the slick way."

"And what way is the slick way?" Sandra asked.

"Ok, if you'll tell me everything, I'll scrub your feet for you and I'll give you a pedicure," Kelly offered.

"Naw, there isn't much to tell."

"Oh, I see that you're going to make me play dirty. I'll do your feet, plus wash your hair, scratch your head, and oil your scalp."

"You've got a deal, baby." Sandra quickly jumped on the offer because there was no way she could resist the soothing effects of one of Kelly's "head scratchings," as she liked to call them.

～

Later that afternoon, after Sandra and Kelly finished with all of the cooking, Sandra decided that she'd surprise Samuel by dropping by with a plate of food. She loaded his plate with macaroni and cheese, greens, slices of roast beef and mashed potatoes smothered in gravy along with large slices of German chocolate cake and caramel cake that she'd baked. The sweet tooth she had was a monster. She wrapped the plate in aluminum foil, told Kelly she would return shortly, and headed out the door.

～

CHAPTER FOURTEEN

Samuel was in the backyard raking up the autumn leaves when he heard someone speaking to him from the sidewalk. "Well, aren't you a sight for sore eyes."

Samuel halted his business of raking the leaves in a pile and looked over his shoulder in the direction where the voice came from.

"You look good with a shaved head," complimented Vera.

Samuel allowed his eyes to give away his thoughts as he admired her smooth caramel skin, seductive eyes, long straight black hair, tight hip-hugging jeans and her black turtleneck, which accentuated her breasts. She stuffed her fingers in the front pockets of her jeans as she stood on the other side of the fence.

"Why are you being such a stranger?" Vera inquired. "You don't call me anymore. We don't speak anymore. I mean, we can still be friends, can't we?"

"We'll always be friends, Vera," Samuel said, wondering how in the world his old girlfriends knew to show up when he had a new woman in his life. "I never said I didn't want to be your friend." Samuel approached the fence so he didn't have to speak louder than necessary.

"Well, friends don't ignore each other like you've been ignoring me, mister."

In the back of his mind, Samuel knew he needed to be forthright with Vera, but instead of saying that he'd met someone and bringing complete closure to their past sexual relationship, he left a door open while he considered whether or not to tread old waters.

"I've just been busy, Vera. It's nothing personal."

"Now that makes me feel much better." She ran her tongue across her smooth chocolate lips in an effort to both tease and excite Samuel. Vera unlatched the gate and stepped inside of the yard. "So, do you think you could make some time for me?"

Vera began working her charms on him by locking her fingers behind his neck and gazing into his eyes, signaling that she'd come over for the purpose of a hot night of sex.

"You know, I haven't been with anyone since you," she said. "I've been celibate for nearly eight months. Don't you want to crack me open and discover just how luscious I feel on the inside?"

Damn! Samuel said to himself. Vera's offer was causing him to struggle. Samuel knew that he needed to back up. He wanted to back up, but the thought of getting some hot juicy pussy that hadn't been tapped for so long was a temptation that he was grappling with. *Vera isn't a bad person,* he reasoned with himself. *We were good in bed together, and no woman has ever squeezed my manhood with her pussy muscles the way she could; not even Sandra.* Suddenly his cock grew stiff, entertaining the thought of being inside Vera once again. Vera could see that she had Samuel right where she wanted him. She caressed his smooth bald head and spoke purposefully in his ear.

"We should go in the house so that you can see just how wet standing here with you and caressing your sexy bald head is making me."

Sandra saw some wench caressing Samuel's head and hugging him in the backyard. Normally she would've been excited when she reached the neighborhood intersection where his home was located. She would've made a right turn, driven about thirty yards to his driveway, parked her car, and entered the backyard to knock on the kitchen door at the rear of the house. Now, she sat at the intersection glaring at the woman smiling at her man. Tears formed in her eyes as a knife plunged into her heart and her emotions. She didn't make the turn, opting to just drive straight ahead and leave Mr. Too Good to Be True alone forever.

Samuel heard Ted open the back door.

"Oh, sorry, Dad. I didn't realize you had company with you," Ted said. "I just wanted to let you know that I made it back."

"Hey, Ted." Vera smiled and waved at him.

"Hey, Vera. How are you doing?"

"I'm good, sugar, and you?"

"I'm doing good," Ted answered her, "Dad, I'm going to go take a shower before I head on out to Kelly's house."

"Ok, no problem," Samuel said to Ted as he closed the back door, leaving him and Vera to their privacy.

"Once Ted is gone, we can do it all over the house," she whispered.

Samuel could see the lust in Vera's eyes and, normally, that would've been enough to make him give her what she'd come for but he suddenly remembered why he'd broken it off with her in the first place.

"How's your son doing, Vera? Did he get his act together yet? Or better yet, do you have the money you owe me?"

The lustful expression on Vera's face began to fade quickly as she attempted to save the moment.

"Why are you bringing up the past, baby? Can't I make it up to you in other ways?" She let her first and middle fingers walk down Samuel's chest toward his stomach. "I'd be more than willing to work off the debt I owe you."

Suddenly Vera was a complete turn-off to him. "You know what, Vera? You need to leave." The entire moment had gone sour in an instant and Samuel wanted nothing to do with her.

"Damn, if you needed the money back that bad, why didn't you just call me up for it?"

"First, I shouldn't have to call you up for money you owe me. Secondly, I now realize that you're not really the woman I want to be with. I have a new woman in my life, Vera, and she's got her shit together. Plus, I'm crazy about her."

Vera got loud. "Who do you think you're talking to like that? I'm not your damn child!"

"Have a good holiday, Vera," Samuel calmly said. "You can let yourself out."

Without saying another word, Samuel walked back into the house and shut the door, signaling that their relationship and friendship had come to an end.

CHAPTER FIFTEEN

Sandra was about to hit the freeway but decided that, at that moment, she was no longer hurt by what she'd seen. She was pissed off by the fact that she'd allowed some nucca she'd met on the Internet to play with her emotions; especially while she was cramping. *The minute I turn my back, I find him with another woman,* she thought to herself. There was no way that she'd allow the relationship to end without first getting ghetto-fabulous and cursing his ass out like he stole something from her, which in reality he had. He'd stolen her heart and then abused it. Sandra did a U-turn in the middle of the street and pinned the accelerator to the floor of her Jeep Grand Cherokee.

"Samuel, I'm about to drop my foot off in your ass!" she hollered out as she sped along breaking the speed limit and not caring if she got pulled over by the police.

"Now, you've pissed me the fuck off! I'm a classy and reserved woman by nature but I've got a mean and ugly side as well. You just got on it. I'm about to get ghetto-fabulous on your ass!" She brought her car to a screeching halt at the front of his house. She grabbed the plate of food she'd prepared for his ass and hustled up to the front door. She rang the doorbell and listened as he approached the door.

"Who is it?" Samuel asked.

"It's me, nucca. Open up the goddamn door."

"Sandra?" Samuel opened the door, puzzled by her loud language.

"Move out of my damn way!" she yelled as she forced her way into the house. She walked into the living room area and uncovered the food she'd prepared for him. Samuel shut the door and walked into the living room where she was.

"Nucca, how could you?" She picked up some food and flung it at him. He dodged the food. "Hey, what the hell is wrong with you?"

"I've been in the house cooking all damn day, thinking about your musty ass!" She flung the roast beef and gravy at him. Samuel dodged the airborne food, which splattered against his white wall.

"Now hold on one damn minute! You need to calm your ass down and tell me what the fuck is going on?" Samuel raised his voice at her.

"That whore you were out there in the yard hugged up with!" Sandra barked at him.

"Is that what this is about?" Samuel smiled and suddenly began laughing as he plopped down on the sofa.

"What's so damn funny?" Sandra was livid.

"You are." Samuel laughed some more. "You come over here with a scarf around your head and flinging a plate of food at me like you've lost your mind."

"And what's so damn funny about that?" She tossed some more food at him.

"Hey, stop that now!" Samuel said, dodging the food, but Sandra quickly reloaded and nailed him right in his left eye with some mashed potatoes.

"Damn! Sandra, stop it now. I'm serious. I'm laughing because I realize you're just as crazy about me as I am about you."

"Yeah right, nucca!" She flung some greens at him, which hit him in the forehead. She flung some more greens but missed her mark and hit the wall behind him. At that moment, she heard the water running upstairs.

"Oh, that bitch is still here!" Sandra howled as she dropped the plate on the carpet, turned, and headed up the stairs.

"Sandra, don't go up there," Samuel pleaded.

"I'm going to give this wench a piece of my damn mind," Sandra said, stomping up the stairs."

Samuel quickly got up to attempt to stop her but stubbed his baby toe on the edge of the cocktail table.

"Son-of-a-bitch!" he wailed out in pain as he hobbled up and down on one leg trying to shake off the pain.

Sandra pushed open the bathroom door, walked over to the shower curtain, snatching down both the curtain and its rod.

"Whoa!" Ted was startled as he stood naked glaring at a woman he'd never seen before.

"Who the fuck are you?" Ted said to the woman, who was obviously stunned to find him in the shower.

Sandra couldn't help but notice how much Samuel's son looked like him. He was just a younger version of his father. She didn't want to look down at his manhood but she couldn't help it. Ted had been blessed with the same tools that his father had.

"I'm so sorry," Sandra uttered, feeling like a complete fool. "I thought you were someone else." Sandra couldn't stop her eyes from blinking. She was about to crack open and cry.

"Who in the hell were you expecting? Santa Claus?" Ted barked at her as he turned off the shower.

"I'm so sorry," Sandra apologized again, and then she turned and hustled out of the bathroom. Before Samuel could make it up the stairs, Sandra had rushed down them and out the front door in a flash.

~

CHAPTER SIXTEEN

Sandra rushed home and pulled herself together as best she could so that she wouldn't ruin Kelly's dinner with her boyfriend. When she returned, Kelly instantly picked up on Sandra's shitty mood.

Kelly wrinkled her face at her mother. "What's the matter with you?"

"Kelly, I'm not in the mood for your whining tonight," Sandra snapped at her but she really didn't mean to seem like she was angry with her.

"I can't believe that you're coming out of a bag on me like this."

"I'm not coming out of any damn bag, okay! Let's just get through the dinner so I can get some sleep."

At that moment, the doorbell rang and Sandra went to answer it.

"That's probably him, Mom. Be nice, okay?" Sandra ignored Kelly's comment and buzzed the lobby door so Ted could come up. A few moments later there was a knock at the door. Sandra opened it.

"Oh, shit!" Ted said when he saw Sandra greeting him at the door, the woman who'd seen him naked in the shower.

"Oh, my God!" Sandra put her hands over her eyes and closed them. Her fear was now a reality and a migraine suddenly began to develop in her temples.

"Let me guess. You're Theodore, right?" she asked.

"Uhm, yes, ma'am, but everyone calls me Ted. And you're Miss Gill, Kelly's mom, right?"

Sandra could hear a bit of uncertainty in Ted's voice. At that instant, she really wished that she were someone else because she couldn't bring herself to look him in the eyes.

"Yes, I'm Kelly's mother," Sandra answered him.

"Should I come in or is this a bad time?" Ted asked politely, but he was really thinking that his future mother-in-law was a goddamn nut; just like Vera, his father's ex-girlfriend, was a nutcase.

"No, please, come in," Sandra said as she moved aside. Kelly came out and gave him a hug and kiss.

"Hey, baby." She wound her arms around his neck.

"Hey, baby doll," Ted responded, feeling nervous and extremely awkward.

Sandra was about to close the door when she was stopped by the sound of Samuel's voice calling her name.

"Sandra, we need to talk," Samuel said, entering her condo.

Sandra tossed her hands in the air in frustration. "How did you get in the building?"

"I walked in the door with one of your neighbors," Samuel answered.

"Dad, what are you doing here?" Ted asked, completely dumbfounded.

"What are you doing here?" Samuel asked the same question. "I didn't notice your car outside."

"Wait a minute, hold on." Kelly raised her hand. "Can someone please explain to me what's going on here?"

"Well, um," Ted spoke. "Your mom sort of came over to my house today and...well...she thought I was someone else, I think, and she ripped down the shower curtain and saw me naked, I mean, she didn't mean to, I don't think."

"Ted, be quiet," Samuel interrupted him. His son was unintentionally making his woman sound like some kind of senseless lunatic.

"Wait a minute, back up a second," Kelly said. "What was my mother doing at your house?"

"I can explain," Sandra said, releasing a deep sigh of embarrassment. "It appears we're in a peculiar situation. I've been dating Ted's father, Samuel, and you've been dating Samuel's son, Ted."

"Hold up." Kelly began laughing. "This is too creepy. Are you the man my mom met on Sistergirls.com?" Kelly asked Samuel.

"Yeah, but Ted's the one who gave me the website address. I was just surfing the net one night. I went to the site and saw her photo."

"So all of this is like total coincidence, right?" Kelly asked.

Sandra sighed. "Yes, it appears that way."

"So, what's the deal with you seeing my Ted naked, Mom?" Kelly asked with a catty tone in her voice.

"I think I can answer that one," answered Samuel. "An old girlfriend of mine stopped by the house this afternoon and, well, quite frankly, tried to seduce me. I think at the exact moment she was trying to convince me to be with her, your mother saw that. But, she didn't see me when I told Vera to leave."

"I drove off," Sandra confessed. "Then I got pissed off because I thought Samuel was playing me for a fool. So, I decided I was going to give him a piece of my mind. I drove back to his house, got very unladylike with him, and in a fit of anger flung food all over his house."

"Yeah, because you've got food all over the walls and furniture, plus you ripped the shower rod right out of the wall," Ted added.

"I'm sorry about that. Trust me; I'm not some whack-o. I'm going to take care of the damage I caused."

"Baby, you don't have to worry about that. It's water under the bridge. I was planning to repaint the front room anyway," Samuel said.

"I got so pissed with Samuel when he started laughing at me," Sandra continued. "You made me feel stupid, and I really felt dense when I thought the woman I saw in the backyard was taking a shower."

"So, Mom, you thought you were going to confront another woman." Kelly could hardly believe her ears. "That's so unlike you. It must be some powerful loving going on to make you want to fight over him."

"Kelly, shut up." Sandra wrinkled her lips at her daughter because, although it was the truth, Sandra didn't want to hear it from Kelly's mouth.

"Baby, I didn't mean to make you feel dumb. That's the last thing that I wanted to do. I was just tickled because at that moment I was happy. When I saw how pissed off you were, I knew that you were as nuts about me as I am about you. I must admit, if I had rolled up on you and seen another man with you, I can't say that I wouldn't have done something outrageous as well. I never intended to make you feel dumb. Can you forgive me?" Samuel approached Sandra, placed his arms around her waist, and gazed into her eyes showing how sincere he was.

Sandra was silent for a moment, contemplating whether or not to let Samuel off the hook. "Only if Gomez promises to never make Morticia feel that way again."

"Gomez promises," Samuel said.

"Who are Gomez and Morticia?" Ted asked, confused.

"That's grown folks' business," Samuel said with a thundering tone.

"And you need to stay out of it," both Samuel and Sandra said in unison.

"Well, excuse me!" Ted said, laughing.

"This is like too damn wild," Kelly chimed, as she laughed and swung her head from right to left. "I mean, I'd expect to hear something like this on one of those raunchy ghetto daytime talk shows. I mean, Ted and I have been talking about marriage. But if you guys got married as well, that would mean that my stepfather would also be my father-in-law, and my husband would also be my stepbrother. Ew, that's sick."

"I must admit it is a bit, extreme," Sandra agreed. "I don't believe I'm about to say this, but there's nothing wrong with that. We're all adults and can keep our business confined between us."

"So where do we go from here?" Samuel asked. "Now that all of our drama is out in the open."

"Might I suggest we sit down and eat Thanksgiving Dinner? I don't know about you guys but my behind his hungry," said Ted.

"That sounds like a wonderful idea," Sandra said, feeling better now that they'd gotten the misunderstanding cleared up.

Samuel chuckled. "Well, Ted, the Edgar men certainly know how to find good women."

"Yup, we just let our fingers do the walking and logged onto Sister-girls.com."

The four of them split open with laughter.

THE END

Somewhere Between Love and Sarcasm

V. ANTHONY RIVERS

~

CHAPTER ONE

After enduring close calls, computer viruses, and strange meetings in the night, I STILL never learned my lesson. I guess I can't help myself. I went to Netscape, typed in "dating" and before I knew it, I was hooked, again. I scrolled down the list of websites. I got addicted instantly to my own fascination. One after the other...I mouthed the words, *chicks with*...Never mind...I continued to scroll. I couldn't stop my fingers from caressing the mouse. I got one that looks like an eight ball. I'm referring to the one used in billiards, mind you.

Nevertheless, I couldn't stop the onslaught of curiosity from oozing its way out of my unconscious actions. I placed in front of me, a sort of welcome mat type of belief that my next internet experience would somehow be different. Different from the last and the one before that...In other words, it would actually work out and I wouldn't find myself needing to rush to my computer and block another person from emailing me or seeing me on their buddy list. I'm about sick of doing that over and over. Pretty soon, my buddy list won't be able to take any more names.

I shake my head in disbelief as I look at what my life has amounted to, once I embraced the insanity of internet dating. My most recent experience comes to mind like a warning sign, telling me not to keep clicking on all these websites. *Don't do it,* my inner voice tells me. I don't listen, at least not closely. *Remember the cloak and dagger style apartment?* I shake off the continued warnings. *That apartment was so dark inside. Then when you went to turn on the lights, you discovered there were no bulbs in any of the light fixtures.*

"Shut up!" I blurted out, continuing to search through websites with an almost demonic expression on my face.

Remember how she kept screaming at the top of her lungs whenever she called out to you? She left you alone in the living room while she was doing God knows what in her bedroom. Was she changing clothes or was she sharpening some sort of blade, to be used on her unsuspecting invited guest?

"It wasn't like that... I don't know!"

And what were you doing in the living room after you decided to open the curtains, permitting daylight to illuminate the room?

"Doing?"

Remember seeing all those thousands of magazines? You wondered in darkness why her apartment smelled like a newspaper stand.

"Yeah, that was the first thing I noticed. Well, after she opened the door and ran toward the back, disappearing on a brotha, I noticed."

Uh huh, and after you'd seen all those thousands of magazines, what did you do?

"I can't believe I'm having this conversation with myself..."

Remember discovering an issue of Ebony *magazine from 1946 with Lena Horne on the cover?*

That part gives me reason to smile. Yeah, I remember that.

You thought about taking the magazine but then suddenly the woman screamed from her bedroom that she'd be out in ten seconds.

"Yeah, and it took me five to run out the door, hop in my car, and drive away!"

And you still wish to continue searching for love on the internet?

I thought for a moment. Should I, shouldn't I, should I...I scratched the stubble beneath my chin until I'd come to my most confident conclusion.

"Yeah!" I proclaimed.

I felt like I didn't have anything better to do. And, there's nothing else that takes as little effort yet has such an enormous amount of potential once my luck actually changed for the better. Who am I fooling? I'm addicted to this stuff and now that I've set myself in motion to go through with another attempt, there's no turning back.

I clicked at the bottom of the screen to go to the next fifteen selections of dating websites. At the top of the list was Sistergirls.com and something about that name caused me to do an unconscious imitation of the Rock. My right eyebrow did like his does. It went up so far, it almost touched my hairline. Well, the one that I used to have. No, my hairline isn't receding or anything like that. I've just recently been styling with the au-natural, Michael Jordanish, Tupac Shakurish look these days. And let me tell it? I look damn good!

Back to my dating search. Once again I gazed at the name Sistergirls.com. My right eyebrow continued to stay airborne.

"Humph, what's this all about?" I asked myself as if I already knew the answer.

I was all giddy as I clicked on the website. The words "Welcome To…" never looked better. I was already hooked, intrigued, and raring to go!

"Okay, how much is this going to cost me?" I spoke in the direction of my computer screen.

Hmm, I couldn't find anything that said I needed to pay in order to browse or even email someone, if I was interested. I smiled. I bit my bottom lip and rubbed my hands together like a fly, eyeing an unattended big plate of juicy watermelon. Let's see. I clicked on the search link, which took me to a prompt that said, "I am a man in search of a woman between the ages of…" I had to click on the age range I wanted. It took me a while to decide because sistahs these days look incredible from 21 to 61. I narrowed my scope, being that I'm a sometimes well-adjusted 33-year-old, or so I'd like to imagine. I clicked on 25 to 41 and moved my cursor to the search button.

"Ooh wee, success!" I whispered out loud.

Names and pictures started filling up my computer screen like chocolate candy rolling by on a conveyor belt. It was a virtual candy parade! Debbie, Valerie, Alisa, Delores, Camille, Kaleesha, Jada... Jada...Hmm...I stopped there. I clicked on Jada's picture and read her stats.

Jada Broussard, 5'9, model type, light mocha complexion, banging body, long hair (all mine), looking for a man not afraid to give a lot and spoil his woman. Must have nice car, nice place, great dresser, good teeth, great career...

Never mind. I didn't need to read any further because this chick only wanted to spread her arms open wide enough to see how much you could give her. Plus, I think she also wanted to make sure you looked good for those rare occasions when you might be seen with her in public. No thanks. I didn't have the funds in my account to supply her habit of me, me, me, give it all to me...Nope, I had to hit the go back function and continue looking until someone else grabbed my curiosity.

I found plenty to choose from on Sistergirls.com. In fact, there were way too many for me to look at without getting a little winded and a little frustrated. In the back of my mind, I kind of wondered why all these gorgeous women were even on the net, advertising themselves for dates. I couldn't really talk about them in a bad way because then I'd just be representing myself as a hypocrite. Nope. After taking a grape soda break, I continued my search while not even considering that I might have something more important to do on a Saturday like washing clothes, washing the car, grocery shopping, paying bills, et etera, et cetera.

Bump all that domestic stuff. I returned to my search, clicking to go to the next page of women. Once again, the names paraded by one after the other. Stephanie, Jacqueline, Pamela, Celeste, Tamara, Julie, Victoria, Karen...For some reason, the name Celeste leapt into my thoughts. I scrolled back up and clicked on the photo to enlarge it. She looked pretty good, kind of sophisticated. I could see no hints of issue-related confusion behind her smiling eyes but I had to remember, I was just looking at a photo on the internet. No telling how much it could've been doctored up or distorted in her favor.

I continued to stare at the picture for a moment. It was like her picture improved the more I stared at it. As I said, she had an um, sophistication about her. Maybe she'd been around not only literally, but figuratively, though I didn't mean that negatively. She just looked like she might've been a little older than myself but that was cool. What was one or two years older going to hurt? It might've been what I needed since everything my age or younger had turned out to be a disappointment.

I took my curiosity a step further and clicked on her stats and interest. First thing that came to mind was that this lady seemed very intelligent. Either that or she just had a lot to brag about and didn't mind doing it. She wrote so much that it was almost intimidating, but then again, maybe that was by design. She was going to flush out all the playas, freaks, and non-intelligent fools that otherwise might follow through with an introduction like "You so fine, why don't you holla back with your number so we can get together?" I didn't think something like that would work with this particular lady. My always-active curiosity was turning into a good healthy dose of admiration as I read through Celeste's dating profile. It read like this:

Hi! I'm Celeste Marshall.

I'm a 39-year-old, single black female. My hair is short and I've been known to change the color every now and again. I won't say what color it is now because if you're the chosen one and we meet, you might call me a liar because the color could be different. I don't like being called a liar and it's one of my pet peeves when it comes to a man in my life. Tell me a lie and I'll invite you to leave. Pet Peeve…Doesn't that sound like an adopted policy in one's life? I assure you, I've always hated liars so there's nothing new about that. Now, before I lose you with my ranting about liars, I'll move on to the next subject.

The rest of me, underneath my gorgeous smile…Well, I don't consider that extremely important but I do understand that the visual is necessary in today's got-to-know-everything-up-front world. Let's just say that I'm put together very well and being that I will soon turn 40, I'm all about nutrition and taking good care of myself. Even my doctor applauds my efforts and says he never has to give me any instructions unless I ask. Hell, most of the time he asks me what my secrets are. I have only one pet peeve about my doctor, though. I recently discovered that he's dating one of my girlfriends so I almost feel like I'm doing something wrong since this man has seen both of us naked. I can't believe I'm sharing this in a dating profile but what the heck! This is such an impersonal form of sharing dialogue and/or meeting someone that it needs for individuals to express themselves as they would face to face, in person. I'm doing just that, though I'm sure I might appear somewhat long-winded. That brings me to my next subject.

What I'm like...I'm very easy-going and yes, I talk *a lot.* I believe that conversation is man and woman's greatest gift. Though I've dated a few quiet men in my past, if they don't learn to speak up, they get the boot. Needless to say, I've run into quite a few and as you can see, I'm now trying my luck here. Let's see, I enjoy going to museums, festivals (especially food and art), concerts (mostly jazz), and movies (foreign and dramatic films). Maybe if you're reading this now, you're either about to move on to the next lady or you're daring and the kind of man that I like. So, for those of you sticking around, I'm looking forward to your email introduction. I hope it's something that will make me smile and even challenge me a little bit. There's nothing more seductive than an intelligent man who's sharp and quick-witted. I've sort of been debating lately if I'm attracted to someone who's sarcastic. I guess I can take it up to a point. I'm still undecided about that personality trait.

What I do for a living...Now this is something that I prefer to keep private and not talk about over the internet. However, I will say that I'm involved in the financial field and recently I've been rewarded to the point where all the hard work it took to get here finally feels like it was actually worth it.

Now for the all-important part...What am I looking for in you, the man? That can sometimes be a loaded question. The most perfect scenario would be that I find someone just like me who likes to do all the same things that I like to do and yet doesn't get on my nerves because we're so much alike. So, for those of you not confused by what I just said, please email me and tell me a little something about you. I know I was somewhat vague in what I'm looking for but I believe that I will know just by seeing an example in how you communicate. I'm not shy at all so if you're not for me, I will be straightforward and tell you. Thank you for reading my profile. Hope to hear from you soon...

Sincerely,

Celeste Marshall

Wow. After reading Celeste's profile, my first thought was to brush her off as some uppity chick trying to describe herself as being the ultimate woman. She just went on and on when most brothas just want some body statistics, sexual orientation and favorite foods. Celeste seemed like she was on some high maintenance tip and probably would have a fit if I did something like take her to a Jack-in-the-Box to get some curly fries. I bet she'd get on her cell phone right away and call a cab. Or, if she was driving, she'd probably give me money for bus fare so I could get home safely, or not. Actually, I take that back. Celeste didn't seem like the type to ever drive a man around on a date. Nah, I kept looking at her picture and rereading different parts of her profile. I debated and thought about it, over and over. Should I? I moved my cursor over the link to respond with an email. I hadn't clicked yet; I just kept teasing the link with the arrow. I had to think some more. I wasn't sure but just like that devil that sits on my shoulder, curiosity was again pulling me by the ear. I responded...

Dear Celeste,

I don't do this often, (*I lied*) but I couldn't help the urge that came over me after reading your profile and yes, seeing your picture. You are indeed stunning. (*I'm trying to sound intelligent*) But, to be totally honest, (*I'm about to lie again*) I am pleasantly overwhelmed by the colorful and exuberant manner in which you described who you are. I find myself very attracted to you and I realize that's a bold statement to make before meeting you in person. I pray my assumption doesn't offend you. The thought of meeting you, Ms. Marshall, already puts a smile on my face.

Well, allow me to cut to the chase (*I'm stupid, trying to sound so intelligent*) and share with you a little bit about myself. I feel like I should remain brief here for fear of any pending embarrassment I'd suffer, should I not hear from you. Please don't think that I lack confidence because I assure you, I'm a very confident young man. I'm a few years younger than you are but I hope that the age difference won't present a problem. I wear a shaved head, similar to Avery Brooks. *(Saying Avery Brooks might make me sound even more intelligent)* Remember him from *Star Trek* and he once played as a detective on a short-lived television series. His gun was too big so they cancelled his show. I'm being facetious, of course.

Physically, I'm a fairly tall person, 6'3" in height with a slim build. I can't profess to be a nutritional guru but I do a great job with seafood and pasta dishes. I'd enjoy cooking for you one evening.

All the activities you mentioned in your profile sound great. However, I am a sports hound so I do require an occasional football game on Sundays and I do become glued to the television when the Lakers come on. I hope my love for sports doesn't warrant a strike against me. I'd never choose a game over an evening out with a beautiful, intelligent woman.

Celeste, I think I'll end here and wait for your response before I go any further. May this email find you in good spirits. Thank you and God Bless…

Jason King

I felt pretty good about my email response to Celeste, even though I was fronting the whole time. Hell, I don't talk proper like that but I was in search of something different. Celeste could bring a whole new meaning to my life. She could be the missing link. She could represent the torch to light up some new path or direction for me to undertake. Damn, I was sounding desperate, like I had no life. If I meet this chick, I hoped I didn't lose my sense of humor. I clicked to go back to the previous page. I wanted to do something to make sure I was still the same old Jason King. I clicked on Jada Broussard's photo so I could take another look. Then I clicked on her email address. Silly me, I just couldn't resist doing this.

Dear Jada,

My name is Jason and straight up, I'm gonna dispense with formalities and all that other whoop-de-whoop nonsense. I'm just gonna be real with you, girl, and speak my mind. You're one fine sista so why don't you holla at a brotha and send me your number so I can call you, aight? That's on the real, Jada, and that's me...

Peace,

Jason King

I clicked on the send button and then started busting up at what I'd written. That lady would either block me from ever writing to her again or respond by telling me something I'd already discovered. Something like, "You are a stupid man!" The only difference between her definition and mine? She'd be deadly serious about it, and me? I'd say it with a lot of self-love and humor. I was just playing with the lady, anyway. I hoped to hear from Celeste. She seemed pretty interesting. She could teach a young man some old tricks and make me feel like I'd discovered something new.

The next few days elapsed into moments defined by myself as pure misery. My ego took a beating each time I signed on to Sistergirls.com and noticed that I'd had no one respond to any of my inquiries. Not even Celeste wrote back to at least say she'd enjoyed my email. I wondered if I'd accidentally deleted my messages or maybe the website screened the emails before it allowed them to reach the intended person. I tried desperately to come up with an excuse. Nothing worked to calm me down. Then I came up with another lame excuse. Like, maybe it's my name! Maybe Celeste, Jada, and a few others took one look at my name and instantly assumed that I might be an ax murderer. That's pretty far-fetched, I know, but ever since those *Friday the 13th* movies had been coming out, I'd been the butt of many jokes. My friends teased me all the time about it and with this whole internet dating scene being such a risk-taking venture, I didn't blame women for being so cautious.

"But, why me?" I shouted in the direction of my ceiling.

I decided to leave the house because with it being the month of August and the temperatures averaging in the nineties, it was still hot, even at night. Not to mention, sitting there looking at my computer and waiting for a response had me feeling like the walls were closing in. I had to do myself a favor and also prevent the inevitable from happening if I did stay home and continue waiting. What would happen? The ambulance would have to come get me because I'd surely lose my mind to all that severe anxiety build-up. Lord knows I didn't want to try to explain to friends, family and co-workers what I was doing at the hospital, sitting in a padded room with a funny-looking jacket on. No thanks. I made the right decision, getting out of the house.

My first stop was 7-Eleven. I decided to get a huge Slurpee and drink so fast it would cause my brain to freeze. I figured a frozen brain would be too busy trying to thaw itself and wouldn't have time to think about something foolish like waiting on some chick to respond to an email and maybe go out with me, and maybe want to *keep* going out with me, and maybe, umm…Forget it. Picture a tall chocolate brotha in the back of a 7-Eleven store, wearing a Rocawear sweat suit with sandals on his feet and wire-rimmed glasses, mixing together the *ultimate* Slurpee. I mean, I used a BIG-O 40-ounce cup and put a little bit of each flavor in it. I topped it off with pina colada. My drink was looking like a psychedelic strobe light. I could walk in darkness and still be seen. Look at me, going to the extreme to keep my mind off that computer. For some reason, I could visualize it waiting for me at home saying, "Come check your email, bro. I've got a surprise for you!"

I took a long sip of my Slurpee until the back of my throat went numb from the coldness. Then I paid for the drink. I bought a couple of Lotto tickets; just in case my luck was more financial than female. I had a smirk on my face after listening to my thoughts. The most I'd ever won on the Lotto was about twelve dollars and I'd celebrated by doing just what I was doing now. I bought a Slurpee and, yes, some more lottery tickets. It's a never-ending cycle. They know it, I know it, but we all do it.

After I walked outside the store, I was met with an interesting surprise. Actually it was more like a shock. I knew I'd recognized this white jeep with the black convertible top that had pulled up and parked two cars away from mine. It belonged to one of my internet dating experiences. Damn, I'd had so many that bumping into one was bound to happen sooner or later. I walked to my car, hoping she wouldn't notice me but, at the same time, I wanted to confirm if it was who I thought it was.

As the door slowly opened, the woman slid out of her driver's seat. My confirmation had been achieved. It was her. Belinda Doss, the woman from the east side of hell. Why that side? Cause they grow trees on that side for her to swing from.

I remember Belinda all too well as an experience I wanted to forget, but couldn't. I'd met her off some other website, not Sistergirls.com, so I was hoping my next experience would be a lot better than that one. But going back to Belinda, on the first of our two dates, she was all up on me, under me, and over me. I know I crave affection and attention sometimes, but this lady took things too far. I mean, even in the restaurant I'd taken her to, she had me feeling off the hook with embarrassment. When I began ordering my food and trying to explain to the waiter how I wanted the meat cooked, Belinda slid underneath the table like a snake and then, after a few bumps under the table causing the silverware to jingle, she appeared between my legs. Belinda smiled but she was also rubbing the top of her head to check if there was any blood. The waiter stood by trying to maintain his composure. I vividly remember him saying, "I think you folks may need a little more time…" After that, he was grinning every time he approached us to ask if we needed anything else.

That was the highlight of my first date with Belinda and I should've paid attention to the warning signs but, as always, what's the single most common reason for most brothas' downfall? Why would I choose to ignore being so embarrassed and put off by her strange behavior that I'd actually go out with her again? If you didn't guess THE BOOTIE then you aren't living in reality. Belinda had a serious body. She was toned where it counted and had a little extra something where it needed to be. Body-wise, she was a ten. But above the neck, she was scratching for delivery of her senses. There was nothing between her ears. She needed a brain transplant and damn…I'm talking about her bad, huh?

At any rate, the second date was pretty much the same. I ended up with a severe case of embarrassment. The moment in question? We were at this hotdog stand called Tail-O-The-Pup. There were a lot of people there for an early evening; just enough to make me run and hide because I used to be a frequent customer. Used to be meaning, after this happened, I stopped going. Belinda looked at me, all sexy eyed, moving her hips to some imaginary music, smiling and approaching me slowly. I stood there with the food and drinks in my hands trying to spot an empty bench for us to sit on. I remember thinking that we'd probably end up eating in my car but Belinda had another thought or desire that she wished to express.

She asked me, "Are you pretty strong?"

"Right now, I'm hungry, shoot…"

"No, really." She giggled. "Let me see how strong you are!"

I didn't know what to expect at that moment. Belinda was acting sort of dumb blondish or should I say, goofy. The trip about it was that her actual physical appearance was nothing like that. Nah, Belinda wore her black hair in a long curly shag and her skin tone looked deliciously mocha. I took my chances with her spontaneous behavior…

"I'm strong, why?" I responded, reluctantly.

"Hold out your right arm," she told me.

"My right arm? Well, let me put this drink down first."

"No, no, no… I just want to see your arm strength. It doesn't matter what you're holding," she said in a child-like manner.

I rolled my eyes and took a deep sigh before going along with her request. I held my right arm up and braced myself for the unexpected. Two seconds later I realized I didn't brace myself enough because Belinda decided to test my strength by attempting to hang from my arm like Tarzan.

"The hell!" I said while on my way, headfirst toward the pavement.

The food from my left hand went flying all over the place and the drink in my right hand hit the ground before I did. So did Belinda, but she seemed to enjoy it until my 200 something-pound body fell on top of her. I could hear a few of the onlookers saying, "Oh my God!" Others just did what I would've done had I seen some stupid shit like that. They laughed. One of the guys from inside the little hut where they make the food stuck his head outside the window.

"You folks all right out there?" His East Coast accent just added more humor to the situation.

I waved him off as I searched for napkins to wipe the combination mustard, chili, relish, ketchup and ranch dressing that was splattered all over my clothes. I didn't fare too well but it didn't matter. My ass was so embarrassed that I just looked at Belinda and told her, "Let's go…" She followed me like a wounded puppy and never said a word as I drove her home, opened the passenger side door of my car from the inside, and then gave her the thumb as if to tell her "get the hell out!" I was serious and I was tired.

Damn, that's a hell of a way to remember somebody. I was lucky that Belinda never noticed me standing over there behind my car the whole time I was reliving our episodes together. She walked inside the cleaners, which was one door over from the 7-Eleven that I'd just walked out of. I could see her through the glass and noticed that she was about to come back outside. After reliving those memories, I decided to avoid any further embarrassment so I jumped inside my car, forgetting that I'd left my Slurpee on the roof. As I backed out of the parking space, I heard my name being called.

"Jason, is that you? Jason!"

I looked in my rearview and sideview mirrors. It was Belinda running toward my car and I could hear her shoes flip-flopping on the pavement. I drove off before she made any attempts to jump on my car like some stunt woman. I saw my Slurpee hit the ground and spill out slowly. That hurt my spirit because that drink tasted really good. I still had my lottery tickets, though, so at least the night wasn't a total loss. I think that weekend the jackpot was supposed to be fifty-five million dollars. If I won that, I doubted if I'd need anybody's internet for anything!

When morning came, I decided to treat myself to a jog around the block. I figured that since I was attempting to make some sort of blind romantic connection, I might as well have myself together in every way. In all honesty, I was just trying to kill time and run out some of the frustration that was causing my heart to palpitate. I still hadn't received any responses on Sistergirls.com. I was really beginning to wonder if my emails even went through. I made a pact with myself that if I didn't hear anything when I returned from my run, I would write to the webmaster and see if there was something wrong with the site. I refused to give up. I was determined to get some sort of response. Something!

I returned from my run about thirty minutes later. I cheated, a little. Maybe I cheated a lot. Rather than run around the entire block, I cut through a couple of neighbor's backyards and did my imitation of the fastest human on earth. I almost bent my door key trying to get back in the house. I'd left my computer on so all I needed to do was sign onto the internet and then type in those magical words. I could type the web address with my eyes closed and that's exactly what I did, just to prove a point, silly me.

There I sat waiting for those lovely words to announce that I've accessed what is now my most favorite link: Sistergirls.com. For some reason I'd felt as though this time would be different. I could feel it in my bones. I must've felt something because my mind was oblivious to the sweat dripping off my forehead and onto my computer keys after that very brisk run that I'd taken. I signed in with my password and crossed my fingers. I needed all the help I could get. I waited. I took a deep breath. Man, it was taking forever for the computer to change screens. *I hate when it does that*, I thought to myself. Then a few seconds more went by before I moved my cursor to the refresh button. I'd lost my patience and wanted to see if it would go faster but before I could click my mouse, the screen had changed and the mailbox icon showed that I HAD MAIL!!! I raised both fists in the air and shouted, "Yes!" I was beyond elated to see that I had some email waiting for me. I rubbed my hands together and used the power of wishful thinking.

"Please let it be from Celeste…" I said to whomever could hear me that granted desperate wishes.

And somebody heard me loud and clear because the email was from Celeste Marshall and in the subject area were the words, "Please forgive me for the delayed response." That had me smiling as if I'd just been awarded everything I'd ever asked for in life.

I clicked on the link to open the email. I felt slightly nervous as a smidgen of panic seeped inside my brain. *What if she's writing me to say, better luck with somebody else!* I'd wonder to myself. *What if she could tell I was faking the funk with all that pseudo intelligence I was trying to put on her?* I continued to panic as little beads of sweat gathered together on my forehead. I closed my eyes and began to convince myself that all the worrying wasn't gonna get me anywhere. The only thing I was accomplishing at that point was raising my blood pressure level. I was about to have folks recognize me as a third-generation heart attack victim. It was time to act like an egotistical male and see what this chick had to say. Yeah!

Jason,

Hi, how are you? What a pleasure it was to read your email. I smiled the whole time because it's so rare, especially on the net, to find a man who can express himself using words from the English language. I don't mean to put anyone down but you should see the emails I've received from other so-called men, writing to me through this website. Jason, it's scary, to say the least.

But anyway, be that as it may, I am really happy you emailed me. First, let me apologize for my late response. I usually check my emails each day but I've been out of town at a conference. I enjoy my work and sometimes they send me to places that I otherwise wouldn't think about going to. This time I was in Albuquerque, New Mexico, and I really had fun. It was hot as the dickens but I survived by staying by the pool when I wasn't attending the conference. Not to mention, there was this bar at the hotel that served a delicious raspberry margarita. That's like my favorite. You could get me to do almost anything if you know how to make one of those! I'm only half-serious so don't get any ideas.

Anyhow, do you have a picture you could send to me? I usually don't ask and it's okay if you decline to do so. I guess to some degree I'm having trouble convincing myself that you're real. Maybe you had someone write that nice email for you? Don't be too offended by my accusation. I'm actually complimenting you in my own strange way.

Well, I'm going to end here and wait for your response. Take your time if you have to but just know this, I am VERY interested. Smile. Until, next time…

Celeste

After reading Celeste's email, I was bobbing my head and shaking my leg. Wasn't no music playing. I was just happy and silently giving myself a high-five for scoring the way I did. My email worked and this gorgeous woman let me know that she was interested. I had to catch my breath, relax, and think about my next response for a minute. How did I want to answer her and what about her request for a picture? I thought it might be better if I didn't send her a picture. I'd rather be mysterious all the way up until we met face to face. Why give her the opportunity to run from me before that special moment? I wanted to have a slight edge going in since I kind of knew what she looked like. I was feeling good about my situation and my chances. *Celeste, Celeste, Celeste*, I sang to myself over and over again.

Dear Celeste,

I'm so happy to hear from you as well. In fact, I'm so excited that I'm responding as soon as possible so you can feel my immediate reaction after reading your email. I had to read the last part of it a few times to myself. You don't mix words when it comes to what's on your mind or what you feel and I like that. Thank you for letting me know that you're interested because I'm pretty sure you can tell the feeling is mutual.

I love the way you express yourself and I thank you for the compliment you gave to me. I really can't believe that anyone would dare send you an email that wasn't filled with respect, admiration and adoration. You seem to be the type of woman that naturally attracts such qualities. (*Was I laying it on thick or what?*)

Celeste, you requested a picture of me and I'm going to do the unthinkable right now. I'm actually declining your request. If we are to truly connect, I would love for it to happen because of what we both seem to love the most, which is communication. I assure you, I have the good looks to highlight my entire package but since we've taken this first step to connect, why not allow the visual to be the climax to what could very well become a beautiful union. That is, if you're willing. I'll wait for your next response…

Jason

As soon as I clicked the send button, I knew I was taking a chance by not attaching my picture to the email. Celeste seemed like the type of woman who typically got what she wanted but I figured that if I could stimulate her curiosity then she'd really be up for the challenge. She'd already confessed to being interested in me so that alone sort of raised my level of risk-taking ability.

Suddenly, as I was inches away from signing off the website, the mail icon lit up. I was thinking, *this must be my lucky day!* Maybe I just needed to be patient all this time and allow a couple days to go by before I'd receive anything. I've always been the type to jump the gun on pretty much everything. You could definitely label me as impulsive. I'm one of those men who never reads instructions. I just rip stuff out the packages and try to make them work. I guess women would say, *typical male!* That's all right, though. I have a 98-percent success rate in not destroying anything.

It was time to find out who else wished to enjoy my company. I was thinking that maybe Jada sent me a response so I smiled with a devilish grin before clicking on the icon.

"Celeste, again?"

I didn't expect to hear back from her so soon. In the subject field of the email it read, "I'm willing, are you?" I smiled. I think I'd been doing a lot of that lately: smiling.

I opened the email and read it…

Jason,

I get the feeling that you're playing with me and to be honest, I like it! A lady never knows when she'll meet a man who challenges her every thought, huh? As they say, be careful what you wish for. You are really something or at least, you appear to be.

Question, would you like to chat right now or am I being too forward? I noticed your email was sent not too long ago so you may very well be online right now. Perhaps you're browsing through the many other photos of lovely ladies but I'm not a jealous person. Smile. Just kidding… Let me know if you want to. I'll remain online for about ten minutes and wait for your response. Chat with you soon, I hope…

Celeste

Once again, I was dancing in my chair, celebrating my already successful hookup on Sistergirls.com. Actually, I could remember feeling like that before so it would've probably been wise for me to stay cool and take it slow. I didn't need to get too excited. *Forget that!* This whole hookup with Celeste was sweeter than some rainbow sherbet ice cream. That's my favorite flavor; next to chocolate. I decided to respond before losing my mind, thinking about ice cream.

Celeste,

I'm still here on the website and would love to chat with you. You'll have to give me a moment to figure this thing out. I imagine that all I need to do is click on something so give me a couple of seconds. Is there a special room I need to go to?

Jason

I clicked to send the email and then I searched for the chat room area of Sistergirls.com. That wasn't hard to find but there was a long list of active chat rooms so I sat in limbo, wondering what I should do next. My email icon lit up. For sure that had to be Celeste. It was and I smiled again.

Hey Jason,

Once you get to the chat room section, you'll notice all the rooms that are currently active. Search for the room that says "CJ Communications" and I'll be waiting for you there. See you soon!

Celeste

I scrolled down until I spotted the title that Celeste told me to look for. I felt a little nervous sensation shoot through my veins before clicking on the link to go to the room. It was a weird feeling but definitely an indication that my excitement was real.

Seconds later, I was in the room and I could see her name. An image of her waiting at a table with only her face illuminated behind some flickering candle shot through my mind. *I could see that happening*, I thought to myself. She'd be waiting for me and I'd be about five minutes late, though her gentle smile would signify forgiveness and she'd shake my hand, allowing me to feel the softness of her flesh. Her scent would travel through the air between us, floating on the light breeze that filled the room.

Suddenly, I heard a chime, distracting me from my daydream...

Celeste: Hello?

It was Celeste, greeting me inside the chat room.

Jason: Hey!

Celeste: I've been waiting for you to say something. Was your computer frozen? Sometimes that happens to me.

Jason: No, I was sitting here trying to figure out where to type in the words.

Celeste: Oh, okay. Well, here we are.

Jason: Yep.

Celeste: I almost want to laugh because I'm feeling somewhat nervous.

Jason: I said the same thing to myself before joining you in here. It's kind of like, now that I'm chatting with you rather than emailing you, I hope I'll have something to say.

Celeste: Laugh. You're doing just fine, Jason. To be honest, I was thinking the same thing but I'm already getting comfortable with you. I really enjoy the way you express yourself and you seem to be a very open and honest person.

Jason: Thanks. It's like you said in your profile, we should be open with our thoughts since this can sometimes be a very impersonal way of communicating. It would be easy to jump on here and tell a bunch of lies but I think the truth shines through, eventually.

Celeste: You are so right about that, wow! You sure you're a man? Laugh.

Jason: Yes, 100 percent sure!

Celeste: You go, man!

Jason: Smile. Why'd you ask me that, anyway?

Celeste: Because of your sensitivity and honesty. So far, you've said everything I've ever wanted to hear a man say. I'm tempted to show your emails to my friends at work but I feel like if I did that, they'd show up at your door before I did. Laugh.

Jason: You flatter me too much, Celeste.

Celeste: Well, don't think I've taken down my flag of caution yet. I just want to give you your props as being a real man instead of a pretender.

Jason: I don't know what to say except, thank you.

Celeste: Question.

Jason: Okay.

Celeste: There's an obvious difference in our ages. I'm 39 and you're?

Jason: 33.

Celeste: That's right. Well, time is more on your side than mine so I'm wondering what do you expect or hope to get out of this, should things progress to the next level?

Jason: I don't know, yet.

Celeste: Not a good answer, Jason.

Jason: Well, it's like this. Anything in life is possible and quite often we come to a crossroad that requires deep thought and confident decision-making. I hope I'm making sense here...

Celeste: In other words, you'll cross that bridge when you get to it, right?

Jason: Yeah, that's another way to put it.

Celeste: Question.

Jason: Okay.

Celeste: Do you have a lot of friends? Do you hangout with the fellas, etc. etc.?

Jason: I have a couple of close friends, why?

Celeste: Because friendship is very important to me and gives me stability in my social life. I have to talk to at least three of my girlfriends each day or I'll feel like something is missing. And on weekends, there's always some kind of get-together over at someone's house.

Jason: Sounds like fun. Do your friends ever try to introduce you to anyone?

Celeste: They've tried but we all discovered that if we were to remain friends, playing cupid would have to cease. But anyway, the point I was trying to make was that any man who wishes to enter my life must recognize the importance that I place on my friends.

Jason: Okay.

Celeste: Am I making you change your mind about me?

Jason: No, why?

Celeste: You're not saying as much as you were before.

Jason: No, I'm just listening or should I say, reading. I didn't want to interrupt.

Celeste: Question. Smile.

Jason: Smile. Okay.

Celeste: One of my girlfriends is throwing a gumbo party tomorrow night and I think it might be nice if we went together. You seem to be a very sociable person, very knowledgeable, and our parties quite often include adult games and conversation, not to mention the food.

Jason: Adult games? Smile.

Celeste: Don't get any ideas. I'm not talking about sex toys or strippers. I'm talking about charades and *Family Feud* type of games where we all can shout out answers and act really silly. We have a lot of fun. You interested?

Jason: Yeah, looking forward to it.

Celeste: Wonderful. Give me your phone number and I'll call you in the morning. We'll make plans then. Maybe we can meet earlier somewhere and then drive from there to the party.

Jason: Sounds like a plan. 555-4866.

Celeste: 310?

Jason: Yeah.

Celeste: Talk to you in the morning. Goodnight...

Jason: Night.

As I watched Celeste disappear from the chat room, I felt a sense of not being totally sure things went well during out chat. I guess I rated it about an eight because toward the end, I was somewhat turned off. The level of enthusiasm seemed to slack off a bit. Maybe she was turned off also when I answered her question with the infamous, *I don't know.* Some women hate those words coming from a man but sometimes, that's all you can give to a question that feels like an uppercut coming from nowhere. Sitting there contemplating tomorrow's meeting had me wondering, *what have I done now?* Maybe it was just me being fickle or panicking now that I'd actually made contact with this woman. Before, it was simple. Just say the right words and email them to her. It wasn't really that hard to figure out what she liked to hear when I had time to think about how I was gonna respond. Now the question was how would I act with no time to respond? She might have to get used to hearing some more I don't knows.

Morning peeked through my window like an unwelcome stranger. It didn't help that I stayed up until 3 a.m. watching some all-night classic movie channel and worrying myself over hooking up with Celeste. I called myself drinking some hot milk to get to sleep but the only thing that accomplished was sending me to the bathroom a few times. They were false alarms, though. The most I got out of each trek to the john was that I left behind trails that one could surely follow simply by using one's nose. We're talking a three-letter word here. G-A-S! Perhaps I'm getting a little too graphic.

Time slipped away once I finally got to sleep. Before I knew it, it was already 10:30 a.m. and I'd successfully rolled over into a more comfortable spot in my bed. I cursed the thought of getting up. Laziness had a strangle hold on my entire being. Nevertheless, it was time to get up or suffer the embarrassment of extremely puffy eyes if I continued to sleep any longer.

It was such a task getting up. I had to do it gradually as though each movement were a giant leap, requiring some sort of applause. I took one more deep sigh and stood to my feet. My eyes were halfway closed as I walked to the bathroom and that's how they remained until I stood under the jet streams of my shower head. That was just what I needed before attempting to wake up the rest of me by drinking a hot cup of coffee.

I was in dire need of some serious stimulants to wake my body up but before I could reach the kitchen, my phone rang. Was it the call I was expecting? It surely was and I no longer needed that coffee. Keeping up with Celeste, bantering on the phone woke me up completely.

"You gonna sleep all day, honey? You sound tired!" she said with the effect of a bullhorn placed near my right ear.

"I'm awake…"

"Hello? Yoo-hoo!"

"I said I'm awake!"

"You don't sound like it, honey. I think we need to do something to *change* that! If you want any chance at being my man, you're going to have to remove all lethargic behavior from your personality."

The words "change" and "my man" stuck in my throat like dried toast. I needed something quick, fast and in a hurry to help me swallow what I was feeling. Something was changing here. There was a difference in Celeste that I'd never picked up on in her emails. I would've probably have used the words "overbearing" and "bossy" right about then. I was sure I'd discover other words floating in the air between us, too.

"This is the last time I'm going to say this, are you there?" Celeste asked as her voice finally seeped in when I paused between thoughts.

"I'm here." I did my best to shake off the warning signs I'd felt. "So, we're going to meet somewhere first, before the party, right?"

"Umm, we already discussed that, honey. Now we have to determine where we're going to meet."

I hate the way she calls me, honey! I thought to myself.

"Do you have a place in mind, Jason? If so, then fess up, honey, because I have so many favorite places around town that I frequent."

She said it again…

I quickly remembered the last time my hand brushed against my right pocket and discovered the absence of any sort of bulge, so I suggested a place that I could afford.

"Hmm, how about we just go to the IHOP?" I said.

Celeste laughed. "Excuse me?"

"House of Pancakes?"

"You're not serious, are you?"

I paused for a moment to figure out which way I wanted this conversation to go. Her reception to my idea was all but lukewarm so I figured if I kept pushing the idea she'd probably determine that I wasn't for her and then we wouldn't see each other. For some reason, I at least wanted to match the visual of this woman to the typed words we'd been sharing. Curiosity is frustrating.

"Listen, Jason, this time I'm going to choose the place, okay?"

"Sounds good."

"Question."

*Damn, here we go...*My anxiety button began to flash a bright red color. Most of the women that I've ever known who say question before actually asking one usually follow up with something to cause serious debate. Either that or make you want to walk in the opposite direction before their words strike the intended target. That's me.

I held the phone gently and cleared my mind of all prejudgment. I waited for her torpedo to launch otherwise known as her, "question."

"Jason, do you believe in scoring points with a woman or just any sort of point system to determine the possibility of a relationship with another person?"

I laughed nervously before asking Celeste, "Meaning?"

"Meaning, I usually start off by giving a person 100 points in their bank, so to speak. Then as we get to know each other that 100 points will either remain as it is or situations will arise causing me to remove points, as is the case right now."

"What do you mean, right now?"

"Well, honey, when we chatted on the computer, you answered a serious question with an I don't know. That's a serious no-no for me. I deducted five points for that."

Again, I laughed nervously. "Five whole points, huh?"

"Yes, Jason."

"So, you've got me at 95 right now, correct?" I asked as if the point deduction wasn't all that bad.

She immediately busted my bubble. "No, you're a little bit less than that. Please let me continue so you can see why. I will give you your chance to redeem all points at the party tonight."

"Oh, okay..."

"May I continue, Jason?"

"Please..."

"Your lethargic behavior over the phone doesn't sit well at all with me. I deducted another two points. I was lenient. Then, my God! Jason?"

"What?"

"You suggesting we meet for the first time at an IHOP?"

"Was that so bad? I thought it would be cool; although I was only half-serious."

"I don't think you were half-serious, as you put it. I believe that if I would've said yes, you might've celebrated quietly over there, thinking I'd be your cheap date tonight."

"Well, I guess you deducted another five points then?"

"I'm sorry. I had to take away eight points for that one."

"Eight? Damn, I'm not doing so good, huh?"

"Your sarcasm isn't warranted, Jason. This is very serious to me."

"I apologize."

"You now stand at 85 points and I'm wondering if you're the man for me. You know what really keeps you in the game and what makes me think that perhaps you're simply having a bad day?"

"What's that, Celeste?"

"The beautiful way in which you expressed yourself in your emails...I read them again this morning before calling you so I can honestly say that I have faith in you as the man I believe you truly are. Now, it's time to put my faith to the test."

"I appreciate that. So, are we still on? We still going to meet somewhere?"

"Yes, I'm thinking right now which of my favorite places would be great for our first time meeting in person. I also would like for us not to go someplace that's too far from my girlfriend's house."

"Okay, sounds good."

"Let me think..."

I listened to the silence that separated Celeste and me. It gave me time to think. About what, I wasn't sure but I was doing some heavy thought processing. Maybe I was trying to mentally untangle myself from this web I seemed to be trapped in. I didn't dare attempt to prevent Celeste from figuring out the best place for us to meet. The clicking of what sounded like her tongue against the roof of her mouth led me to believe that there was some seriousness involved in her decision-making. I kept quiet and waited. I closed my eyes and silently prayed that in person, she'd be more down-to-earth and a lot easier to talk to. I might be stretching it a little with that request.

Moments later I could hear Celeste clear her throat. Perhaps it was time for her to make a special announcement. Maybe the girl needed some fanfare before she enlightened me a little. I'd begun wishing she could place me on hold and allow me to listen to an elevator music rendition of "Can't Hide Love." I was thinking to myself, *give me liberty or tell me where the hell we gonna meet!*

Celeste spoke to me, finally. "Hello, Jason?"

"Yes?" I responded while yawning at the same time. "Whew…" I let out at the tail end of my yawn.

"Did you sleep at all last night? Never mind, don't answer that. I jotted down a couple of places we could meet. Tell me what you think and give me your honest opinion, okay?"

"Okay."

"First place is Maple Drive. My girlfriends and I go there quite often for drinks and appetizers. Have you ever been, Jason?"

I wasn't sure if I wanted to answer her question truthfully. I knew about the restaurant but, to be honest, it never appealed to my price range. Meaning that spending my whole paycheck on appetizers wasn't my idea of fun. Now if she just wanted to sit in the patio area, assuming that they had one because this is Los Angeles and I don't know of a restaurant that doesn't have outside seating. But assuming that and recognizing how great buttered bread goes with a glass of water, Maple Drive Restaurant sounded like the perfect spot.

"You're not answering, Jason, so I'll give you my second choice and then you tell me which one appeals to you more."

"Sorry bout that, what's your second choice?"

"I was thinking about this new place in the Hollywood area called the Patagonia Grill. If you haven't been, it's to die for, seriously. I love the potato and onion-style tortillas that they have. But actually, wherever we go, we're not going to really eat anything because we have to leave room for the delicious gumbo that my friend Palencia is making. Speaking of which, she's probably slaving over the oven right now as we speak. Please, whatever you do, make sure you finish everything on your plate at tonight's party because she will be offended if you don't. I'm sure she'll make that announcement several times throughout the night."

I just held the phone and listened to Celeste go on and on. I wasn't familiar with her second choice of restaurants at all. If it were left up to me, Celeste and I would've met at a mall, parking lot or any place where we could just look at each other and determine if we wanted to go further. I guess that's a typical male remark but I just didn't see why a restaurant was necessary considering we had a party to go to where the main idea was eating gumbo. Celeste wasn't making sense to me. There was enough frustration building up inside of me to where I was gearing up to give her a piece of my mind.

Celeste asked, "So, have you decided?"

"Yeah, how's the atmosphere in that grill? Is it laid-back enough for us to talk and be heard?"

"Yes, very much so…"

"Okay, let's meet there."

"Patagonia?"

"Yeah…"

"Great!"

I'm so weak. Who was I fooling about giving her a piece of my mind? Nobody!

"Celeste, you have the address?"

"Check your email before you leave the house. It'll be there, and Jason?"

"Yes?"

"I look forward to seeing you tonight. By the way, make sure you dress California comfortable!"

"California comfortable?"

"Casual, but fine, honey… See you soon!"

"Yep, soon…"

As I hung up the phone, my excitement fizzled a little. I'd still planned to go through with meeting Celeste but I just wasn't trying to jump through any hoops to be with her. At least, not anymore, I wasn't. I took my time in getting ready. I watched a little television. I played with different shirt and pants combinations to see what would work best. It took me a long time to settle on something to wear. I felt like wearing all beige that night. I laughed at myself. The nights had typically been hot all that month and Celeste did mention being comfortable. I had this beige shirt and pants combination that usually looked pretty nice on me. I also threw on a little silk undershirt that would be exposed after I left a few buttons on my shirt undone. A gold chain, a nice watch, some cologne and I was good to go.

It took me about thirty-five minutes to get to the Hollywood area and find the restaurant where Celeste wanted to meet. Then it took me another ten minutes to find a place to park. I had to settle on one of those five-dollar-every-two-minutes parking lots. I almost cursed out the attendant but I didn't want to waste the energy. Deep down, I knew that I was gonna need plenty of stamina for that night.

I walked at an even pace as I made my way to Patagonia's. I had a sneaking suspicion that Celeste would probably be inside already. I wished I was more familiar with the place because then I could blend in and not be noticed. However, I had no clue what to expect so for me it was all about taking a deep breath and going for broke.

As soon as I walked inside, I noticed the off-white décor and a gorgeous Middle Eastern-looking lady waiting to show customers to their seats. After she asked if I was dining alone, I told her that someone was expecting me. She stepped aside and gave me a smile, along with her permission to search for the person awaiting my arrival. I glanced across the room as I took one step after the other, making my way around tables in my path. The fact that there were but a few black people in the restaurant made it quite easy to determine that Celeste was the lovely darker-toned lady sitting alone with her fingers interlocked underneath her chin. It was one of those classic *I'm waiting on some guy who's two seconds late* positions. I approached slowly and respectably. I wasn't sure if Celeste was happy to see me or if she was gonna reach over the table and snatch my chest hairs off. Reading her mind was beyond impossible. I smiled nervously and said hello.

"Celeste?" I asked.

She nodded. "Jason. My, aren't you handsome..."

She didn't get up. Not that I expected her to but she kept her hands in the same position as before though her eyes shifted down and then back up. I could tell she was checking out the goods. Maybe I'd earned back a couple points. I was tempted to just stand there and do a table dance or something. Maybe then I'd recoup my 100 points and be able to start fresh. Her little rating system sort of bruised my ego a bit so I felt compelled to win my honor back somehow, if you will.

As I sat down, I noticed the burlap seat covering on the chairs. It made an interesting sound that took me by surprise. Celeste noticed my reaction, teetering on embarrassment.

She said, "Same thing happened to me, honey."

I relaxed a little and gazed into her brown eyes. We had a nice little rapport going on, though our date was about five seconds old by that point. I said a silent prayer to myself. *Where the hell is that waitress?* I figured another voice might alleviate the uncomfortable silence between Celeste and me. She cleared her throat and finally took down her hands from beneath her chin.

"So...Jason?"

"Yeah...Celeste?"

"You have trouble finding the restaurant?"

"No. I probably had more trouble finding a place to park around here."

"Really, where did you park?"

"About a block away..."

Celeste turned and noticed the waitress approaching the table. My attention was so focused on reading her expressions that I'd become oblivious to our surroundings. Her voice sounded really seductive in person, yet at the same time it was laced with that sort of ultra intelligent vibe of a sistah who should be running things on Wall Street. She softly greeted the waitress. The tone of her voice was so hypnotic to the point where there was dead silence for a moment. I missed my cue to order something so I had an audience of two waiting and waiting until finally I heard the sound of a clearing throat and gentle laughter.

"Oh, is it my turn?" I asked, trying to play the situation off.

"Yes, honey, we've been waiting…"

"Sorry about that, I was thinking."

Celeste smiled and so did the waitress.

"I'll just have some water with a lemon in it, for now."

"Live dangerously, Jason! Come on, honey!" Celeste chided me.

That time her voice sounded annoying. I gave her a smirk and then glanced at the waitress. "That's all I want for now. Let me hold on to the wine list."

"A margarita for you, ma'am, and water with lemon for you, sir?"

Celeste and I nodded in unison to the waitress. She was all smiles. I guess because she'd gotten our order right. I had myself in a quiet state of paranoia because I couldn't really tell how things were going. We both seemed to have our guards up, which is normal for a first-time date but it's just interesting to me how two people can open up and tell their life stories in an email but as soon as they meet that person face to face, almost everything becomes a secret.

"So, Jason! You looking forward to the party tonight? I already told Palencia about you and she had me laughing because she asked me how big you are?"

"How big I am?"

"Yes, and before you react the same way that I did, I assure you, she was actually talking about your weight."

"Oh."

"Yes. That girl always keeps me on the edge of embarrassment but she's pretty harmless…"

"Why did she ask about my weight?"

"In her words? She said it was because she wanted to know if she should put your gumbo into one of those huge cake mixing bowls!" Celeste laughed.

I didn't really catch the joke but I enjoyed the sound of her laughter so I smiled.

"I guess I should tell you a little bit of my history and then you'll know why Palencia made that comment. You see, my last internet date was with a very heavy gentleman. Nathan was such a teddy bear, but…"

"Oh really…you been on very many internet dates?"

"Umm, I think you just interrupted me in mid-sentence, Jason. Certainly, you should apologize, don't you think?"

I sat across from Celeste, unable to say anything. She caught me totally off guard because the look on her face reminded me of how my grandmother looked when her lips got really tight. I started to look at Celeste's hands to see if she was gonna smack me next.

"Gee, that just irks me, Jason. Please don't interrupt me again, honey. Now where was I?"

Saved by the waitress, I thought to myself as she approached in the nick of time. I needed something to flush down the lump in my throat. Then before she could get away I ordered something a little bit stronger, well, a lot stronger!

"You think I could have a rum and Coke?"

"Sure. Are you two ordering dinner tonight, perhaps appetizers?"

I looked at the woman who would be boss, sitting across from me. Celeste glared. I figured she was still fuming behind my interruption. I had a mental picture of about ten points being deducted and another five about to slip off, just because.

Celeste took a deep breath and released me from the hangman's noose of her intense stare. "I will have the grilled chorizo sandwich, please."

The waitress nodded her head, pleased with the selection that Celeste made from the menu. "And for you, sir?"

"I'd like to try the caramel crepes…"

Celeste laughed. "You're getting dessert already?"

"Yeah, what's so funny?"

"Jason, you have some peculiar ways about you, honey."

"No. I just don't want to ruin my appetite for later, that's all."

"Uh huh…"

"By the way, I interrupted you from talking about your last date?"

Celeste sighed as if I'd said the wrong thing, again. "If you were listening closely you would've heard me say it was my last internet date, Jason."

"My bad…I'm truly sorry. I didn't realize there was a difference."

"Now you're doing the same thing you did in the chat room last night, being sarcastic."

I shrugged my shoulders, took a deep sigh and wiped the sweat from my bald head. I watched as Celeste's mouth opened again.

"Question…"

I looked to the side and rolled my eyes, undetected by Celeste.

"Hold that thought…" she said. "I need to visit the ladies room for a moment."

"Okay, I'll be here."

"Yes, you will, won't you…" she'd responded as a cold chill lingered behind her parting glance. I could feel her paying me back for my sarcastic jabs. She hated those, and me; I got off on that.

After Celeste excused herself to the bathroom and left me by myself to listen to mumbled conversations and stare at the paint on the walls, my intuition told me that she went to give her preliminary report to her best girlfriend about the date. I hoped she was being truthful and just said that it was much too early to judge how things would go. I hadn't given up yet; even though I pretty much assumed my points were now hovering in the mid-fifties somewhere. I had to laugh about that and take a powerful sip of my rum and Coke.

I noticed from the corner of my left eye, Celeste was returning to the table. It wasn't a surprise that she was fumbling around to put her cell phone back inside her purse. I played the part of a gentleman and stood up as she approached. I waited patiently when she took her time in sitting down. She didn't take all that long in the bathroom. It must've been a very short conversation.

"Everything okay?" I asked.

"Everything is wonderful, Jason."

"Great. I believe you had a question before you left?"

"Yes, but for whatever reason it vanished from my mind…" she responded before sipping her margarita. Celeste had a very relieved smile on her face.

"Well, Celeste, I have a question for you."

"Okay. Ooh, here comes the food…"

I turned and noticed the waitress who had become the star of the evening so far because each of her visits to our table loosened some very tense moments.

Celeste surveyed both her plate and mine. "You sure you only wanted dessert, Jason? I don't want to be accused of torturing you, honey."

"You're funny, Celeste. But hey, I think I'll end up bringing more of an appetite to the party than you."

"Maybe so, Jason, but you're a stranger and Palencia will forgive me if I ask for a doggie bag. I don't even wish to imagine what she'd do to you..."

Celeste winked at me before taking a bite of her chorizo sandwich. She acted as if she were one up on me in the battle to see who was supreme, Mr. Sarcastic or Ms. Perfect.

"Jason, did your question vanish or would you still like to ask it?"

"Well, my question had to do with your point system and where I currently stand..."

Celeste laughed. Her head jolted forward as she continued to chew and chuckle at the same time.

"So, you want to know if I deducted any more points?"

"Yes, I'm curious if you did or not..."

"Jason, I mentioned to you over the phone that you'd have your chance at the party tonight. This meeting at the restaurant was only to become familiar with each other from the standpoint of seeing if there was a physical attraction. You are very appealing; though I could've taken away points for your tardiness."

"I figured you did..."

"No, I didn't. I guess one of us needs to work on our self-esteem, huh?"

I pretended I didn't hear Celeste and focused on the sweet taste of my caramel crepes. It went down a lot better than the oneupmanship game playing we were doing under the guise of being two intelligent people.

After about ten minutes of concentrating on what was on our plates, Celeste finally broke through the barrier of silence that separated us. She smiled as she spoke to me. Occasionally she'd make eye contact and would hold it for a few seconds but most of the time she'd speak while looking away or at the food on her plate.

"Jason," she said. "I must warn you about something before you get to the party..."

"Oh, what's that?"

"Well, Palencia sort of does her homework before her parties actually happen..."

"And that means what?"

"You interrupted me again..." Celeste sang the words, making me feel like a little child on the other end before she continued in a more serious tone. "Palencia does her homework, meaning that she finds out who is attending the party and then she creates name tags with special nicknames on them, according to each individual personality. I'm not sure what she'll have for you, though she did ask me questions."

"Hmm, that's scary..."

"How so?"

"I don't know yet, but I'm sure I'll find out."

Celeste held up her glass as if to make a toast to an interesting evening. I didn't hold up my glass but in my moment of glancing at her from across the table, I wondered what the hell she was up to. "Tit for tat" had new meaning in our presence and Celeste seemed very talented when it came to not revealing her next move. Case in point...

"Thanks so much for choosing this place, Jason. I guess I'll see you at the party. Here are the directions on how to get there..."

After that, Celeste handed me a piece of paper. I could tell she printed it off the Mapquest.com site. I've used it several times myself. She winked at me after I accepted it and then walked away before I could ask her, "Am I paying for this?" Let's just say she walked faster than I was able to think and react...

It was pretty easy to find the house where the party was located. The directions Celeste printed from Mapquest were right on point. At least this time I didn't have to pay for parking but I did have to search long and hard before I could work my parallel magic on the tiny space I found about a half-block away. I was so happy that the Larchmont area of town wasn't too far from the Hollywood location of the restaurant that Celeste tricked me into going to.

Her friend's house was gorgeous. I noticed the well-manicured lawn as I walked up toward the entryway between the perfectly-cut hedges. I looked forward to going inside and meeting the owners of the house. I figured they had to have a style all their own to be living in such a gorgeous, two-story, Spanish-style house. I loved the huge door that I was about to bruise my knuckles on. I was tempted to speak in clichés and say, "They don't make doors like this anymore!" but rather than say that, I proceeded to knock. A tall white gentleman, juggling a wine glass and his already tipsy behavior, greeted me at the door.

"Oh, look everyone, it's Tupac!" he announced before walking away and roaring with laughter.

I could hear in the distance someone saying, "You're absolutely nutty, Charles, just nutty!" I assumed they were talking about the white gentleman and his sense of humor.

I continued to stand in the doorway, unsure of where I should go or if it was safe to enter. I knew I had the correct address but with me being a stranger in a very expensive home, I didn't want to chance setting off any "who are you?" type of alarms. From what I could see thus far, most of the folks appeared to be either white or Hispanic. There was just a sprinkle of black folks around and even one brotha who looked like Bishop Tutu in a dashiki. I thought about approaching him but my efforts were intercepted by this Debbie Allen look-a-like with an apron around her waist.

She looked me up and down and said, "I don't know you. Were you invited by someone?"

"Yeah…umm, I was invited by Celeste Marshall?"

The woman laughed. She held out her hand as she introduced herself.

"My name is Palencia. I'm *sure* Celeste has told you goo-gobs about me, most of which are probably not true."

"Goo-gobs…Well, she's mentioned you and um, I feel like I know you already."

"Oh really, well, if you feel that way then I'm gonna have to beat my girlfriend because she must've told you way too much!"

Palencia laughed and smoothed out her apron. I liked her almost immediately. Maybe it was because of her uncanny resemblance to Debbie

Allen. She even had that ballet dancer's expression on her face when it was her turn to listen to me speak.

"Celeste said good things about you," I assured Palencia. "She also mentioned that at your parties, you give out name tags that sort of fit the personalities of your guests. I noticed on homeboy's tag that greeted me at the door, it said life of the party?"

"Oh, you mean Charles?"

"I believe so. Someone did call him that name after he announced me as being Tupac at the door."

Palencia smiled. "Yes, he's out of control sometimes but he's harmless. He's also my husband so I'm sure you'll bump into him many times throughout the evening."

"Your husband?" I asked with a tinge of embarrassment written on my face.

"Yes, it's been fifteen years now, most of it spent in this house."

"It's a gorgeous house, too…"

I glanced around at the immediate surroundings until resting my eyes, once again on Palencia. Again, I liked her. She seemed pretty cool; a down-to-earth woman.

"Ooh! I have to get back to my gumbo. I'm making two kinds and if they don't taste perfect, I'll call Taco Bell and have them cater this party!" She laughed.

"You're funny…"

"Listen," Palencia said as she reached for a basket located on a small table near the front door. "Let me put your name tag on, and then feel free to mingle. Check out the house; there's little snacks and drinks in the living room and outside in the back so just have fun!"

"Have you seen Celeste?"

"I saw her when she arrived but after that, she disappeared. She's completely at home here so for all I know, she could be upstairs rummaging through my closets, looking to see what new outfits I bought."

"You two have been friends a long time, huh?"

"A *long* time! But anyway, there, you have your tag now so I'm going to get back to the food. It was great meeting you. Enjoy, mingle!"

Palencia walked away and disappeared after she turned the corner headed in the direction of the kitchen, I assumed. After she vanished from sight, I turned to get my bearings on where I was and which direction I should walk toward. I felt totally like a stranger and the house was so immaculate that all I could do was walk carefully and keep my distance from small, artistic objects. This place felt like a museum, it was so clean. The floor in the entryway was shiny and then once I stepped down in to the living room, I noticed the paintings on the walls and the beautiful white drapes opened wide revealing a lovely patio area.

I caught a glimpse of the buffet-style table near a huge fireplace in the living room. As I made my approach, an older Hispanic woman smiled and pointed at my name tag.

"That's amusing," she said with a slight accent.

Her tag read, "Don't mess with wisdom." I didn't see the humor but I figured she was a woman to be respected so I smiled and continued toward the table.

While scooping up some finger sandwiches and wondering if I should try the wine or settle for punch, a bearded man kept looking in my direction and laughing to himself.

"That, my friend, is funny," he said, pointing to my name tag, which I still hadn't looked at.

He asked me, "Is that your company? Have you profited much from your dot com business recently?"

I frowned. "What do you mean?"

"On your name tag it says "Sistergirls.com" so I'm assuming that you're advertising your business. What is it, a dating service or some sort of woman's organization?"

"The hell?" I reacted simultaneously as I looked at the name tag attached to my shirt.

Soon after, the bearded man began laughing.

"My, you seem surprised! Palencia never fails at getting a laugh at someone else's expense. Look at my name tag…What do you see?"

I took a look. "Um, Black Santa Claus?"

The man laughed. Okay, he did have a long beard but that was kind of corny. He excused himself and I picked up a glass of punch.

"Okay y'all!" Palencia announced as she approached the entrance to the living room, pushing a cart with two huge cooking pots. I assumed they contained her gumbo creations. "I want everyone to enjoy the gumbo. It's a family recipe and I don't want to see any leftover food on anyone's plate! There's folks starving in other countries so y'all aren't about to make me feel guilty by throwing away some good food!"

Nervous laughter filled the entire room as no one could figure out if Palencia was being serious or making a joke. I couldn't tell either. I watched as she stood there with her hands on her hips, talking to the small crowd of people. Then, before she could finish her announcements, I looked in the direction of the spiral steps that led to the second floor of the house and there stood Celeste. Long-lost Celeste finally showed her face. I almost got mad at her because she had me walking into this house not knowing one soul and feeling like I truly didn't belong. It was her friend Palencia that had saved her ass. Of course, I didn't have the nerve to say all that to Celeste, but I definitely thought about it.

I stared so hard at that woman I think it caught her attention. She looked to her left and spotted me in the crowd of folks, laughing at Palencia making more idle threats about finishing everything on our plates.

"I don't even want to see any bones on your plates!" she shouted as she exited the room.

Her husband, Charles, mimicked the way that she'd sashayed out the room and everyone laughed. Old dude had jokes that never quit, it seemed.

"There's plenty to eat, everyone, so don't be shy. We love pigs so throw caution to the wind and fill your bowls!" Charles told the crowd, which was now converging on the pots filled with gumbo.

I could smell Palencia's creation and I have to admit, my taste buds were becoming aroused. I wasn't able to get a clear shot at the gumbo but I did notice a direct path, leading to where Celeste was standing. I chose to take that route instead and find out what she'd been up to since arriving, probably before me.

"Ms. Celeste, I've been wondering where you were…"

"Trying to keep tabs on me, Jason? I gave you directions."

"Yeah, to the house but there was nothing on the map that said Celeste is over here or right there..."

"Humph. Well, have you enjoyed the party so far?"

"I haven't really been here long enough to reach an opinion about it."

"How long do you need, Jason? Maybe you're not used to parties like these."

I wasn't sure I liked what Celeste was implying so I left it alone.

"Anyway, now that I'm here, Celeste, do I get to spend more time with you? We are on a date, aren't we?"

"Well, Jason, it's like this...I have to see how a man acts and reacts in certain surroundings that are most familiar to me. You seem to be a good sport about your name tag but still, you act as though you don't belong in this setting."

"Don't belong?"

"Just observing your behavior, honey...Now Nathan, on the other hand, seems a lot more comfortable and has made himself at home, completely."

I had to do a double-take on the name she'd mentioned. "Excuse me, Nathan, you said?" I frowned.

"Uh huh... I said Nathan, why?"

"Didn't you mention someone named Nathan at the restaurant?"

"Yes but, at the time, you interrupted me, remember?"

"I didn't think I interrupted you but umm, you're telling me that this Nathan dude is here, at the party?"

"That's correct, Jason."

I gave Celeste my most intense *wait a minute* look as I held up one finger to make my point a little stronger. "You mean to say that you invited both of us?"

Celeste answered me without making eye contact. "I don't mean to say anything, Jason. I invited you both and that's how it is."

"This is some crazy shit," I mumbled, standing close to Celeste while glancing around the room.

"Excuse me?"

"Nothing...Will I end up meeting this Nathan dude?"

"I don't think I need to introduce the two of you because I noticed you talking to him a moment ago."

"I did?"

"Yes...He's the one with the beard."

"Black Santa Claus?"

"That's him, though he looks more like a teddy bear to me."

"Ain't that some shit?" I muttered softly.

"Did you say something, Jason?"

"No, I think I'll just go get some gumbo and make the best of this night."

"Don't go too far, Jason. The highlight of the night is about to happen."

"What, you invited another dude to the party?"

"I don't wish to discuss that with you. I was just referring to the game of charades we always play after everyone is full from the food."

"Oh, charades, how fun..."

"Maybe you should lose some of your sarcasm and realize that life doesn't always revolve around you. If you try hard enough, you never know what rewards might come your way."

"Oh, you mean like a date number two with the wonderfully gifted Celeste?"

"I am not going to talk to you when you're like this, Jason King. You can feed some other woman your sarcastic gibberish and see if she likes it. At least Nathan is respectful despite his overactive enthusiasm for food. I'll talk with you later, honey..."

Celeste left me standing at the bottom of the stairs, thinking to myself that this *wasn't* happening. She was coming off as a woman who met none of my criteria for being everything that I'd wake up hard to each morning. I almost had to take that statement back because dare I say it, Celeste was fine! The way she walked away from me with so much *Sistergirl* attitude flowing through her veins reminded me of that girl from Spike Lee's old movie *She's Gotta Have It*. Celeste had that "Nola Darling"-style walk about her; even though she'd probably never admit to having so much black in her genes. I'm kind of mean for saying that. Maybe I'll just take away points from my own damn self for that bit of criticism. Or, hell, maybe not...

After an hour went by of idle chitchat amongst partygoers and the somewhat musical sounds of everybody slurping on some very hot gumbo, Mr. "Life of the party" made an announcement.

"Charades, anyone? Time to see who can come up with the best non-verbal descriptions amongst us all..." Charles offered.

His challenge seemed to excite everyone. I could immediately tell this was a party favorite with them all. It instantly brought attention to which individuals were party veterans and which ones were newcomers like myself. I stepped into the background so as not to be asked to join in. I was more comfortable in being a spectator. I spotted Celeste smiling and portraying to be an eager participant in the festivities. Charles chose to go first, letting everyone know that he wanted to get the ball rolling.

Charles began holding his nose and running in place. Different people started to blurt out answers.

"You're dancing!"

"There's a fire!"

"Too much smoke in the room!"

"President Bush in Afghanistan!"

The room erupted into laughter as everyone turned to look at this heavyset white dude shrugging his shoulders and raising his glass in the air. He reminded me of a political science professor in school I once had with really radical views. I imagined this guy's politics were cemented during the '60s. He had that ex-hippie look about him.

After the laughter settled down, the gathering of people continued to blurt out answers as it didn't seem like anyone was coming close to what or whom Charles was imitating.

"You're running from some God-awful odor!"

Charles stopped for a moment and said, "You're close..."

"Yesterday's headlines!"

Again everyone turned to look at the heavyset dude. Charles laughed before telling him, "This is not political satire, Russ, I assure you..."

The room quieted for a moment as Charles continued to do whatever he was doing. I kind of sat back and just laughed at how goofy he looked. I glanced around the room and noticed Palencia. She was a sexy lady. She seemed borderline embarrassed by her husband's antics but that didn't stop her from showing a hundred percent support. Then I noticed Celeste really into the game, trying to figure out what Charles was doing. She didn't blurt out any answers but she looked like she was really studying his movements.

Celeste started to beg. "Charles, why don't you just tell us? I think you have everyone stumped in this room…"

A few unh-huhs and sure-dos filled the room and Charles looked pleased, to say the least. He folded his arms proudly and surveyed the area to see if all eyes were on him. Charles attempted to relieve everyone from suspense.

"You people give up so easily!" he said before erupting into laughter. "Let me just repeat once more for those of you giving your gumbo most of your attention, I wasn't doing political satire. As a matter of fact, I was making fun of my gorgeous wife."

"How was that making fun of Palencia?" Celeste questioned.

"Well, her ritual each morning is to light candles, start her bubble bath, light incense, spray her favorite perfume, use her favorite body lotion, and smoke some weed. Oops! Sweetheart, I didn't mean to say that!"

Shocked expressions and thunderous laughter filled the room as Palencia stood off to the side with her mouth wide open. She couldn't believe what her husband had revealed but, at the same time, she didn't try too hard to deny anything, either.

"Question?" Black Santa Claus yelled out.

"Yes, Nathan…" Charles responded in a welcome tone of voice, meaning they'd probably met before.

I was coming to the conclusion that Celeste hadn't been totally honest with me about her situation. A tinge of jealousy was giving me hot flashes.

"So, Charles, why were you running and holding your nose?" Nathan asked.

"Because that's the mental state that I'm in each morning when all those odors collide with each other. I just want to hold my nose and run!" Charles laughed.

Light chuckles ensued and everyone finally got the joke.

"Okay, who wants to go next?" Charles asked the small crowd. "How about you, Russ? You're welcome to do some political humor, if you wish…"

"Oh no, I don't think I could successfully follow you, Charles," Russ responded.

"Celeste, you always come up with something creative…"

Celeste perked up. "No thanks, Charles, but I would like to ask my new friend sitting back there by the name of Jason King to see if he can stump all of us…"

Charles stretched his neck as he attempted to see whom Celeste was referring to. He and I weren't really introduced so he didn't know my real name.

"I don't believe I've met this Jason King person, Celeste. Where is he?"

Celeste stood up and pointed me out. I hated her for that.

"Oh, okay, you're talking about Tupac. Nice to meet you, Jason. Please, come to the front and have a go at it. We welcome new talent and ideas to our parties. Please."

As I stepped over feet and legs in my path, noticing so many unfamiliar eyes watching my every move, I began to hate Celeste even more. Each step I took, I thought about the time and wasted effort I'd made trying to hook up with the woman. She probably had me at the party to make Nathan jealous and wake his butt up to the fact that she could find a new man without any problem. That's what I thought was going on. I bet more than just my bald head was reminding folks of Tupac. I was developing a serious attitude. My eyes changed from an innocent glance to an angry glare. I turned to perform my charade.

My first motion was to form my hand into the shape of a gun. I held it to my head and pretended to pull the trigger. Some in the room gasped a little and others either smiled or laughed nervously. It took a couple minutes before anyone began blurting out answers.

"Suicide attempt!"

"Vietnam!"

"O.J.!"

"Rap music!"

"People with too much money!"

"Enron!"

The guesses came left and right, one after the other. I just stood there with my pretend gun pointed toward my head and my eyes staring directly at Celeste. She stared back and probably wondered what I was doing. I would've given anything to be a mind reader so I could've heard what she was thinking. Celeste looked uncomfortable. She didn't make any attempts to guess. She just stared. I was beginning to feel strange, standing in the middle of someone's living room with my fingers to my head. My attitude was lifting but I felt as if I had a point to make. Charles brought the attempted answering to a halt.

"Okay, you stumped us completely though I must applaud you for standing so still. You, my friend, are quite an actor!"

Nathan chimed in with his own remarks. "Yes, Mr. Sistergirls.com, please tell us what your charade is all about before one of us feels the need to call 9-1-1."

Nathan chuckled and that inspired me to answer.

"Internet dating…" I responded as the room collapsed into silence and I took that as my cue to exit.

I smiled at Palencia on the way out because she was really cool and then, without hesitation or a breakage in my stride, I left that gorgeous house and never looked back. It was nighttime and I felt as though the moon followed me all the way home. Then I thought to myself that maybe in the sky there was this mystical spotlight shining down on my every move, bringing attention to a sincere but desperate brotha. I gave it my best try. Was it my last try? I don't know but I've been down this road before. Sistergirls.com represented a new beacon of hope for me but was it really the answer and could it give me what I'd been searching for? As I turned into my driveway, I wrestled with thoughts of never turning on my computer again. I needed to overcome my addiction and stop going online so much.

When I walked through the front door, I had a mental picture of my to-do list, which read like a who's who of past due notices. Then I caught a glimpse of the stacks of magazines and sale papers propped against my living room wall. I'd been seriously ignoring the real world because of all that internet dating stuff. I'm glad I didn't have an animal or some goldfish to feed because they would've probably been dead at that point.

As I stood in the middle of my own living room, I had every reason in the world to pick up my laptop sitting on my dining room table, march through the kitchen and out the back door where I'd find a big black garbage can. But, you want to know some insane shit? Despite what happened at the party, experiencing another failed dating attempt, or my surreal images of me throwing away my computer, nothing pulled at me stronger than the thought of signing back on and going right back to Sistergirls.com.

I submitted to the intense gravitational pull of my zero-percent willpower. I waited a few seconds and noticed I had mail waiting for me on the website. I had another chance and I felt great about that. Maybe I'd given up too soon just because things didn't work out with Celeste. I was excited again. My eyes readied themselves for the beginning of something wonderful. I clicked on the Sistergirls mail icon and read my one and only email.

It was from Jada.

"Yes!" I celebrated, clutching my fist and raising it high.

I immediately determined that she simply hadn't signed on to the website recently and that's why it took her so long to respond. I scrolled down to the body of the email, below the subject line which had no title. It read:

Dear Mr. Jason King,

Your ghettoized email was really stupid. I'm blocking you from making any further attempts at emailing me. You should get a life...

Sincerely,

Jada Broussard

Ouch! That bruised more than just my ego. I unplugged my computer without even signing off. I walked through my kitchen, out the back door and proceeded to do what I should've done before my feelings were hurt. Seconds later, a loud crash could be heard at the bottom of my big black, no longer empty garbage can. I walked back inside, brushing off my hands as though I'd done some serious work outside. I glanced at the empty spot on my dining table and realized what I'd done. I decided to go to bed, knowing that I'd probably toss and turn all night until discovering relief by retrieving a broken laptop computer from my garbage can, outside. Goodnight, for now...

LIFE HAPPENS

RIQUE JOHNSON

Christmas Eve 2002
6:53 PM

Jessie was surprised when Tyrone suggested they enter the jewelry store. Their date was to consist of dinner and a movie. The dinner had already taken place. He'd allowed her to choose her favorite restaurant as well as the movie for them to see. She knew that he wasn't particularly fond of "girlie" movies, but Tyrone didn't object to her choice. She reflected on the fact that throughout their relationship, Tyrone had pretty much gone with the flow of things. When she thought about it in realistic terms, she appreciated that she'd been spoiled by his pampering.

She watched a salesperson spring from her seat upon recognizing Tyrone. Jessie followed him to a jewelry case on the other side of the store where he approached the salesperson.

"Back so soon?" the salesperson asked.

"I told you that I'd be back," Tyrone stated.

"This you did," she said, passing a glance at Jessie.

"Oh," Tyrone said, looking at the salesperson's nametag. Tyrone had always been terrible with names. "Lin, this is Jessie. Jessie..."

"Hi, Jessie," Lin stated, cutting Tyrone's words short. Lin extended a hand for a handshake.

"Pleased to meet you," Jessie replied during the greeting.

"Wait until you see what he has in store for you."

"Honey, what's this all about?"

"Well," Tyrone replied. "I think it's time for us to take our relationship to the next level. Therefore, I've picked out a few rings for you to choose from."

Lin unlocked a drawer under the showcase and produced a small pouch. She emptied it and put the rings in separate holders. Jessie's arm flew around Tyrone in an appreciative hug. Tyrone embraced her tightly as he lifted her from the floor in joy.

Jessie's index finger moved back and forth between the rings as if it were some sort of Geiger counter; measuring the level of excitement each ring made her feel. Her mouth was open in awe during the process of lifting one of the rings from its holder. Tyrone chuckled within. Actually, his heart smiled as he watched his soon-to-be fiancée being pleased with the engagement ring she selected.

The ring was about two and a half carats in size, brilliant looking, nearly flawless. His girlfriend was holding her hand out in front admiring the ring. Tyrone knew that she adored it by the way her eyes glistened, but when a smile as brilliant as the perfect sunset splashed across her face, he knew that this was the one. He also knew that she loved it and that there was no point in revisiting the other two rings.

Jessie nodded. "Can we get it?"

Tyrone instructed Lin to put the other rings away. Somehow, he'd already known that her choice in rings would be the one he favored. But, to be on the safe side, he let her choose from three rings similar in quality. He felt proud to have her as his mate. His soulmate was how he thought of her.

"Rone," Jessie said overly excited. "Isn't it absolutely gorgeous?"

"It's wonderful, just like you."

"Shall I wrap it up?" Lin asked.

Tyrone passed a glance to Jessie. "You answer that."

"No," Jessie stated. "I'd like to wear it now."

Tyrone nodded to Lin and gave her a credit card. "Ring it up."

Tyrone tenderly held Jessie's hand in his, removed the ring from her finger and gazed into the sparkling diamond like it was a crystal ball. He twirled it between his fingers and the dancing sparkles sent his thoughts to their wonderful beginning.

One year and eleven months earlier

Tyrone walked into his home, tired from a hard day's work. As he flopped onto the sofa, he realized that he was more than that. He felt exhausted. He had to think hard to recall a time when his work had had a similar effect on him.

Tyrone Taylor was a Network Engineer, Manager of Network Operations at the largest IT firm in Washington, D.C. He was six feet two inches and boasted a powerful-looking chest. Today had been one to remember; there had been a massive sick-out. His supervisor was on vacation and all but two of his employees had called in sick. Therefore, he had to get into the trenches and pull cable throughout a multistory building. His fingertips were sore from picking the tips off the tiny wires inside the cables to make the RJ45 connectors. He clinched and opened his fist several times in succession as a means to relax the tightness in his hand. He looked at the telephone in disgust when it rang and thought, *Damn, I just sat my ass down.* After a day like today, all he wanted to do was to rest a minute and pour himself a glass of wine. After four rings, the answering machine picked up and Billy's voice came through the speaker.

"Yo, T, Billy...pick up if you're there."

Tyrone hesitantly snatched the cordless off the kitchen wall and returned to the sofa.

"BB," Tyrone replied, "what's up? You sound kind of anxious."

"I'm a little psyched right now."

Billy was Tyrone's coworker, Manager of the Network Security side of the house. He called himself a brother, even though he could pass and blended quite well with the white folks. Tyrone had nicknamed him "BB," which stood for Black Billy because he had never encountered a Black man with such a country name.

"So, who is she this time?" Tyrone asked. He knew that every time Billy met someone, he'd call him to brag; even though Tyrone felt that it was to get his approval.

"Her name's Gwen," Billy commented. His enthusiasm made Tyrone shake his head from side to side. "She's my age, very cute, fine and...did I say that she was attractive?"

"You started with very cute. And, how did you meet Ms. Right?" Tyrone asked, knowing that he was in for a long story. All of the others had been and with Billy being all giddy, he knew that he was in for the long haul.

"Over the internet..."

"You're kidding," Tyrone interrupted.

"Nope. There's this site...Sistergirls.com where single Black professionals can go to hook up. If you see someone that interests you, you can send that person an email, do the instant message thing or chat online. Hell, you can do file sharing, if you are into that kind of thing. I'm telling you, bro, the site is tight. In less than a week, I met Gwen...got my hookup," Billy stated boastfully.

"How do you know that she is all that you make her to be?"

"Well, she sent me pictures of herself. We've chatted online and just now, I talked to her over the telephone. Man, she sounds lovely."

"It sounds like she has her hooks in you."

"I'm telling you, you should check it out. I know that you'll like someone there. Unless," Billy stated with a chuckle, "you want to get back with crazy Diane."

Tyrone made no verbal comment but thought, "Hell no" with that idea.

"I just thought that I would pass the information to you, my brother. If nothing else, you can see some pretty headshots of some beautiful Black women."

"I might check it out."

"You won't be sorry. Gotta go. Holler at you later."

Billy hung up without hearing Tyrone's goodbye. Tyrone thought about it and realized that he didn't have an interest in finding a woman over the internet. "They're all a bunch of want-to-be players, trying to get their freak on," he stated aloud.

As he poured himself a glass of wine, he recalled how excited Billy was. He felt happy for him because he knew that Billy's luck with women was bad. He turned on the radio; WHUR was thirty-five minutes into the "Quiet Storm." Of all of the songs that could have blessed his ears, "Superstar" by Luther Vandross had just started. The song had meaning to him. Besides feeling that Luther is the greatest crooner of all time, the song reminded him of when he'd met the only woman he'd ever loved unconditionally. He wished that the song would repeat itself because he found himself lost to the sentimental feelings it stirred within him. It made him feel lonely.

He sat on the sofa with his head back and stared at the ceiling. *What the hell?* he thought.

When the Sistergirls.com web site loaded in his browser, he was amazed how professional-looking it was. He thought that it was neat, the way pictures of couples that came together after meeting on the site popped up as the page loaded.

"Want to meet your perfect man or woman?"

Tyrone looked at that question on the web page with skepticism. Especially, when under it, the next line was "Sign-in here."

"Here we go," he thought, "this is where I have to pull out my credit card."

He continued nevertheless. The next page was where he chose the user-name TT41. He created a profile of himself and described the qualities that he was looking for in a woman. After the registration page was completed, it took him to where the action was.

Now, we're getting somewhere, he thought.

When the thumbnail pictures of the available women loaded, he gave Billy his props. The women he was looking at were indeed gorgeous.

"Ninety percent of them anyway," he announced aloud. Tyrone clicked on a picture of a woman, "Wanda35" and a larger version of the thumbnail displayed with her vitals below it. He repeated this process several times and became fascinated with the fact that most women were looking for the same thing: a man that was trustworthy, attractive and working. He thought that since this was a site for professionals, that stating a work requirement was rather redundant.

Tyrone checked to see what some of the men had to say and became very amused. He then closed the browser, shut down the computer and went to bed without having dinner.

Oddly enough, the next day from work, he went back to Sistergirls.com. He told himself that it was because he wanted a few laughs but, when he started looking at the pretty women again, he admitted that he found some of them to be quite attractive. He clicked on the "online chat" icon and a java applet started a chat session window. On the right side it listed the number of people currently chatting.

"One hundred eighty-nine people chatting at one time," he stated to himself. "There is a lot of lost productivity in here."

Tyrone sat and watched the conversation of various users and found the laughs he was looking for. When work called him away, he would scroll through the previous conversations and catch up on his reading.

"This shit is like a soap opera. Some of these users must know that people know that they are lying."

On several occasions, he wanted to type "bullshit" in the chat room but refrained until someone made a comparison between Will Downing and Luther Vandross.

"Will Downing is a Luther Vandross want-to-be," Tyrone typed.

He watched someone respond back, **"Will Downing can outsing Luther any day."**

This was another time where he wanted to type "bullshit," but he didn't. He continued to debate the issue for most of the afternoon. Ultimately, he decided that the Will Downing lovers were idiots.

At the end of his workday, Tyrone was about to shut down his computer when he noticed an instant message from a user in the online chat room at Sistergirls.com.

"**You're truly a Luther lover,**" the message stated. "**I've never seen anyone so defensive about Luther,**" the instant message continued.

"**I just think,**" Tyrone typed, "**that for our generation, he is the best we have.**"

The user, JJ39, responded, "**There are others that can come close.**"

"**Yeah, close, but no Luther. Someday, I'll make me a CD with all of my favorite Luther songs.**"

"**They sell that in stores.**"

"**No, that's not what I'm thinking about. The greatest hits CD had most of what I want, but not all. It had a lot of stuff that I didn't want. Imagine putting together a CD with all of his favorite songs that you like...a CD with only the songs that are dear to you. That would be fantastic.**"

"**I guess when you put it that way, the CD would hold a certain sentiment for that person.**"

"**As soon as I can find someone who has all of the Luther songs on my intricate list, I'll truly discover how sentimental it is.**"

"**Intricate?**"

"**Yes. I have particular songs in mind that would make the CD perfect for me.**"

"**Check this out,**" JJ39's next instant message read.

The next thing Tyrone saw was "Accept incoming file." He received the text file, opened it in WordPad and became amazed. Not only did the file list contain nearly three hundred mp3 songs, it had Luther, past and present. Songs from the Chilites, Blue Magic and the Dramatics all pleased his eyes. Tyrone thought that he had died and landed in mp3 heaven.

"**That's pretty impressive. You collect a lot of music?**" Tyrone's instant message said.

"**Something like that.**"

"**Mind if I get some songs from you?**"

"**Not at all. I guess some of my mp3s satisfy your list.**"

"**Absolutely. JJ39,**" Tyrone sent, "**How do I do that without having to** bother you? I'm new to this process of downloading through Sistergirls.com."

"It's simple. Right click on my username, select 'file list' and another window will load listing the files I have. Pick the ones you want...then choose 'download.' "

"That sounds simple enough. Thanks, mate."

Tyrone queued all of the songs from his delicate list for downloading and several more favorites from other groups he liked. When he clicked the "download" button, a sense of satisfaction consumed him. He smiled and reared back in his chair to gloat.

As his sense of satisfaction faded, he looked to check the status of his downloads and noticed another instant message from JJ39.

"TT41," the instant message read, "that's an interesting choice of songs you're getting."

Tyrone replied back to JJ39, "All classic slow songs. Thanks for being here today."

"No problem."

"I see that you like the old stuff."

"Is there anything better?"

"Not for me...it beats that rap stuff today's generation is listening to."

"Yeah, they have fallen prey to something I don't completely understand."

"In my opinion, it's simple. The music industry uses sex and violence to sell records. Hell, Hollywood has been using this formula for years."

"True. True."

"Don't get me wrong, I can get into the old school. Kurtis Blow, Grandmaster Flash..."

"Let's not forget Kool Moe Dee."

"Rap was clean, fun and easy to dance to back in the day."

"Back in the day. LOL...you make it sound as though we're old geezers or something."

"What is so funny about 'Back in the day'?"

"I was in the mall the other day and I heard a teenager say that. This person couldn't have been more than thirteen or fourteen."

JJ39 waited for a response from TT41 for a couple of minutes. Later on, toward the end of the workday, Tyrone responded.

"Sorry, mate, duty called...you still there?"

Tyrone ran a couple of reports while waiting for a reply. After the reports completed, he shut down his computer and headed home.

The next day, he and Billy arrived at the office front door simultaneously. Billy had a huge smile on his face.

"You still feeling good about the woman you met on Sistergirls.com?" Tyrone asked.

"Yep. I talked with her on the telephone before I came in. Have you checked it out yet?

"I went there yesterday. Some of the faces I saw were attractive."

"I told you. Sistergirls.com and all of the others that follow will replace the telephone chat lines that were so popular a couple of years ago. So, did you talk to anyone?"

"No women, but I did talk to this guy and downloaded some mp3s from him."

"Man, you've got issues. You go to the hottest place there is to meet someone and all you do is download music from some guy. If I didn't know better..."

"Don't even go there. I told you that I'm not into dating women over the internet."

"Whatever, man. I'll talk with you later."

In his usual fashion, Tyrone checked with his people, assigned tasks to accomplish today's goals and began preparing next year's budget. His screensaver suddenly disappeared. It was triggered by an instant message from JJ39.

"U there?"

"Yep," Tyrone replied back. "Sorry for yesterday. I'm doing the internet thing from work."

"Me too..."

"So, where exactly are you?"

"NYC."

"Nunna Your Concern?" he replied back with his face frowned.

"LOL...I'm cracking up here. NYC stands for New York City."

Tyrone laughed to himself and replied, "I'm not totally up on this short text stuff."

Tyrone saw another "LOL" come back. He knew that LOL stood for Laughing Out Loud, but didn't really understand why JJ39 would find that amusing.

"I think the term is 'Instant Messaging,' " JJ39 sent.

"If you think that is funny, you'd die if I told you what I used to think BRB stood for."

"I gotta know."

"Burping...I couldn't understand why people were always burping."

"I'm glad that you're not here because the lady next to me gave me a strange look when I laughed again. TT41, how could you translate BRB into Burping? You know that it stands for 'be right back?' "

"Yes. As I said, I'm new to this instant messaging thing. The odd thing is that I work with and around computers every day."

"May I ask, what do you do?"

"Let's go to chat mode. It is better for an extended conversation. Got time?"

"I have a few minutes."

"Now, where were we?" Tyrone typed.

"I'd asked you, what kind of work you do?"

"Network Engineer...Computer."

"Computer geek?"

"Not really. We install wires to allow office computers to communicate with each other and access the internet. Obviously, knowing how a computer and its hardware works is a vital part of the job." Tyrone waited a few seconds before questioning, "U there?"

"I was waiting to see if you were finished. Put two carriage returns at the end of your sentences. This way I'll know you've finished what you're saying."

"Sounds good...your turn."

"I work for a law firm. I'm a legal assistant."

"I bet that's interesting."

"Most times, some of these legal papers I type are captivating."

"How fast do you type?"

"Somewhere between 123 and 130 words per minute."

"Damn, you can fly."

"You have to realize that I've been going at this a long time."

"And how long is a long time?"

"Pretty much since I got out of college. TT41, got a question for you."

"Shoot."

"What does the TT in your nick stand for?

"Tyrone Taylor...and JJ?"

"Jessie Jenkins."

"It's nice to meet you."

"You, too. I guess our similar interest in music is the basis for our extended conversation."

"You can't go wrong with slow songs.

"I have to agree with that. So, how did your date go last night?"

Tyrone read Jessie's instant message, confused. He reflected on their previous conversation but couldn't recall ever mentioning having a date.

"Date? What makes you think that I had a date last night?"

"Well, the mp3 songs you downloaded. They had to be used for a romantic evening. Either that or Luther's slow songs are as dear to you as you've stated."

"The second part is more precise. However, I'll admit Luther's the perfect person for a romantic evening, but again, I wanted them for my personal use. Kind of a trip down memory lane."

"This SBF has had that technique used on me."

"Excuse me...you're female?"

"Single Black Female. You?"

"SBM. I assumed that Jessie was a male's name."

"Most people think that."

"Well, in that case, it is a real pleasure to meet a woman with such a fine taste in music."

"Likewise."

"So, what do you like?"

"I like tennis, basketball and professional football."

"You sound like a dude."

"I was a tomboy growing up. Back to you. What do you like?"

"I like football, even though it has pretty much been replaced by golf."

"That's cute. You want to be another Tiger Woods."

"No, I like the sport of it...even though golf is the most challenging thing I've ever done."

"All of the golfers I know say the same thing."

"Mellow music, sports...what else are you willing to tell me?"

"What more is there to tell?"

"Whatever you're comfortable with telling a virtual stranger."

"Nice pun. The virtual world of the internet and virtual stranger. I'm 39 years old."

"I guessed that by the 39 in your nick."

"If that is true, then, your age must be 41."

"Yep. I'm glad that I didn't say any of those male talk things. I may have embarrassed myself and upset you in the process."

"Good thing; even though I don't offend easily."

"Jessie, are you going to be at Sistergirls.com tomorrow? I have gobs of paperwork I need to get done."

"For the next couple of days it won't be possible. I'll be out of town."

"Vacationing?"

"Work. My boss and I are leaving to prepare a legal brief for one of our clients."

"I see. I guess I'll catch up with you later then."

"I'll be online later this evening from home."

Tyrone paused for a few seconds. A strange feeling swept over him, prompting a smile.

"In that case, I'll be sure to look for your nick when I get home."

"I'll be home at approximately seven. Look for me sometime after that."

"Sounds like a plan."

"TTYL."

Tyrone replied with the same four letters, assuming that they meant "talk to you later." Jessie sat at her desk with somewhat of a frown on her face. She was puzzled as to why she'd thrown the suggestion to Tyrone that she'd like to talk with him later. She had never dreamed of meeting someone over the internet. For the most part, she thought that it was disgusting. However, there was something about the dialogue they shared. And, she admitted to herself that Tyrone's lack of "male talk" as he put it, helped her decide that he wasn't a prick.

Well, she thought. *Not as this moment.*

When she arrived home, she prepared herself dinner while fighting the temptation to go to Sistergirls.com immediately. After all, it was just after seven and she didn't want to seem desperate. She realized that it had been some time since she'd had a serious relationship or any relationship for that matter. She laughed when thinking about how long it had been since she'd made real love.

"Hell," she stated aloud. "I've probably earned my virginity back."

As she ate her meal, she found herself staring at the computer monitor in anticipation. When she thought about it honestly, she was eager to talk with her internet acquaintance.

A four-hour drive southbound, Tyrone entered his home hurriedly. Traffic had seemed unusually slow on the way home. Either that or his need to get home on time to chat with Jessie was the catalyst for his impatience. He wasn't completely sure. All he knew was that thoughts of her inundated him during his ride home. The questions that plagued him needed answers, hopefully to calm the butterflies they caused. He was extremely excited, too excited, to the point of having to take something to settle an overly zealous stomach. He followed that with a gin and juice, relieved himself and sat in front of his computer.

"**How was the rest of your day?**" was Tyrone's first instant message to Jessie who was already on Sistergirls.com.

Instead of a message reply, Jessie initiated a chat session, in which Tyrone immediately accepted.

"**The rest of my day was hectic. I had two long briefs to type. My eyes got tired. I guess I'm getting old and should have them checked.**"

"**I know what you mean...when I have to make the RJ45 connections, I sometimes have a hard time seeing where the colored wires go.**"

"**Age will do that.**"

The unanswered questions forced Tyrone to ask something completely off subject.

"Why did you tell me that you'd be on Sistergirls.com tonight?"

"To be honest, I really don't know. I've asked myself that over and over."

"And what did you come up with?"

"As I said, I don't know. Maybe it was the way we've communicated."

"Can I be honest with you?"

"At this point, I don't see a need for you to be dishonest with me."

"If I'd known you for years, there would be no need for lying."

"I've always said, when you start the untruths, it becomes harder to remember the ones you've told. The stress involved in remembering who you told what to is not worth it."

"Exactly," Tyrone agreed. "And my memory is shot."

"You were about to share an honest thought."

"Oh, see, I told you that my memory is bad. I was about to tell you that I had to take some Maalox to calm my stomach."

Jessie supported her head with a palm on each side of her face with her elbows on the computer desk. She tried to make the relationship between Maalox and anything they talked about. "You ate something for dinner that didn't agree with you?"

"LOL. The Maalox is a result of me being nervous about talking with you."

"Don't be nervous. We can continue in the same fashion as we did at work."

"I know, but that question I asked you keeps messing with me."

"Why did I tell you that I'd be online tonight? It is basically the same as saying that I wanted to continue our conversation."

"That's pretty much how I decoded it."

"Well, my newly acquainted virtual friend, I enjoyed our dialogue and thought that it would be harmless to continue later."

Deep down, Tyrone felt there was a lot more to her explanation than what she revealed but he didn't press the issue.

"What do we talk about other than music and work?"

"I guess the best thing to do is to go through the typical questions first. Our responses should lead to other questions."

"Good point...who's going to start?"

"I will," Tyrone typed. "Let's see, I know your profession, I know your age, hum, what color are your eyes?"

"Dark brown and I make them green when I feel like a change."

"Colored contacts? I once saw a woman with those designer cat-eye ones."

"That's a bit extreme."

"Do you wear contacts though?"

"No, the green ones are just for show."

"Does that mean that you're an exhibitionist?"

"Me? LOL...I dislike drawing attention to myself."

"Do you get comments on your green eyes?"

"Sometimes."

"Is this not drawing attention?"

"I suppose that's true. People wouldn't notice if it weren't for my skin color."

Tyrone didn't know how to respond to her last sentence, so he simply typed, "??"

"I'm dark, real dark...or as my girlfriends say, 'I'm blue-black.' "

"Green eyes on a person as dark as you've described would definitely invite attention."

"Yeah, especially when my facial features are European. You know, pointy nose, small lips, and straight hair."

"Sounds like an interesting combination."

"If I were a dog, I'd be considered a mutt."

"That's funny. Wait...LOL."

"Describe yourself."

Tyrone paused for a second to consider how to go about describing himself. He has looked in the mirror for years and never thought about how to say that he has this and that.

"Stunned you?" Jessie typed.

"I'm not accustomed to detailing things about me."

"Okay. Let's play questions and answers. What color are your eyes?"

"Brown."

"Your hair?"

"Black with gray coming on strong."

"Salt and pepper?"

"Yes."

"Nose and lips."

"The funny part about my nose is that it looks pointy from the profile view and semi-wide from the front."

"James Amos type."

"The guy from *Good Times?* Not that wide. My lips are normal for a Black person...full but not overpowering."

"Have you ever been married?"

"Once. Divorced now, though."

"Were you crushed by the ordeal?"

"Pretty much. I loved her and thought that she loved me. Three days into the marriage, I found out that she only married me to get back at someone else. On the fourth day, I had the marriage annulled."

"People go through a great deal to prove a point."

"Have you ever been married?"

"The irony of it all is that my marriage was just as short as yours."

"Oh?"

"Really, mine is best described like this. Have you ever seen the commercial where this dorky guy calls his wife into the room saying, 'Look honey, the video of my bachelor party.' "

"That's a strange commercial; especially when he says, 'It's embarrassing.' "

"Well, on the third day of my marriage, I found his video. Actually, it was left in the VCR. He was probably showing it to his friends that didn't make it."

"Was it that bad?"

"Before I answer, did you have a bachelor party?"

"Yes."

"Was it extreme?"

"Yes, it was the first and only time I've ever been drunk."

Tyrone watched Jessie type, "**Girls involved?**" then backspace both words and replace them with "**Strippers?**"

"**No girls. The guys and I played poker all night and I had too much to drink. Boring, huh?**"

"**That's respectable. My dumbass ex-husband had strippers and the whole nine yards.**"

"**Most bachelor parties include strippers, lap dances and that kind of stuff. It's some ritual designed to have the male let his hair down before a life-long commitment.**"

"**I agree with that and think that it's healthy to a certain point.**"

"**Then, what was so bad about your ex's tape?**"

"**The SOB,**" Jessie typed. She suddenly realized that just thinking about it angered her all over again. "**I didn't mind when he pinned dollars on an almost naked woman or received several lap dances until he came in his pants. But, my ex went too far. He ended up having sex with this woman. As far as I can tell, two others did too but the main one was him. It was pretty disgusting...like watching a porn movie.**"

"**I agree, that was way too far.**"

"**THANK YOU.**"

Tyrone was new to the internet chat thing but someone told him early on that all capital letters meant that the person was yelling.

"**My ex tried to convince me that he was just sowing wild oats before marriage. I didn't buy it, so, like you, on the fourth day I started proceedings to have my marriage annulled.**"

"**I'm sorry to hear that.**"

"**I'm not. It probably saved me trouble down the road.**"

"**Hmm, we like the same type of music. Both of us had quick marriages. I wonder what else we have in common.**"

They both removed their hands from their respective keyboards and looked at their monitors anticipating a question they'd like to ask.

"**Chinese food,**" appeared on the top and bottom of their split screen.

"**Okay,**" Jessie continued first. "**Now, I'm freaked out. What made you type that?**"

"Not sure. It seemed like the next logical thing to talk about is the kinds of food we like."

"I agree, but, neither of us put it into a question. It was just a random thought."

"Stranger things have happened. Who would have ever thought that I'd be chatting for hours with someone I don't know...a female at that, with similar interests?"

"We've been chatting for hours." Jessie looked up at the clock and realized that the length of their chat had been extensive. "Tyrone, I gotta go. I have to pack for an early flight."

"Okay, sorry to keep you."

"There's nothing to be sorry about. I've enjoyed our virtual date."

"Me too. Would it be too forward to ask you for your email address? I may have a message waiting for you when you get back."

"I don't see why not. Most people don't know about my marriage."

Greeneyes@aol.com was the next thing that Jessie typed.

"AOL? You downloaded all of your music on a dialup internet account?"

"No, I have a DSL. I'm just used to using AOL."

"You're a better person than me. I can't stand all of those popup ads and that 'you've got mail' voice irritates me."

"It takes some getting used to. I don't know if I'll have time to drop you a line but give me your email address anyway."

Tyrone gave her the information. Afterwards, they exchanged a few more words before saying goodbye and signing off.

As Jessie packed her things, she couldn't help but think about Tyrone. Not only their conversation, but about him. Was he truly as nice as he seemed? Part of her hoped so; the other part needed it to be true to restore her faith in men.

Tyrone didn't shut down his computer after signing off. He simply turned off the monitor and went to his bedroom. However, after he slid between the sheets and closed his eyes, his virtual date with Jessie made the sleeping attempt wasteful. He thought of how she described herself and found that the combination intrigued him.

He sat up with his back against the headboard and oddly spoke aloud. "Yeah, but it's more than her perceived beauty. There's something about her...us. Our openness has to mean something."

He thought how foolish he felt talking in the darkness, so he made himself comfortable between the sheets again.

Whatever it is, he thought. *I'm willing to explore.*

Jessie dropped her bags onto the living room floor, made a mad dash to the bathroom and thought how nice it was to relieve herself. She had a relatively short flight back but she refused to use the toilet on the plane. It was early afternoon and she guessed that Tyrone would be at work. She thought about him frequently while away. Part of this realization troubled her.

Men, she thought. *No, this man...why are you in my life?*

That question kept repeating over in her head each time she had dinner with her boss and while she prepared the documents for court. She turned on her computer, clicked on an icon and "You've got mail" invaded her ears. She smiled as she recalled Tyrone's words about the voice being irritating. It seemed to be a redundant piece of information since she was checking to see if anyone had sent mail anyway. The only email she received was from Tyrone. It was a simple greeting that thanked her for her time. It stated that he had enjoyed their conversation and hoped that she'd find time to have pleasure on her business trip. It also contained one simple question, "Shall we have another 'virtual date' soon?"

Jessie realized that she was the first to use the term "virtual date" and at the same time realized that that was exactly what they had done. The questions, the finding out things are typical of two people on a date. She replied back to his email, closed the email program and went to the Sistergirls.com to see if Tyrone was online.

It was not long before, **"How was your trip?"** popped up as an instant message. Tyrone accepted Jessie's chat request.

"Not bad at all. My fingers are a little sore from typing, but otherwise things went well."

"Maybe things will get back to normal now that you're back to work."

"I'm at home. I got in maybe an hour ago. I return to the office on Monday."

"Cool, a three-day weekend. By the way, I'm listening to the CD that I made with the songs that I got from you."

Tyrone continued with the small talk for a few minutes. Jessie didn't understand why he hadn't commented on her little surprise. He typed something of which Jessie didn't consciously read. Instead, her patience forced her to typed, "Well?"

Tyrone watched the single word for a few seconds and then noticed two carriage returns.

"Well...what?" he replied after his queue to type.

"What do you think?"

"Jessie, I'm lost."

"It's obvious that you haven't checked your email in the last few days."

"Not since I sent you one. Hold on."

Tyrone checked his personal email from work. He recognized all of the addresses except one with the subject named "Me." He opened the email which contained no text but an attachment. He clicked on the jpeg file and a picture of a gorgeous dark brown woman appeared with a caption of "Hi, it's me, Jessie." Tyrone pushed away from his desk, stood and stared at her likeness with one of his hands covering his mouth. When he sat down, he realized that the same ill feeling as before swept him.

"I knew," he typed slowly, "that your description of yourself seemed unique but you are more beautiful than I'd ever imagined."

"Thanks for the compliment. I was wondering why it took you so long to say something about my picture. Trying to give a girl a complex?"

"Not at all. You know if I'd seen it before, it would've been the first thing I would've said. Actually, I looked for your picture on Sistergirls.com but you haven't posted one yet."

"I'm not sure that I will. I don't want some creep out there knowing what I look like. Besides, I checked for your picture as well."

"I'm probably one of the newest users on Sistergirls; I just haven't had the time to post it. But, in this postcard thing, you even went all out."

"What do you mean?"

"Wearing your green contacts."

"I thought that I'd show you my alter ego...even though I got embarrassed later."

"Embarrassed? You look wonderful with green eyes."

"Yeah, but with one of them in. I was shopping for," she paused to consider the best way to continue, "female products in CVS and noticed this machine that allows you to send digital postcards. Since I was on my way to meet my boss, I had my day-timer with your email address. I found a place to put in my eyes but after I sent the picture, I somehow only removed one."

"You didn't meet your boss like that?"

"I did. It was the first thing that she noticed. A lot of laughs came out of that."

"I bet it did." Tyrone had a certain relief that her boss was a she. "So, when is our next virtual date?"

"Tonight, if you'd like. I'll be home about the same time as before and will be on Sistergirls shortly after that."

"Somewhere in the seven o'clock hour then?"

"By the way, do you have a picture that you can send me?"

"I have a couple of digital ones that I can attach to an email."

"Do you mind?"

"Not at all. It'll be the first thing I do when I get home."

The rest of the day seemed as long as the green mile for Tyrone. He struggled with the notion that Jessie might not like his picture. His only fortitude was that either way, he'd be okay. He thought that it would be cute to have a pet name for her. "Dark Cherry" was the first one that entered his mind because somehow he felt that she was dark on the outside and sweet on the inside. A better one, "Nubian Queen," danced in his mind. As the thought ran though his mind a second time, he smiled because it felt perfect. Perfect for her.

He viewed the pictures that he had of himself and wished that he had a better selection to choose from. Of the two pictures he had, he was smiling in one and the other was what he considered his normal expression. He had always had a problem with smiling in pictures and therefore, chose to send the one without. He typed a small note in his email, attached the photograph, and positioned the mouse pointer over the send icon.

"I'm not insecure about the way I look," he said to himself. As if the other side of his brain listened, it replied, "Then, why are you holding your finger above the mouse button? Push it, chicken."

He shook his head as a means of banishing what he felt were irrational thoughts, clicked the send icon and smiled within.

"Well, Jessie," he stated aloud, "this is me."

Tyrone prepared himself a light meal and ate in silence. A contradicting thought ran through his mind.

"So, this is where the 'you've got mail' thing comes in."

The wait was taxing on him. He remembered that he had told Jessie that he'd send the picture but had no recollection of her saying that she'd be online tonight.

"Tyrone, this is stupid," he announced to himself while looking into the bathroom mirror. "Either she likes you or she doesn't. Don't sweat it."

He was sweating it because the more he thought about it, the more he realized that he was taken by her. Her adorable picture, the way they met and the conversations they'd shared were things that made their encounter special. But, the wave of emotions that possessed him when they chatted was strongly convincing him that something tangible could be in the wings.

He sipped on a glass of wine and checked his email for a reply. After approximately forty-five minutes of waiting for a return email, the dumbest thought occurred to him. Actually, it was the logical thing to do all along. He nervously joined what he considered their live chat room on Sistergirls.com and within seconds, an instant message appeared before him.

Tyrone smiled when he read, **"Anyone care for a virtual date?"** He started typing his reply but before he could complete his sentence, Jessie was requesting a private chat session.

"How is your evening thus far?" Tyrone typed.

"My evening is going well. I got off work early so the traffic was moving well. But, the best part is, you kept your promise and sent me your picture."

Tyrone asked her a question but he truly wasn't prepared for an honest answer. "You really wanted to see what I look like?"

"Yes. I was eager to put your face with the typed words. And," she paused for effect, promoting a question mark from Tyrone, "you're a handsome fellow."

"Thank you," he replied back but was actually thinking, "Whew!"

"I'm surprised that no one has snatched up a handsome guy like you."

Tyrone suddenly filled with confidence. His chest swelled as he felt a weight lifted from him.

"I have to admit," Tyrone typed, "that there are people interested in me but..."

"I know what you're about to say," Jessie interrupted. "You have no interest in them."

"You hit it on the nose."

"That kind of stuff happens to me all of the time. It becomes flustering."

"True. When I saw your picture, I wanted to ask you why there wasn't a significant other in your life but I didn't want to be presumptuous."

"It would have been appropriate...and there isn't. What about you, handsome?"

"I'm not involved at the moment. I haven't found the right chemistry."

"That's important to you?"

"Very much so. I believe within the first ten minutes of meeting someone, you're able to determine if the two of you will get along."

"Are you referring to people meeting in person?"

"In most cases...there is chemistry between us," Tyrone typed confidently.

"What brings you to this conclusion?"

"By the simple fact that we've established this extended dialogue. We could've easily concluded our conversation after discussing our music choices."

"So, we have virtual dates because of our virtual chemistry?"

"I guess that's one way to look at it."

"My next question could be interpreted as leading." Tyrone's eyebrow raised but he waited for Jessie to continue. "Actually, I'm more curious now that I've seen your face. What does the rest of you look like?"

"The rest of me?" Tyrone typed with a smile on his face. "Well, I'm six feet two inches tall; one hundred ninety-eight pounds, but my build is not proportional. However, I consider myself in good shape."

"Six-two, One-ninety-eight, sounds like you're in good shape, but the non-proportional thing is what I don't understand."

"I do push-ups and crunches a couple, three times a week, so my chest is more developed than anything else."

"A man with muscles."

"I'm not bulky, I consider myself toned and I have four of a six-pack."

"LOL...that was cute."

"I'm working on the other two."

"Wow, a working, articulate...in-shape man. If I were searching, you'd be ideal."

Tyrone stared at the words before him. He admitted to himself that he had a certain curiosity about where all of this was leading. And, he realized that her picture had provoked a greater desire to get to know her. In the short time before he responded, he tried to rationalize his fondness of their virtual dates. It came to him that getting to know her meant eventually meeting her to see if the typed words would manifest themselves into what he felt about her. He thought that he'd really like to hear her voice.

"You on shut down?" Tyrone typed.

"If you mean do I need to restore my faith in men, then, yes."

Again, Tyrone stared at her written words, this time with puzzlement. He wondered what the purpose of their communications was because he felt at the minimum, they were starting a friendship. A distant one, nevertheless, a friendship.

"Sounds like a lot of drama is intertwined in that," he responded. "Let's talk about it."

"Not much to talk about. Heartbreak...hardened heart, that kind of stuff."

"I'm sorry to hear about that, but actually, when I said let's talk about it, I meant, can I call you or you call me?"

This time, Tyrone's words caused Jessie to stare at her monitor. She felt that he'd finally made an aggressive move and she had mixed emotions to prove it. She too had enjoyed their conversations, their virtual dates but strangely she was not sure if she was ready to talk to him.

Tyrone typed a question mark. Jessie thought about the fact that it was her who initiated their conversations outside the work arena. *It was me who sent the first picture*, she thought. *So why am I tripping about talking to him?*

While she rationalized the array of feelings presented with his statement, Tyrone's next move surprised her even more.

"It appears," he typed, "that you have issues with me calling you, so call me at 202-258-7437."

~

"Yes," Tyrone stated as he answered the cordless telephone.

The unique way that he accepted his call caused Jessie to pause before responding with written words.

"You always answer your telephone with yes?"

Tyrone spoke into the handset instead of typing his reply. "Jessie?"

"I don't have issues with you calling me."

"So, it is you," Tyrone spoke with more enthusiasm. "It's so very nice to hear your voice."

"Same here, Mr. Baritone...sounds like you need to be singing bass in a group."

"My voice is deep, isn't it? The strange thing is my voice before puberty was very high."

"Most guys' voices are like that then."

"Yeah, but for the longest time people thought I was a girl when I answered the telephone. Then one day I woke up with this grownup voice."

"Can you sing?"

"Give me a shower and a bar of soap as a microphone and I'm good to go."

"Is that a yes?"

"Actually, I can hold a tune but I don't consider myself a singer. Truly," Tyrone says while changing the subject. "It is a pleasure to finally place the voice behind the words.

"I'll admit that I was a little nervous about verbally talking to you. The strange part is, I've enjoyed our…

"Virtual dates," they both spoke.

"Common sense," Jessie continued, "says that talking with you would be the same."

"How did you feel about sending me your picture?"

"I was excited about that…maybe because I knew that it was an unexpected surprise."

"That it was…even though I kinda blew it by not retrieving my email before you got back."

"No big deal," Jessie typed.

"Thanks," Tyrone typed back.

Jessie spoke, "Got a pen?"

"I have."

"Write this down."

Tyrone listened for Jessie to continue but his eyes caught both her home and work numbers being displayed in their chat window. He wrote her numbers down on a pad next to the monitor.

"Secretive," Tyrone spoke.

"No," Jessie spoke. "I'm combining two technologies. Just keeping you on your toes."

"I see," Tyrone typed.

"I guess that I should be on my toes, too," Jessie spoke. "So, what do you want to talk about?"

"Well, now that I've heard your voice, I'd like you to keep talking to me. It's you who has the nice voice."

"My voice is too soft."

"Exactly, you have the voice of a radio personality."

"You're kidding?"

"Seriously, you'd be perfect for one of those 'quiet storm' type shows where they play slow, romantic music. Hell, I could even listen to you read a dictionary."

Tyrone saw **"LOL"** appear on his computer screen and, at the same time, heard Jessie break into the laughter she just typed.

"That was stupid," Jessie spoke.

"Yes, but it made you laugh...even though I was serious."

"In that case, it was a sweet thing to say."

"So, Green Eyes, what's on your agenda for this weekend?"

"Green Eyes. Is that your name for me?"

"According to your picture, you look stunning with your eyes in."

"Thanks, but I don't wear them every day."

"All I'm saying is that they give you an exotic look."

Tyrone strangely felt that he should type his next thought.

When Jessie read the words, **"I honestly love the sound of your voice,"** she spoke. "Thank you, again. I thought that we were beyond that."

"We were. The thought materialized and I expressed it."

"Do you always speak...type your mind?"

"Isn't it the best policy to live by?"

"I suppose it is."

"Now that all of the small talk is over, do you want to discuss your distrust in men?"

"You don't want to talk about that," Jessie spoke and at the same time typed, **"Painful."**

"It had to be," Tyrone typed back. "Most heartbreaks are," he spoke.

"Can we talk about this another time?"

"Surely, but please understand, that if you ever want to talk about that...or anything, I'm a good listener."

Tyrone's words moved her in some way. She felt disoriented, pleased and nervous simultaneously. She couldn't understand why.

"You'd do that for me?"

"Yes. You see, I'm a man. By virtue of that, your distrust automatically includes me."

"I didn't mean to imply that I distrust you."

"None taken. It's just, if our friendship is to flourish, trust has to be present."

Jessie didn't respond immediately, delayed once again by the effect of his words on her. She had to come to grips with what she was feeling. She hadn't thought about men in quite some time and this man trying to be her friend tested the security she hid behind.

"I suppose," Jessie spoke slowly, "that our virtual dates and now the telephone conversation is heading to a friendship."

"I thought that we were already virtual friends."

"That we are."

"Then becoming friends is the next logical step. Wouldn't you agree?"

"Yes."

"Then, again, if you ever want to talk about any issues concerning you, call me anytime. Please believe that I'd call you," Tyrone stated, assuming that she'd take an anytime call from him.

"Have you ever thought about hooking up with someone that you met over the internet?"

"Until recently, the thought never crossed my mind. I have this friend named Billy to thank for introducing me to Sistergirls.com. Our experience has shown me that maybe, just maybe, it isn't so bad."

Jessie was fully aware of what Tyrone was implying; she typed a colon and a right parenthesis in the chat window.

"The notion," Tyrone spoke, "has always contained the possibility of deception. What if you'd sent me a picture of someone else?"

"How can you be sure that I didn't?"

Tyrone typed the same smiling face that Jessie previously gave him. He spoke, "Your story about one green eye was too detailed for it not to be you."

"You got me there. So, what else do you want to talk about, muscle man?"

"Nice nick you've given me," Tyrone typed.

"I think that it will work for you," Jessie typed back.

It was then that Tyrone noticed something different in the chat window. "Hey," Tyrone spoke, "you've changed your nick to 'green eyes.'"

"I liked it, so I adopted it."

"Or, should you be called one green eye?"

They both laughed at Tyrone's joke. He used the comment about her eyes as a lead-in to his next question.

"What does the rest of you look like?"

"My turn, huh?"

"Exactly."

"I'm five-ten..."

"That's pretty tall for a woman," Tyrone interrupted.

"I know and I'm not going to tell you my weight. Just know that I'm not overweight."

"Can I use the same term you used for me?"

"What's that?"

"Fit? You in shape."

"I will tell you that I'm not overweight. I walk at lunchtime most days. I definitely have Black ass-sets," Jessie typed. "You should be able to guess what my top looks like from my picture," she spoke.

As if it were a hidden command, Tyrone viewed her picture and stated, "Judging from the picture I'm looking at, you look great."

"I wish some of this butt could be transferred to my breasts. In other words, take two inches from off my butt and put it in my breasts and I'll be close to that old Commodores song."

Tyrone typed, **"You're not giving yourself enough credit."** He switched to the telephone, "If I understand you correctly, you look damn good."

"I told you that I wasn't overweight."

"What size shoes do you wear?"

"Tyrone, you know that women don't like to tell their age or shoe size...even though you already know the first part."

"So, the problem is?"

"I'm not telling you," Jessie joked. "What size shoes do you wear?"

"Not a chance."

"So, what's the saying about men telling their shoe size?"

"I don't know of one, but I'm not falling into the size of a man's shoe is the size of...well, you know. Besides, the measurement is more accurate when compared to the size of a man's hands."

"Do you wear large gloves?" Jessie typed as a joke.

"Cute," Tyrone spoke.

"Well, muscle man, I have to get off this telephone. It's well after midnight. My bill is going to be outrageous."

"My apologies. The proper thing for me to do is pay for it."

"I can't accept that. It's just one of those things that happen when two distant people try to get to know one another. Besides," Jessie joked, "I'm sure that you will get your turn."

"You're right about that...or we can stick to our virtual dates."

"Let's do that and keep the length of our phone conversations down."

"All bets are off when we're talking from work. Those calls are free." Tyrone chuckled.

Their phone conversation ended. They continued with another lengthy goodbye in their chat session, but each ultimately shut down the chat feature on Sistergirls.com feeling good about their talk. Tyrone removed his clothes and slid under the sheets with his mind racing a hundred miles per hour. The continuing thoughts of Jessie made his sleep attempt a wasteful effort. He held his eyes tightly closed and tried concentrating on the word "sleep." After a long frustrating moment, his eyes sprung open in the dark. He found himself sitting in the darkness, inspired. He turned on the lamp on the nightstand, pulled a notepad out of one of the drawers and notated his thoughts. He went to his computer, started his email program and typed.

Jessie thought that she'd heard the "you've got mail" sound very late that night. She had just crossed the line into slumber and was not about to get out of bed to see who had sent her a message. The next morning when she saw that it was from Tyrone, she smiled while thinking that he too had trouble sleeping. The subject of Tyrone's email was "I speak my mind. Sometimes I shouldn't." She became very intrigued and went on to read what the email contained.

"The darkness of the vast room surrounds me in a quiet still.

Blackness as far as the eye can see all but encompasses the

orange glow of the digital clock.

Its futile attempt not to be enveloped by the black hole reminds me,

As long as there is light, there is thought.

Yet, my mind would be blank without thoughts of you.

I close my eyes, visions of you blanket my lids with your

picturesque beauty.

I see your face, radiant and stunning,

calling me.

Is it the wonder of you that attracts me,

or is it that I wonder about you?

I should not wonder about the tenderness of your embrace,

the softness of your kiss,

nor the passion that your eyes reveal.

Yet, I'm drawn to these things as if they speak my name."

Early the next morning while Tyrone was getting dressed, his telephone rang. He answered the telephone and an elated Jessie was on the other end.

"Tyrone," Jessie stated. "When did you write those words?"

"I couldn't sleep after talking with you. I lay down and the next thing I knew, I was writing what I sent you."

"It's beautiful. It displays true emotion."

"Maybe I should've kept those emotional thoughts for some other day."

"They are at the right time. You had already warned me that you speak your mind. Don't change that."

"Outside of it revealing secret desires...well, not so secret anymore, did you truly like it?"

"I'm touched. I've never had anyone write poetry for me."

"I'm just concerned that it was a bit forward. I don't want to offend you."

"You didn't, don't worry. I told you that I loved it and it is a wonderful gesture. So, relax."

Tyrone and Jessie continued to have their virtual dates for the next nine months. During this period, Jessie's job took her on two- and three-day trips on several occasions to prepare legal documents for their clients. While away, Jessie found time to chat with Tyrone on the telephone and through Sistergirls.com.

Their communications became in-depth and more personal. Each revealed the kind of things that would be the basis for a true friendship. Both of them had thoughts in the back of their minds indicating that their communications were directing them into a relationship. However, neither would admit it to the other. Tyrone was sure that he didn't want to be the first to disclose his feelings.

While at work, they had gotten their chatting down to a science by using a mixture of telephone calls to each other as if it were business.

"So," Jessie typed. "How was your lunch?"

"Great and usual."

"Your lunch hour is always usually good?"

"Well, I usually have nothing more than a protein shake. The best part is a statue of an eagle that I enjoy viewing."

"What's so special about it?"

"It's a huge monstrosity, wings spread, seemingly soaring through the air, protecting all."

"You sound passionate about it."

"I am. If you're ever in town, I'll have to show it to you."

The momentary pause they experienced was related to the fact that over the months of talking, this was the first time the chance of meeting each other had been expressed.

"I'd love to see it," Jessie typed in their private chat window.

Tyrone viewed her words with excitement. He didn't know if he was overstepping his bounds, but he needed to hear her voice to see if it expressed the same exuberance.

"You're serious," Tyrone stated after Jessie answered his call.

"Hey, Rone." Jessie chuckled. "I'd love to someday see the statue that steals your lunch hour."

"That's it?"

Jessie laughed again. "But, the main reason would be to see the man who has fallen for a statue."

"You know, that would take our relationship," Tyrone paused, and selected a less leading word, "...friendship to the next step."

"I believe that we both are aware that it is the next step in our progression."

"Wow!" Tyrone stated with too much glee for his own liking. "I finally get to meet you."

"You're funny," Jessie said after picking up on his childlike enthusiasm. "So, how do you want to do this? Me travel to New York or you to D.C.?"

"We can talk about it later. I'm getting the 'come here' signal from my boss."

"Okay. I'll call you or catch you online from home."

"Talk to you later, Rone."

"Until then, Green Eyes."

Tyrone sat at his desk for the remainder of the day with no sense of purpose. His thoughts were focused on continuing the conversation with Jessie. Somehow, the thought of meeting her had stirred his already mixed emotions. He forced himself to calm down and get through the rest of his day.

Tyrone sat on his sofa sipping on a glass of wine. The glass of wine was symbolic; it represented his time to unwind, rest, and reflect on how he could have made his day better. This day, he felt that it could not get any better. He had already joined their favorite chat room and had the cordless telephone next to him in anticipation of Jessie's call. When the telephone rang, it startled him, it woke him.

"Tyrone," Jessie greeted. "I'm sorry to call so late. My boss kept me after-hours."

He glanced at his watch and noticed that it was nearing midnight.

"It's okay. Work happens. Besides, it's always a pleasure to talk with you."

"Thanks for being understanding."

"So," Tyrone stated, getting down to business. "Where were we when we last talked?"

Jessie still sensed his excitement.

She stated, "Discussing our meeting plans," with a hint of amusement.

"I think that I should come there. I'll take the travel burden."

"That won't be necessary..."

"Something wrong?" Tyrone interrupted.

"Something is right. I found out from my boss that we'll be in your area in about a week."

"Really! You're coming to D.C.?"

"We're going to a place called Annapolis somewhere in Maryland. Is that far from you?"

"It's less that an hour's drive. How long will you be there?"

"At least two days."

"Let me know which days or day you have available and I'll be sure to come to see you."

"I'll know more details tomorrow. We can discuss our plans then."

"Great. You excited?"

"You already know that I travel a lot. But, this time I'm excited about meeting you. It has been almost a year since we started talking. Our meeting now is appropriate."

Her words struck Tyrone as impersonal. His feelings had grown beyond a fondness to a genuine caring for her. He further admitted to himself that the thought of "what if" had been tied to her name for quite some time.

"Rone, have you ever wondered what would happen if we met?"

"All the time."

"Me, too. This virtual friend considers herself your friend and if I'm true to my feelings, I'd admit that I like you more than I care to acknowledge."

Tyrone shook his head in confusion. He believed that her previous statement and the ones that had just blessed his ears contradicted themselves. He chose to ride on the good vibes from her latest words.

"Well, in that regard, we feel the same way," Tyrone stated.

Tyrone's words warmed her in ways she hadn't expected. Suddenly, the realistic chance of a long distance relationship struck her as a real possibility. In ways, it scared her. In ways, it enticed her. They knew that their feelings were real but, they also knew that a cautious exploration of them would be required.

Life Happens

Annapolis, Maryland

Tyrone met Jessie in the lobby of her hotel on a Wednesday evening. As he walked through the door, he inhaled and exhaled deeply to release some nervous tension. He had more than a week to prepare for their first meeting, yet, his nerves caused him to have butterflies in his stomach. His palms were clammy and he felt his own perspiration.

He spotted Jessie sitting on the couch next to the hotel's registration area. Moments ago, she was standing waiting for Tyrone but she found herself pacing nervously. She realized that her knees felt weak so she sat to calm herself. Seconds after she'd crossed her legs, Tyrone had walked through the hotel's entrance. Jessie waved her hand to capture his attention. She saw a huge smile splash across his face as he approached her.

Tyrone walked up to the standing Jessie and extended his hand for a shake. When Jessie's hand fell into his, he pulled her close and hugged her.

"Very nice to finally meet you," Jessie stated as she patted his back.

Tyrone's embrace was firm and tight. He replied, "Likewise."

When they separated, Tyrone marveled at how good she looked. He realized that the pictures he had received didn't do her proper justice. He felt that she was much more beautiful in person.

"You look wonderful," he expressed.

"Thank you. I don't see an unbalance...I believe you stated that things were not proportional."

Tyrone thought for a moment and smiled.

"You know," he stated, "that your analogy about the Commodores song is on the money. She's a brick..." Tyrone playfully sang.

"...house," Jessie continued.

"I'm sorry, was that a sexist thing to say?"

"I told you, I'm not like that."

"Thanks. Maybe, I'm just being overly paranoid."

"Ten months, two weeks and three days later, we meet face to face."

Tyrone was impressed that she could recite such a detail.

"Close to a year. Shall we?" he suggested while extending his arm toward the exit.

Tyrone drove a few blocks down the street to a harbor area. Moments later, they had walked down a pier and were both resting their arms on the railing looking into the water. The oddness of the situation was that they had just met for the first time but to each, it felt as though one or both had been away. Each never realized how much they'd missed one another until their reunited moment.

"It's peaceful out here," Jessie commented.

"Yes, the water has a calming effect. Oh," Tyrone stated as if he'd forgot something. He passed her a postcard. "This works better for me."

"This is your statue," she stated with excitement. "It's huge."

"You should see it in person. It is much more impressive."

"I'm sure that I'll see it up close one day."

"While I waited for you, I was thinking that we've talked about everything under the sun."

"True, because of this, I feel that I know you pretty well."

"I guess our next step would be to experience what we believe we know about each other."

"Makes perfect sense to me. There is one subject we've never brought up," Tyrone said, turning to face her.

"Sex," they both recited at the same time.

"We've avoided that conversation like the plague," Jessie continued.

"I didn't want to give you the wrong impression of me and, this distrust you have for men probably has something to do with sex."

Jessie's head lowered. She didn't confirm or deny his suspicions.

"Do you want to talk about it?" Tyrone asked.

"Not really. I don't want our first meeting to be filled with emotional drama."

"Okay...but you need to understand one thing about me. I'm a man, but I'm not all men."

"Rone, I know this. This is what you've displayed through our communications. Otherwise, I would've stopped talking with you a long time ago."

"I hope you believe that because I stand committed behind everything I've ever told you."

Jessie grabbed one of his hands, turned and looked at the water again.

Tyrone gazed across the water in the same fashion as Jessie. After a moment of silence, Jessie spoke. "I do like making love."

Tyrone's head turned toward her. Under the moonlit night, he could see that her face contained a certain amount of distress.

"I don't like having sex," Jessie continued, still affixed on the water.

"Jessie, if this particular subject is troubling, please don't continue. Let's go inside," Tyrone suggested. "Care for something to drink?"

They entered a dome-shaped building with windows completely around the exterior and took a table with a view of people's personal boats.

"If I guess what you like to drink, would that make you smile?" Tyrone joked.

Jessie smiled before answering. "You don't have to try to cheer me up. I'm okay."

"It's my civic duty."

"Okay, what do you think I like to drink?"

"Bellini, on the rocks," Tyrone stated confidently.

"I must say, I'm impressed. We talked about that months ago."

"I listen well and try to retain most things that interest me."

"Now that we've met, do I interest you?"

"Very much so. Shamefully, for quite some time now, since our initial chatting days on Sistergirls.com."

Jessie looked directly into his eyes and hoped that he would repeat the sentence.

"It's true," Tyrone stated for more assurance.

Almost instantly, her eyes watered and tears began to fall. Her tears came as a surprise to Tyrone. He noticed that her watering eyes never broke their stare into his; therefore, he held her hands and watched as she released a secret pain. Shortly, her eyes closed. Tyrone could see that they were being held tightly. She removed her hands and stood up abruptly.

"I have to get out of here," Jessie cried.

"Jessie," Tyrone stated with concern. "Talk to me. We've already shared some intimate details. Let's expand on that and let me help with what's bothering you."

"You can't."

"I can try. How do you know if we don't try?"

"Why do you want to be involved with a person like me?"

Both of his hands held her face tenderly. He looked into her swollen eyes and stated, "Because I care about you. I care for you."

Tears streamed down her face again. "You don't understand," she stated with a trembling voice. "I care for you, too...that's part of my problem."

Tyrone's eyes widened with more confusion. "We can work this out," Tyrone pleaded. "Please sit down and let's talk."

"I'm so sorry, Tyrone. This isn't how I envisioned our first meeting. Just being next to you magnified all that I've felt for you."

"That can't be a bad thing."

"Everything that I hoped and feared bombarded me. How can a person be swept away by someone they laid eyes on less than an hour ago?"

"When you answer that, you'd be answering for both of us. We met over the internet, established a dialogue that manifested itself into one," Tyrone held up his pointer finger as if he were counting, "us sharing our inner-selves. And, two," his middle finger joined his other finger, "the whole nine yards, the music, the chatting and the phone conversation became the basis for the feelings we both share. I wasn't looking for this, but it's here. I don't know about you, but I don't want to let ten months, two weeks and three days go without finding out what we can be."

Jessie was sitting with mass confusion evident on her face. Whatever haunted her was still there. He could see that she was trying hard to contain herself. However, she was sitting and Tyrone felt that was a start.

For the first time, Jessie became aware that several people were watching them. She glanced at one couple as if to say, "What, you've never been troubled?"

"Don't mind those people," Tyrone said upon noticing her expression. He took a deep breath and changed the subject. "If I guess what you want to drink, would that make you smile?"

Jessie smiled as much as her troubled emotions would allow.

"Better yet, if I guess your shoe size, would that make you smile?"

This time Jessie's smile contained teeth.

"There they are," Tyrone joked.

"Shall I examine your hands now?"

"You also remember things said to you months ago."

"That Bellini would be nice."

"Coming right up."

Tyrone returned with two identical drinks, prompting Jessie's comment.

"I hope that one of those is yours. I'm not that depressed."

"I thought that I'd try my first one."

"I promise our next meeting will be different from this. That is," she stated with uncertainty, "if you want to see me again."

"I'd love to."

Jessie nursed her drink for quite some time. Afterwards, she asked to be taken back to the hotel under the premise that she'd like to finish getting herself together. When they exited the bar, Jessie paused for a second and suggested that they walk the few blocks back to the hotel. Without hesitation, Tyrone extended his elbow. Jessie hooked her arm with his and started a unified stride down the street. About halfway to her hotel, Jessie spoke for the first time since she'd suggested the walk.

"Thank you," she stated sincerely.

"For?"

"Taking this stroll with me."

"Not a problem at all. Thank you."

"For?"

"For this."

Tyrone stopped his stride, guided her into his arms and gave her another strong hug. Jessie fell into his embrace easily, willingly. This time her hug was firm and captivating. It was emotional. Tyrone understood everything it contained as well as her silence. She released her embrace, slowly and hesitantly.

"That felt good," she stated.

"It was absolutely perfect."

Jessie gazed into his eyes, smiled inward, but spoke no words as she started walking. They held hands in a comfortable silence. When they approached her hotel, Tyrone inquired if she'd be available for a real dinner tomorrow. Jessie graciously declined the offer, stating that her work would occupy her remaining time.

Tyrone acknowledged that he understood, but deep down he was disappointed. Part of him wanted to continue the good feeling he had in her presence. The other part wanted to explore the emotional breakdown she'd had earlier. He knew at that very moment, if there were any chance of a relationship with her, her demon would have to be put to rest.

Jessie stood in the hotel's lobby gazing at Tyrone. She was uncertain of what to say to him. Her jumbled thoughts produced nothing more than a glimmer of a smile.

"Are you okay?" Tyrone asked.

"I am...I will be. Please accept my deepest apologies for my behavior earlier."

"I would normally say a catchy phrase like 'Life being Itself' to summarize things like that. Now, my pet phrase is, 'Life Happens.'"

"That just about covers it."

In the moment of silence, Tyrone knew that nothing more needed to be said that night. He felt that she needed time to sort out her feelings. He gave her a tender hug and tilted her head to give her a polite kiss on the cheek. Jessie intercepted his attempt. Tyrone was about to apologize for his actions when Jessie's lips met his. A stunned Tyrone felt the softness of her lips, but oddly enough didn't know if he should proceed. Jessie pressed her lips firmly against his, her mouth parted to begin a passionate kiss. Tyrone wrapped his arms around her and fell into the kiss as if he'd made the first move. He felt her heat. She felt his passion, his longing for this embrace. The kiss lasted for moments as if two lovers had been reunited. Jessie ended their embrace and gazed at Tyrone with a difficult to read expression.

What he wanted to say, he held within. Instead he commented, "For a person who doesn't like drawing attention, you have a strange way of showing it."

"I don't exactly know why I did that. Maybe it was to answer the questions you had in your poem."

"You remember that. That was a long time ago."

"You don't forget things that touch you."

"As you've touched me," Tyrone spoke softly.

Jessie closed her eyes, inhaled as if to fill herself with the essence of his words.

"Jessie?" a woman spoke.

Jessie's delicate moment was interrupted by the familiar voice. A look of panic splashed across her face. She backed away from Tyrone, looked at the woman, threw a glance back to him, turned and ran away. Tyrone's mouth fell open with no words leaving it. His arm extended as in reaching out to her.

"You can leave now," the woman stated while lowering his arm.

Tyrone frowned his face in confusion. He had noticed the woman watching them since they'd entered the lobby. He thought that she was attractive and made her to be as tall as Jessie. Up close, he knew that she was taller. He couldn't place her. *Italian*, he thought. She boasted long shiny black hair and a figure to be proud of.

"How do you know Jessie?" Tyrone asked.

"I should ask you the same, but I'm her boss."

"Hello, I'm Tyrone," he stated, extending his hand. His hand hung for a few seconds before he realized that his handshake effort was wasted.

"I need to go check on Jessie," she stated, turned and walked away.

Tyrone stood awed. Confused. Hell, he didn't know what he was feeling. He jogged back to his car and drove home partially wondering what he had gotten himself into. His telephone was ringing as he entered his home.

"Tyrone, it's me, Jessie."

"I was hoping that you'd call. What's going on? Is there something I should know about?"

"Other than being embarrassed when my boss called my name, nothing."

"Are you sure? She seemed overly protective of you."

"She calls herself watching after me. She's the only person who knows my pain."

"I'd like to be the second."

"In time, Tyrone, in time."

"I hope so. I'm concerned about you. Having seen the demon that troubles you, I can't help but want to try to help."

"I truly appreciate your concern. I'll get my act together because I don't know how long you'll stick around with so much drama going on."

"I don't know what to say."

"Don't say anything...just be honest with me."

"Honestly, I enjoy the way you kiss."

"Considering the fact that it was you who initiated our moment of heat, I should say that I enjoyed your surprise move. It was everything that I dreamed of, everything my words described. Thank you."

"I just wanted to explain my actions. I hope that you understand."

Tyrone understood, but not completely. He understood that she had skeletons in her closet and ascertained that something terrible had happened to cause her pain when she tried to care. He didn't understand the awkward feeling that he had with the boss experience. There was something about the way her boss resisted him that made him feel uneasy. There was also something lingering in the balance he felt with Jessie's explanation.

"I do have a question for you. You may feel uncomfortable answering it."

"Considering all of the drama earlier, any question you may have shouldn't be a problem."

"Would you like to see where all of this leads? Are you willing to explore what our chance meeting has in store for us?"

Tyrone knew that both questions asked pretty much the same thing, but he wanted to be sure that Jessie knew his intentions. Jessie held her breath as if it would help her formulate an answer to his inquiry. Part of her screamed "yes." This part was willing to dive in headfirst and continue their journey to something tangible. The other part realized that diving in headfirst meant that it would be a swim all upstream.

"Tyrone," she spoke slowly, 'Life happens' is what you'd say. I'm adopting a saying as of this moment. 'The future waits for no one' is something that applies to this moment...to us."

"I like that and you're absolutely correct. However, I don't want to assume anything so please tell me, are we going to go for it?"

Jessie paused before answering.

"I'm not going to run away from this golden opportunity. Yes, Tyrone, I'd like to see what we can become."

"Me, too. I'm feeling good about this."

"Where do we start?"

"I started from the word become."

"Thank you for understanding and believing in me."

"As long as you believe in us, I can believe in you."

Tyrone and Jessie made a concerted effort to see each other every weekend. They each traveled every other weekend, respectively visiting each other. As if their weekend trips weren't taxing enough, they stayed in hotels while on their visits, all in the name of building a strong foundation. Somehow, they managed to refrain from intimacy. They actually had laid down on several occasions but neither would go further than heavy necking.

They showed off their city's attractions all in the process of discovering "what if." When all of the words had been spoken, when their hearts had examined all of the things surrounding "what if," they allowed time to transform "what if" into "this trip" as it related to intimacy between them. Today, Jessie was to stay in Tyrone's home for the first time. The intimacy they had talked and teased about was to take place. Tyrone knew all that he needed to know. His next step was to put his plan into action.

Jessie's knock on Tyrone's door came earlier than expected. However, he was delighted.

"Green Eyes," Tyrone said, giving her a tender hug. "You're early."

"I know. I hope you don't mind."

"Don't be foolish. The earlier the better."

"It looks as though you have company."

"You mean the van in the driveway. He's here to prepare our evening."

Jessie's expression clearly showed that she didn't understand.

"Please sit," Tyrone requested. "I want this evening to be memorable so, I've planned something different."

"This is to be our first special evening. I bought whipped cream."

Tyrone chuckled. "I know that the evening will be special...memorable is what I'm after."

"Okay, what is his role in this?"

"I hired him to pamper us. He will be a waiter, a cook and a servant."

"Stop joking."

"I'm not; he will take our meal request, prepare it fresh and serve us slippers after dessert."

"When you said that we'd have a nice dinner, I never imagined anything like this."

Tyrone escorted Jessie to the living room where the table was dressed to complement the evening. A huge arrangement of oriental lilies served as the centerpiece. A long candle burned at each end of the table and assorted sizes of wine and champagne glasses surrounded the place setting that donned a decorative folded cloth napkin. A small bouquet of roses, two red, two white and two pink was in her assigned seat. As she picked up the roses, her smile indicated that she was pleased. She smelled the flowers, and then caressed her face with the soft petals. The person for hire—in the capacity of servant—entered the living room, cut the bottom end off each rose and placed them in a water-filled crystal vase.

Being ever the gentleman, Tyrone pulled her chair out, seated her and then himself. Under the napkins was a small laminated menu of their meal choices. Jessie seemed impressed that their dinner choices were seafood, steak or Italian.

"None of this is precooked?" Jessie asked.

"That's correct."

She almost laughed when he rang a small bell that sat on the table. In a matter of seconds, the person for hire dressed like a waiter appeared.

"Are you ready to order?" the waiter asked.

"I believe so," Tyrone stated.

"What can I prepare for you, Madam?"

"And, you're going to cook any one of these meals fresh?"

"Any way you like."

About twenty minutes after their order was taken, Jessie had to see for herself. She walked into the kitchen and saw all fresh ingredients being masterfully prepared by the person for hire who now wore a chef's outfit. She thought that Tyrone had gone overboard upon noticing that the noodles that came with her seafood were being made from scratch.

She joined Tyrone in the living room again, shaking her head while stating, "Unbelievable."

Their food was served to them with the professionalism of an upscale restaurant. The food was delicious; Jessie told Tyrone so. After the dessert, the person for hire removed their dishes, cleaned the kitchen and turned on some slow jazz. They sat cuddled on the loveseat and lost themselves in conversation. An hour's time had passed; the servant reappeared out of thin air.

"Shall I prepare the bed or bath?" he asked.

He did manage to keep a straight face when the shocked look appeared on Jessie's face. Tyrone smiled and directed his comment to Jessie.

"He is not going to be here for that. He will run bath water or turn down the sheets."

"Oh," Jessie stated still stunned.

"Which one do you prefer?"

"I'd like to take a bath first," Jessie said, somewhat embarrassed.

"What fragrance would you like for your water?" the servant asked.

"Which ones do you have?"

"Name one."

"Jasmine."

"Jasmine it is."

Jessie nodded in agreement. The servant disappeared into the bathroom. In a short while, the pleasant aroma of her fragrance filled her nose.

"Rone, I don't know what to say. This is one for the record books."

"Have you enjoyed your evening thus far?"

"The food, the wine, the atmosphere were all perfect." She raised a brow. "Any more surprises that I should know about?"

"There's nothing more up my sleeve."

The servant returned from the bathroom and presented Jessie with a long satin robe and matching slippers. After she accepted the items, the servant asked Tyrone if he would need his services further. Tyrone thanked him for the excellent service as he packed his things, then departed.

Tyrone knocked on the cracked bathroom door.

"You can come in," Jessie instructed.

Tyrone found Jessie sitting on the side of the tub. She was wearing the robe while enjoying the atmosphere of what seemed like a thousand candles.

"I was wondering why I could smell jasmine in the living room. The candles are jasmine scented as well."

"Are you pleased?"

"Very. Are we sharing this bath together?"

"Only if that is an invitation. I plan to shower after I bathe you."

"You want to do what?"

"Bathe you."

She smiled before stating, "You're kidding, aren't you?" Tyrone gave her a firm look. "You aren't. I'm not completely comfortable with that."

"Your comfort level is just your shyness talking."

Tyrone extended his hand, helped her stand and gave her a caring hug. He could sense her nervousness and hoped that she couldn't feel his. He had rehearsed this moment countless times in his mind to figure out how to successfully start intimacy between them. He felt that the dinner was a great prelude to the moment, a form of hands-off foreplay. But, it was time for hands-on and he desired it to be as perfect as the food they'd tasted.

Tyrone kissed her neck tenderly and followed her jaw line around with small kisses until he reached her lips. He kissed her passionately, hungrily. Jessie responded with the same fervor that swept Tyrone. Her nervousness transformed into heavy breaths that he felt leave her nose. His hands ran down the front of her, across her breasts in search of the robe's silky belt. He released the knot and opened the robe with both hands. His massive hands touched her on both sides of the waist. One of Jessie's hands seized his, seemingly stopping a movement that never happened.

Her actions were too late; the kiss that fueled their passion simply willed her hand away. Tyrone caressed her skin gently with his fingertips before moving them up the side and over her shoulders. He pushed the garment off her shoulders and realized that her skin felt as smooth as the robe. As the garment hit the floor, Tyrone gave her a loving hug to accompany the continuing kiss. Jessie felt weak, vulnerable and shy. But, all of the things that they had talked about, the teasing, the necking, had come to fruition and she couldn't let anything steal this moment.

Tyrone unexpectedly lifted her into his arms, took a couple of steps and lowered her nakedness into the bubbly hot bath. Jessie acted like she was playing with the mounds of bubbles but Tyrone knew that she was trying to conceal her breasts. He grabbed the loofah, lowered it into the water and silently began washing her back. The silence captivated the moment, it captured her, surrendered her will to the hidden desire within. He laid her back and rested her head on the top of the oval tub. When Tyrone washed her breasts as delicately as one might wash a newborn's head, he felt her body quiver.

Jessie closed her eyes and inhaled as the bath took his hand toward her womanhood. She felt his movement stop; he left the loofah touching her heated desire and kissed her softly on the lips.

"I think," he stated softly, "that you can handle this part. The rest of your body is clean."

"Thank you for your gentle touch. My bath was sensual," she replied.

Excitement and disappointment ran through her being. Part of her wanted him to continue, knowing that the thought of his fingers dancing in her wetness enticed her. The other part of her felt let down.

"How far can I go?" Tyrone asked.

"As far as you like."

Tyrone picked up one of the candles, tilted it and let a drop of wax fall onto her exposed breasts. The hot substance ignited every sensory organ she had. It made his tongue feel as hot as a flame itself. He induced the wax treatment again, this time directing a single drop of wax to one of her nipples. Jessie let out a passion cry that invited Tyrone to squeeze the wax before it dried. Her legs crossed as if she were trying to keep her wetness contained.

"Squeeze tightly," Tyrone instructed softly into her ear. "Keep squeezing until you can feel yourself being massaged."

Jessie did as instructed. His seductive instructions combined with her timed muscle contractions that invigorated her clitoris made her feel like an orgasm was near.

"I don't want to have my first one with you like this," she cried.

Jessie stood up with the intention of getting out of the tub, but Tyrone held her spellbound as he removed his clothes. "Magnificent" ran though her mind as she gazed at this being. She wanted and needed him. It had been so long since she'd had the touch of a man. The distant memories of how it felt to have a man fill her womanhood seemed to come alive with vigor.

Tyrone stepped into the tub and hugged her. His hardened member touched her skin. The simple act caused her knees to weaken. It motivated her to grab the loofah and wash his entire body. It wiped away her bashfulness, causing her to bathe his manhood without a hint of restraint. She stroked his hardened member with the loofah on one side and her soft tongue on the other. When she took him into her mouth, she felt rejuvenated, she felt complete and a greater sense of what they were doing overcame her in a wonderful way. Tyrone felt her tongue swirling around him and almost lost his sense of purpose. He sat into the water and Jessie joined him. They cuddled, caressed and kissed for moments in the tub before heading into the bedroom.

～⌒

Three months later.
Christmas Eve 2002
7:27 PM

Jessie's hand tenderly stroked Tyrone's face. It broke his trance from the ring; however, he was still feeling the effects of his transported thoughts.

"Honey, are you okay?" Jessie asked.

"I'm fine. I was just thinking about us and how we got to this point," he commented as he placed the ring back on her finger.

"You must have," Jessie joked. "You went into la-la land for a quick moment."

"I'm sorry, precious, but now it's time to ask, will you marry me? Will you be my lovely bride?"

"Yes, yes!" Jessie screamed. "I'd love to marry you."

Lin watched their exchange with a great sense of satisfaction. She felt excited and happy for them. She felt proud to be part of their special occasion. She congratulated them and gave Jessie a "you go girl" hug.

"What about me?" a woman's voice asked.

Tyrone couldn't recall immediately; although he was sure that he'd heard the person speak before.

"Vicki!" Jessie sounded astonished. The panic look on her face placed a troubled expression on Tyrone's face. She held his face tenderly with her hands and kissed him gently on the lips. "Tyrone, honey, I promise that I'll handle this," she stated compassionately. "And, I will explain everything to you later. Please trust me on this; I beg you, Rone, please."

Tyrone didn't know what to say; his thoughts had become scrambled by the mixed signals generated by his now troubled heart. He nodded with an expression that Jessie identified as a hurt one. He drew off the reflection he'd experienced moments ago, shook his head and walked away without a comment.

Jessie walked out of the jewelry store distraught. She didn't know why, but she was going to find out why her boss was here. But, most importantly, she wanted to put an end to the nonsense.

Jessie and Vicki stood in the mall parking lot in a stare-down. Jessie stared at her defiantly. This time she didn't run when she was caught with Tyrone. This time she stood firm and stood up for what they'd grown into.

"What the hell are you doing here?"

"I'm here to keep you from making a mistake."

"If I'm making a mistake, it's mine to make. It is my life. My new life is with Tyrone. Understand that."

"I can't just simply let you go like that. You are my life...I love you."

"I love you too," Jessie snapped, "but not in the same way as I used to. Not in the manner that would allow me to continue a relationship with you. I haven't for a while. I've told you this time and time again."

"Jessie, we can work this out. Please give us a chance."

"Thank you for giving me a chance...for taking me in when I was down and out and showing me how to care for someone. I appreciated all of that, but I've changed. I fight every day to keep my trust in men, to keep my trust in Tyrone. I won't let you ruin that. I've come too far; Tyrone and I have come too far. You can see that," she stated, boasting her ring to Vicki.

"Jessie, please. I've been good to you but more than that, you've been good for me. This is how I developed a love for you."

"No," Jessie stated, grabbing one of her hands with an intense glare into Vicki's eyes. "Don't you see, things aren't the same? Look at me and tell me the things that you used to say when you looked at me."

Vicki searched her face with her eyes and dove into Jessie's pupils as if they were the fountain of youth. No matter how hard she tried, she couldn't see the emotions that Jessie's eyes displayed in the past. For that matter, she couldn't see compassion for her at all. Suddenly, she felt ill. Everything she feared and hoped not to be true had become clear. Tears fell from her eyes.

"I'm sorry, Vicki," Jessie stated with sympathy. "I never meant to hurt you."

Jessie's only recourse was to turn and leave before tears caught up to her. Vicki slid down the door of her car; an emotional outburst accompanied her tears. Jessie looked back once at her but continued to her new life.

Tyrone heard Jessie when she walked into his house. He didn't stand or turn his head when he heard the door close.

"Tyrone," Jessie stated. "We need to talk."

"I'd imagine so. Care to explain what went on in the jewelry store?"

"There's no easy way to say this, so I'm just going to say it...I used to be gay or think that I was."

A look of "Oh, no you didn't say that" formed on Tyrone's face.

"Then why were you participating on Sistergirls.com?" he questioned her. The question repeated itself as a thought.

"I don't know. I hadn't intended on meeting anyone, meeting you... hurting you. Hell, I still haven't posted a picture of me on the site. When I realized that we communicated so frequently, I said 'what's the point' and didn't think of it again. Believe me, all I wanted to do was to chat with the black professionals on Sistergirls. Send a couple of emails, instant messages and just enjoy the wide range of conversations that appeared in the online chat room."

Tyrone wanted to say more. He wanted to lash out at her and express how confused he was but he let Jessie continue.

"Then I found your compassion for Luther Vandross compelling. It made me want to talk with you," she stated on the verge of tears. "It wasn't until we'd established a serious dialogue, when I realized that I wasn't gay. I didn't live the gay-lesbian lifestyle or feel that I was the dominate or passive one in the relationship I had with her. I just had sex with a woman."

"Your boss?" Tyrone whispered under his breath.

"Yes."

"You are the most gorgeous woman I've ever met. How could you have possibly turned that way?"

"My ex-husband. I've blamed him for my interest in women for years. Recently, I've discovered that 'Life Happens,' " she said with her fingers making quotation marks, "and I used my thirst for women to hide from my pain and get back at him."

Tyrone remained silent but his inquisitive expression told her to continue.

"Do you remember my story about my ex's bachelor party videotape? Well," she continued without giving Tyrone a chance to respond. "That next evening, we were to make love. We had a few drinks to set the mood right and had just gotten naked...doing the kissing stuff, when another woman entered our bedroom. She took off her clothes and joined us in bed. He shared the both of us. She shared the both of us and I even dabbled in a lesbian act for the first time."

"I'm confused. Had you ever thought about doing this before?"

"No."

"How did...?" Tyrone started, but Jessie held up her hand and cut his words off.

"I found out the next day that he had spiked my drink with that drug called ecstasy, in the name of living out one of his fantasies. I didn't know what I was doing. I can't remember what the woman looked like. If you asked me was she black or white, I couldn't tell you. All that I was aware of was that I was being touched, kissed, sucked and fucked...and I didn't know how or couldn't bring myself to stop it under the effects of the drug. The next day, my fourth day of marriage, I asked him what had happened and he thought that it was cute to detail all of the things I did under the influence. I smacked his face and filed for a divorce the very same day.

"Vicki caught me when I was weak and vulnerable. She became the perfect opportunity to get back at my ex. I've never hated anything or anyone, but I hated him for what he did to me. I even let him catch us in bed just to rub it into his face."

Tyrone wiped a tear from her cheek. He still had no words for her but he could see the pain that she was reliving.

"I swear to you with God as my witness, I ended...tried to end it with Vicki the same night in Annapolis. I have avoided her, stopped going on business trips with her because those were primarily the times when we were together. She is married. She continued to try to sway me from you since that time. And, I truly had no idea that she would follow me here. All I know is," she said with tears leaving both eyes, "she is not in my heart now. You are and forever will be. I love you. I want to be with you. I want to marry you."

Jessie lowered her head. She felt that she had spoken freely, truthfully and had finally gotten rid of her demon. She was relieved to have told Tyrone about what troubled her because she realized that not telling him ate at her. But, at the risk of losing him, she had remained silent.

Tyrone turned her head toward his, gazed into her green eyes and stated, "I love you, too."

Fifteen months later.

Tyrone and Jessie left their Washington, D.C. home, headed for their three-month-old baby girl's baptism. The occasion was to be witnessed by several couples that Sistergirls.com brought together and some others that were considered on the fence, afraid to truly commit to each other. It was to be a testament to them that "Life Happens" no matter how you may meet.

THE WANTING

MICHAEL PRESLEY

~

CHAPTER ONE

"Damn, damn, damn!" Ron Wingate slammed his hands on the steering wheel. He looked at his watch. He had five minutes to get home. He was two blocks from his house when he saw an ambulance up ahead. He looked in the rearview mirror, trying to decide if he could reverse and come in from the north on Wilmore Street. He quickly realized that wasn't happening. There were at least six cars behind him. He looked to his left and then to his right. There was an empty space behind the Toyota RAV4 parked on the other side of the road. He put on his left signal and reversed until his rear bumper hit the car behind him. He put the car into drive and turned it all the way to the left and went slightly forward. His left bumper connected with the back of a brand-new Audi A6. He waited for a reaction from the Audi's driver; there was none. He put the car into reverse and turned to look behind him. The Jeep had moved a few inches forward. He put the car into park and jumped out.

Inside the Jeep, a big black man was in the driver's seat next to a tiny Indian woman. In the backseat, two young boys were playing video games. Ron knocked on the driver's window. The man rolled down his window.

"The next time you move your car forward, I will come back here and kill you and your family," he said.

The man quickly rolled up his window and put his car in reverse.

Ron went back to his car and put the Volvo into reverse, rolling back until his car rammed the Jeep's bumper. He revved the engine while the car was on the man's bumper. Once more he did the steering wheel as far as he could to the left and pulled in behind the RAV4. He got out and looked at his car. The left front wheel was on the sidewalk. With his briefcase in hand he started a slow jog down the street. He glanced at his watch and the jog became a powerful sprint. As he approached the blinking ambulance light, he saw the remains of a motorbike in the middle of the road. His glance quickly took in the firemen looking up into a big tree planted during the greening of New York City about ten years ago. He ran another block until he came to a red-faced two-family house with about sixteen concrete steps that led to the top floor. He ran up the steps three at a time, taking out his keys before he reached the top.

"Hi, Ron." His wife, a beautiful 32-year-old woman, greeted him at the door. "Look at me. I've finally started going to the gym."

"Talk to you later. I have to go upstairs," Ron said, focusing on the steps.

"Take off your shoes," she said as he ran up the carpeted stairs.

"Not now, Marge." He stopped briefly to look at her. Like the man in the Jeep Cherokee earlier, she didn't say a word.

He went past the master bedroom, then the kids' room, to a small one that had a brand-new shiny gold lock. He quickly unlocked the door and ran to the black computer located on the right side of the room about six feet from the window. He threw his briefcase to the floor and pressed the power switch on the computer. As it began to boot up, he started removing his clothes. When he saw the icons appear on the screen he quickly clicked on the one with the Internet Explorer symbol on it. He sat and waited patiently for instant messenger to load. A pop-up display came up that said he had an urgent message from Allan Walker, his boss. He watched the message disappear.

Hi, are you there? The instant message had come from a Keisha.

Yes, I'm here, he typed as he exhaled.

You're late. You know I can't stay on for too long.

Please don't go. You know how much I missed you, he typed, his hands nervous with anticipation. **I'm really sorry I'm late but...**

We don't have time for apologies. Did you print out the picture I sent you yesterday?

You are so beautiful, I made twenty eleven-by-seventeen copies of it at Kinko's. The worker also said that you were gorgeous.

Thank you. You know I can't stay on here for too long because he is on his way home. If you see that I exit abruptly, don't instant message me.

Life is so unfair. Why can't two people who love each other be together? He got up and ran to his briefcase. He put it next to the keyboard and flipped it open. The pictures that he had stared at all the way home were now in his view once more.

In time, honey, we will be together in time. The money that you've been sending me is helping me arrange my exit from this prison. I hate my husband so much. I feel like I want to puke when he touches me.

I understand you because I'm going through the same thing. Marge has been doing everything to get me to love her again but it is not working because my love is with you. I can't believe how we met.

It was pure fate, my love. I have never been on a chat site before I went to www.sistergirls.com.

You are a true sister. My office here is full of African-American paintings and I have never met anyone who is so knowledgeable about African art and history. It's like you spent your whole life studying our culture. I can't wait for us to teach our children about our history.

Did you see that special in the Times newspaper about Emmett Till?

Yeah, you know I went and got it once you told me about it, Ron typed. **Isn't that horrible, the way they killed that young boy? I don't think he even whistled at the white woman.**

I don't think he did either. Did you hear about that senator? Ron and his coworkers had spent the day debating who was best for black people: The Republicans who say that they don't like blacks or the Democrats who pretend they like you.

Did I hear about him? The man's face has racist written all over it. I think if he had his way we would still have colored restrooms.

Let's not talk about that anymore. I have been going crazy thinking about your big thing inside of me all day today. I can't wait, Keisha wrote.

Tell me what you're gonna do with me again, Ron typed, leaning back in his chair.

Look at my picture.

Yes, I did, he said, gazing at the picture and the computer screen.

Forget that. Hold on; let me bring up my picture on the screen. I wish I had a camera to connect to the computer. I know you sent me money for one but I had to buy food because he left me without anything to eat again this week. I'm telling you, this man is evil.

Why didn't you tell me? I would have sent you some more money.

That's okay, I'll make this do.

I'll send you the money anyway.

Don't force yourself. I know your wife and kids need money, too. Can you see me?

Oh, this is so much better. I can see you and write to you at the same time. Now tell me what you are going to do with me.

You see those beautiful, juicy lips.

Yes. He adjusted himself in the chair.

Oh no. He's home. I have to go.

"Damn," he said as he slapped the computer screen.

He put his clothes back on and walked out of the room.

"We're in here!" Marge shouted.

He took the only seat left at the head of the table, directly opposite his wife. The twins, Jeff and Sonia, sat next to each other on his right.

"Your boss has you doing a lot of work at home these days," Marge said.

"Bills have to be paid, food has to be put on the table. Your job at the day care can't support us."

"But, Ron, you need to spend some time with me and the kids, too. Look at the time we're eating. It is almost ten o'clock. We waited more than half an hour for you to get out of that room." Marge started to serve the food to the kids.

Ron dished up his own food.

"I can't help it if I have to work. Saturday we are going to Philly to present the project."

"No, you're not. Saturday you promised the kids you're going to come to school to watch them play in the band."

"I can't this Saturday. You guys understand?" Ron asked, looking at the kids.

"Mommy, can I be excused?" Jeff asked, his eyes filled with tears.

"Me, too," Sonia said, trying not to look at her father.

Marge looked at them. "But you guys didn't eat anything."

"Mom, we ate late. We'll be okay." Jeff got up and left the table.

Marge looked at Ron, who said nothing.

"Goodnight, guys. I'll come by and tuck you in after I'm finished cleaning up the kitchen," Marge said as the kids left the room. "You don't have anything to say," Marge said, looking directly at Ron.

"What is there to say? They don't want to eat." He put the last morsel of food in his mouth and pushed back his chair.

"That's it. You don't care about what's happening in your family. It's all about that computer upstairs and your job. Keep it up, Ron. The kids need a father, and I need a husband. If you aren't up to the task, I'll find someone who is." Marge started to gather the dishes on the table.

Ron got up and slammed his chair back against the table. He went over to where his wife was standing. He stood behind her, his hands firmly on the arms of the chair she'd recently vacated. "Woman, let me tell you something, I hate threats. If you feel there is a better man out there than me, go ahead, you and those kids you spoil to death. Take them with you. I think that would be the best thing you did in all your sorry life. And tonight sleep on the sofa or wherever. Just don't come into the room."

Ron sat in the bedroom listening to a Miles Davis CD he had purchased at Tower Records. He thought about life without Marge and the kids, just him and Keisha, his soul mate. Yes, life would be very good. He lay back on the bed, a big smile on his face.

CHAPTER TWO

"Ron, you are a fool," Cedric Miller said as they sat in the employee cafeteria. "Let's go outside. I need a smoke. These days you always have to walk a mile to take a drag."

The men got up and walked outside into the cold Brooklyn night. Cedric pulled a pack of Marlboro Lights from his jacket pocket and lit one up.

"These light cigarettes actually work?" Ron asked.

"Yeah, they work. When you fall on your face from lung cancer, you fall lightly. Sorry for calling you a fool. I guess we are all trying to kill ourselves." Cedric pulled deeply on the cigarette and pulled his shirt collar up to his ears.

"I'm not trying to kill myself, Cedric. I'm trying to put life into it. I'm dying living at home with my wife and kids. This woman is a lifetime dream." Ron pulled out one of the pictures he had printed earlier from the computer.

"Let me see the thing you're throwing your life away for," Cedric said. Ron handed the picture to him.

Cedric took the picture and stared at it. "I know this girl," Cedric said, pointing his cigarette at the picture.

"How?" Ron asked with concern in his voice.

"I could be wrong but I think I saw her somewhere before. It had to be somewhere interesting. Otherwise, I would not have remembered her," Cedric said, handing the picture back to Ron. "Ron, don't give up your family for instant messages."

"It's much more than that. I'm going to meet her on Saturday at the Kew Inn in Queens. She's paying for the hotel and everything."

"Be careful. Call me and give me the room number and the time you're going to be there. Take your own condoms. There are some crazy freaks out there. I know brothers who get caught out there. One more thing, Ron. You didn't give that girl any money, did you? "

"No," Ron lied. "Let's go back in. I don't want to be sick on Saturday. Keisha said she has big plans for me."

"Just be careful, bro."

"This woman is different, man. She has so much going on. We connect on so many levels, and if on Saturday the physical thing matches as well as our spirits, it's over. I want so much more from life than a home. I want to live," Ron said as he opened the door for Cedric.

"Be careful," Cedric warned again.

~

"You want the luxury suite, Room 300. Take the elevator to the third floor and make a left," the hotel manager said as he pointed Ron to the elevator. "You are a lucky man, my boy. I saw your beauty an hour ago. Call me if you need help."

"Thanks," Ron said as he headed to the elevator. In his right hand he held an overnight suitcase and a garment bag that contained his gray business suit. He felt his hands shaking as he held on to the overnight bag. The ping signaling that the elevator had reached the third floor echoed in his mind. This was it. He had so many thoughts running through his mind. What about all the stories that filled the news with people being hurt by people they meet on the Internet? Would Keisha drug him and steal a body part? Was her husband waiting in a closet to rob him? So many questions! Ron knocked on the door with the number 300 etched in bright orange.

The door opened and there she was, his sleepless nights. If only Cedric could see what was in front of him now. Keisha was a breathless beauty. The pictures on the Internet were good but they didn't do her justice. This was what a man envisioned when he thought about a perfect woman. Her African braids rested lightly on her shoulders. The caramel color of her skin left no room for blemishes. She stood in front of him dressed in a long open robe. The red bra and matching panties she was wearing must have been specially ordered. Her stomach was flat and inviting.

She reached out for him with a smile, which he quickly reciprocated.

"Come in," she said. The raspiness in her voice could have brought thousands of men to their knees.

Ron's knees buckled as he felt the softness of her hands and the sexiness of her voice. He looked up to the ceiling and prayed that if there were a God, he would receive one night of sin before he was smitten.

"Your picture does you as much justice as a black man on trial in slavery days."

She reached up and put her hand softly on his lips. "Don't say a word. You see the petals on the floor. They are for you. Tonight you are my king."

The room was warm and cozy, unlike the chill in the New York air.

Keisha knelt down on the floor and took off his shoes and socks. She held on to his hands as she walked him over to the bed. As he stood in front of the bed she finished undressing him, then she had him sit down on the edge of the bed.

"I'll be right back," she said. As she walked to the bathroom she reached over and turned on the CD player, which was located on the nightstand. The African drums that filled the air transported him to another time. The beat was slow, then it became fast, then turned slow again. Each beat took him back to the motherland he had never known. She came back into the room minus the robe, but carrying a small washbasin. She set the basin next to his feet. She lifted his feet and put them in the basin.

He never knew a woman could be so gentle. Slowly she started to wash his feet, taking special care to get between his toes. When she was finished, she pushed the basin aside and lifted his left foot to her face.

Cedric had once asked him if a woman had ever sucked his toes, and he had shaken his head "no." After tonight, he was sure that he wouldn't be shaking his head anymore. But instead of her sucking on his toes, she took the middle toes of his right foot, parted them, and began to lick between them. He had never had so much blood go into his manhood so quickly before. It was as if she had hit a nerve that connected directly to it. It didn't take long for him to explode all over himself as he went through convulsions. The orgasm had started after the third lick and before she had licked between his toes for the tenth time, he had exploded.

"There are five orgasmic veins in the body. This is the first and the weakest one," she said, her voice connecting with his soul.

Exhaustion and weakness left him with his mouth wide open. He just looked at her. He watched as she took the basin and went back into the bathroom and returned with clean water and another towel.

"Now we will work on the second."

She pushed him back on the bed. "Turn over," she said in that drive-you-nuts voice.

He obeyed.

She took her fingers and started rubbing behind his right ear.

Ron couldn't believe it. He was getting excited again.

She replaced her fingers with her tongue as her hands moved to the top of his head. "There is a muscle in the brain that goes directly to the penis or vagina that causes an orgasm."

"Um-huh, don't stop," Ron said as he felt himself getting more and more excited.

He felt her nipples as she laid her body directly on his back. He felt her hands move to the back of his head to a small crevice he didn't know existed.

"In here is where you find the orgasmic brain muscle," she said as she pushed her right finger into the crevice and rotated it.

Ron felt the bullet of pleasure shoot through him at the speed of light.

"Oh…" was all he managed to say as once more he ejaculated, sending spasms through him. When she got off him he could barely turn over onto his back. Ron forced himself to see the silhouette of her nakedness through cloudy, weak eyes. Even though he hadn't drunk anything when he came in, he felt like he was intoxicated. Was he losing it? He wondered.

"I see you'll only be able to handle three orgasmic muscle touches," Keisha said as she sat directly on top of him. His penis lay motionless below her vagina.

He wished he could command himself to get hard so that he could enter her.

"I don't know if I could do one more," he mumbled.

"You can talk. Therefore, you still have enough strength for one more,"

Keisha said as she began tracing her tongue down his chest. Her vagina moved up and down over his lifeless penis. She ran her hands down his body as she moved so that her lower body now rested by his ankles. She moved her hands to about two inches above his penis, reached down, and squeezed.

"Please, no more," Ron said, trying to stop her as he felt himself getting excited again. She massaged the muscle as his penis began to grow.

"Do you trust me?" she asked.

"Yes, I do," he whispered.

"Because after your next orgasm, you will lose consciousness," she said.

"When I..." he started and, as before, he didn't finish his sentence. He was losing strength in his upper body. It seemed like all his remaining energy was now in his penis. He had started to go in and out of consciousness as she kept rubbing him. For a moment, he could see her, and then he couldn't. He saw her raise her hand high in the air. He tried to lift his hand to stop her but it didn't move. He wanted to shout but the orgasm that had started deep in his stomach was moving up. As she brought her hands down, the orgasmic force that shook him didn't come out of his mouth; instead it came out of his anus, mouth and nose. The world had become black, and it was a beautiful world.

Ron woke up to the pounding on the hotel door. A woman with a thick European accent shouted that it was time for checkout. He lay in the bed looking around the room for her. She wasn't there. He put his hands to his face feeling the stickiness on his moustache. He reached over and touched below his ear. It was sticky, too. As he got up to walk to the bathroom, he felt as if his buttocks were glued together. He walked with a funny gait. Maybe she was taking a shower. He walked into the empty bathroom. He turned on the shower and sat on the toilet. His butt became unglued. He looked straight ahead at the towel stand. Written in a black marker was the message:

Sorry I had to leave. I will IM you. But soon we will love forever.

As he showered, the remains of a million lives went down the drain. When he got out, he smelled himself. Her scent was still with him. He smiled; he wanted that scent on him for the rest of his life.

Ron didn't put on his business suit as he had planned before. He didn't take another shower to let the scent of his indiscretion fade. No, he wanted Keisha to be with him for the rest of his life. He didn't care what happened with him and Marge. He knew what he wanted. He and Keisha hadn't spoken much but she told him that she would do what was necessary for them to be together. He promised her that he would do the same. As he slowly walked up the steps to his house, he dreaded seeing his wife and his kids. They were standing in the way of his total happiness.

He opened the door and walked in. "Marge," he called out. The house was empty. He went into the kitchen to have a drink. Saturday had left him totally dehydrated. He poured himself a large glass of water and slumped down on the chair at the kitchen table. He saw the note nicely folded in the middle of the kitchen table. He picked it up.

RON,
WE WENT TO THE BAND RECITAL. YOUR FOOD IS IN THE OVEN. HOPE YOU HAD A GREAT TRIP. SEE YOU WHEN WE GET BACK.
LOVE, MARGE

He threw the note back on the table, went upstairs and flopped down on the bed. Sleep came very fast for him.

"Daddy, Daddy, wake up!" Jeff said as he shook Ron.

"Look, Daddy, look what we won," Sonia said, pulling on Ron's arm.

"Ron, the kids were great. You should have been there," Marge said, sitting next to Jeff.

Ron sat up on the bed in a daze. He didn't know how long he was asleep but it could not have been that long because his eyes were burning.

"Keisha," Ron said as he looked at his wife.

"Who is Keisha, Daddy?" Sonia asked.

"Kids, go on to bed. I have to talk to your dad." Marge's voice had suddenly changed.

"Mommy, Daddy smells funny," Jeff said as he exited the room.

"Ron, do you want to tell me what this is about?" Marge asked a few minutes later, standing about a foot away from the bed.

Ron slid his feet off the bed so that they rested on the floor.

"I'm sorry, Marge," Ron said, looking up at his wife's troubled face. "This just isn't working."

"Sorry about what, Ron? Are you sorry that you have been treating us like shit for the last few months? Is it the fact that you spend more time locked in that room with the computer than with the kids and me? Are you sorry that I can't remember when the last time was we had sex? Please, Ron, tell me exactly why you are sorry." Tears had begun to fall down Marge's face. "I made so many excuses to the kids for your behavior. I kept telling myself that things were going to get better. I hoped that you would snap out of it. Tell me, Ron, what did we do wrong?"

"Nothing. You did absolutely nothing wrong. I'm just at the point in my life where I want to satisfy this craving. I have never experienced true love until I met Keisha. She satisfies my body and inner spirit. For me not to follow my heart, I would die a million deaths. I know my behavior has been strange lately but it's because of my transformation. Keisha has actually brought a new person out of me. I'm stronger and better than I used to be. Now I look forward to living instead of dying of old age." Ron reached over and laid his hands on his wife's shoulders. She slapped them away.

"I understand," he said. "I hurt you and the kids and I'm sorry for that but if I don't follow true love, I will live above my grave."

"Ron, do you know what a fool does?" Marge asked.

"What are you talking about?" Ron looked puzzled.

"A fool chases his own shadow, and that's exactly what you're doing. And you know what happens when you catch your shadow? You realize it has no substance. Go ahead, Ron, leave your family and go with your true love. The kids and I will be okay."

"I'm sorry, Marge, but I just can't live without her anymore." Ron reached out again for his wife but she stepped back.

"Tomorrow, the kids and I will be gone." Marge fumbled with the door-knob, finally jerking it open. "And that will be end of our life. My lawyer will contact you so you can start your new life with nothing at all because I want everything, including the house, the car and your unearned income."

Ron lay back on the bed as Marge slammed the door shut. He looked up at the ceiling. She could have it all. With Keisha he had everything.

CHAPTER THREE

They're gone. Now it's just you and me. Ron's fingers moved swiftly over the keys. Next to the keyboard was a half-eaten box of pizza. On the floor behind him was the mattress from his room. Marge had left everything that was in the room. She had taken everything from the kids' room and the rest of the furniture in the house but she didn't take a thing from their bedroom.

I'm planning on telling him everything this evening. Thanks for the $5,000 you sent me. I already gave the divorce lawyer a down payment. I don't care what my husband does. I know we'll be together, Keisha typed.

I'm in the computer room with a half-eaten box of pizza and my mattress thrown on the floor, and I feel so happy. Just to be able to instant message you fills my day with joy. My productivity, everything is going much better at work. I finally made a believer of Cedric after I told him about our night at the Kew. Ron picked up a cold slice of pizza and bit into it.

I know I didn't talk much at the hotel but we don't get enough time to be together physically so I wanted to make every touch a memory. Most people don't know about the different muscles in the body. There are so many different ways we can please each other besides the usual penis penetrating the vagina or oral sex. A long time ago, in Africa, men and women used to make love without exchanging body fluids unless they wanted to reproduce. There are so many different pleasure zones in the body that are right at people's fingertips but they are too lazy to look for it. Ron, the internet has all our secrets. It has a million times more knowledge than the smartest man in the world. Let me not bore you. Did I satisfy your physical craving?

Yes, you did. You touched muscles I never knew I had, he typed, a big smile on his face. I have never had feelings like that before. You touched places that I didn't know existed.

Oh, baby, you always say the right thing. Wait till I get out of here. We will have the rest of our lives to be together. I have so much more to show you. Don't forget I told you that I would be going to my mother's house when I leave here, so you won't be able to contact me for two days. Once I get settled at the hotel, I'll call you. It shouldn't take more than a week. Did you send the rest of the money?

Keisha, you have to be very careful. A man can become very violent if he feels that he's been hurt. I sent you another $2,000 on Friday. You should get it tomorrow. Check your PO Box.

Ron, I don't know what I would've done without you. You are such a strong man and so giving. Thank you for being there for me. You showed me what it is to be loved and for that I will be eternally at your service. Imagine what happened at the hotel happening every day for the rest of your life. I plan to serve you like the king you are. I want to talk for hours on end with you as the sun comes up until night is no more.

No, Keisha, you satisfied that wanting in me. From that day I met you on sistergirls.com you have been giving me a reason to live. Whatever I had at that time was nothing when it was put up against what you had to give. Give me a chance to make you happy the way you have made me. I didn't realize I was a drowning man until you sent out a rope and I held on to it. You have shown me things I know I would never have realized were there without you. Be careful, my love, and remember whatever happens, I will be waiting for you. These words I speak, I have never uttered them before and I don't think I ever will again. Tonight I pray for your safety and our love.

He is coming now, my love. Wait for my instant message. Soon we will be together forever.

Ron stared at the computer long after Keisha had logged off. Two women, one named Helen and the other Rita, invited him to view their webcams but he wasn't interested in viewing anyone's picture. Keisha's beautiful face was the only one he was interested in seeing on the monitor. He had given her money to get a webcam installed but she was unable to do it. But soon he wouldn't need a webcam or instant messages. In a few days, she would be with him for the rest of his life.

CHAPTER FOUR

Ron paced his office floor, glancing quickly outside, then to the monitor. Four days had passed since the last instant message from Keisha. This waiting was wrecking his life. He couldn't concentrate on work. He had told his boss that he needed the next two weeks off, and his boss obliged. Ron's work of late had been superb. He picked up the pocket computer he had bought the day before so that he could send and receive instant messages while on the road. The computer cost him $1,000 with the software. Ron heard a knock on the door and he went and opened it.

"You ready for vacation?" Cedric asked as he walked past Ron.

"I won't have a life if I don't receive an instant message soon."

"What happened to you, Ron? You look like you're on crack or something," Cedric said.

"I haven't heard from her in four days. I think something is wrong."

"Do you have her cell phone or beeper number?" Cedric asked.

"No. She couldn't give it to me. Her husband checked them regularly. We only communicate through instant messages and email. But she was going to leave her husband. Cedric, we're going to start a life together," Ron said, keeping his eye on the monitor.

"She can't just pick up and leave like that, Ron. She has to file for divorce and all that stuff." Cedric took a seat in the chair opposite Ron's.

"I gave her money for that," Ron said.

"You what!" Cedric said, quickly getting up off the chair and getting in Ron's face.

"It's not what you're thinking. Keisha is not like that. I'm no fool. You think I would let some woman rip me off?"

"I'm not saying anything like that. Money ain't nothing where happiness is concerned. All I'm saying is that you gave up a lot for this girl to not even email you to say everything is okay."

"I know, man, but maybe she can't get to a computer. Maybe the husband went ballistic and killed her. If I don't hear from her by Monday, I'm going to the cops," Ron said, picking up some papers off his desk and slipping them into his desk drawer.

"Ron, all you have is a picture and her Internet info. The cops won't be able to find the girl with such limited info."

"Come on, Cedric. We are in 2003. The cops could find someone with only a nickname, if they wanted to." Ron put some papers into his brief-case. "I guess this is it for two weeks. I took this time off so that Keisha and I could go look for someplace to rent. You know I can't stay in that house. Marge wants it, and with laws today, she most likely will get it." Ron turned on the pocket computer and typed in a few words.

"What's that?" Cedric asked.

"A pocket computer that you can receive and send instant messages from while you're on the go." Ron shut down the computer on his desk.

"Well, I hope she gets in touch with you, my friend. Call me if you need anything." Cedric gave Ron a hug and went back to his office.

Ron locked his office door and held the pocket computer by his side as he started to walk down the hall.

The cold water ran down his face, jolting him awake. He rubbed his eyes over and over. He peered through the running water at the small computer screen. He passed the rag under his arms and around his private parts. He rubbed his eyes and squinted at the monitor. He dropped the rag and ran to the pocket computer that he had resting on the sink in the bathroom. There was an instant message for him. He wiped the water from his face with a clean rag that was hanging on the rack in the bathroom. Through his bloodshot eyes he read:

Come watch me on my new webcam my father gave me for my eighteenth birthday. Evelyn.

He slammed his fist on the sink. "Leave me alone!" he shouted, grabbing the computer and falling to the floor with it. He looked at the time. It was 4:00 a.m. It had been eight days since he'd last spoken to Keisha. He hadn't slept in five out of those eight days. His beard was uncut, his hair was in knots. Ron took the pocket computer and went into the office, which now held the same clothes he had worn for the last three days. He got dressed, keeping his eyes on the small computer screen.

"It's time to go to the police," he said to no one in particular and walked out of the room; the computer in his hands.

The sergeant at the front desk told Ron to go back and see the Internet detectives whose names were on the door. Ron walked past a few closed doors with different titles, including robbery and homicide. An officer in uniform passed him with a prostitute in handcuffs. The prostitute licked her lips at Ron. Ron shuddered. He stopped at a freshly-painted door and rechecked the names with what the sergeant had given him.

DETECTIVES ROSCOE AND SCRIPT, INTERNET DIVISION

Ron knocked hard on the door with his right hand. In his left, he clutched a brown envelope.

"Come in," a female voice crackled through the closed door.

Ron turned the doorknob and walked in. There were two desks in the room. A white woman with bright red hair sat on the one to the left and a young black man sat at another desk about four feet from her. Each person had a chair in front of them. Before Ron could ask anything, the black man spoke.

"I'm Detective Script. This is my partner, Detective Roscoe," he said, pointing over at the redhead. "Please come in and have a seat." He pointed at the chair in front of his desk.

Ron introduced himself before he sat, clutching the brown envelope.

"The report said that you were concerned that a woman you met on the Internet might have been hurt by her husband," Script said, turning over some pages on his desk.

"Yes. Her name is Keisha, and we have been in a relationship for a few months now. I have her picture here if that will help," Ron said, offering the brown envelope to the detective.

"Sure, let me take a look at it." Script reached over and took the picture from Ron.

He took the picture out of the envelope and looked at it. He raised his eyebrows as if he had seen the picture before.

"You've seen her?" Ron asked.

"Roscoe, come over here and look at this. I think we have another one," Script said.

Roscoe walked over to Script, her red hair bouncing as she walked. She joined Script in looking at the picture.

"Another one," she said as she straightened back up and walked back to her desk.

"Is she okay?" Ron asked, easing up off his chair.

Script and Roscoe exchanged looks before Roscoe spoke. "Where did you say you met the lady in the picture?"

"On a chat line on the Internet, Sistergirls.com," Ron answered.

"And did you and the woman do anything else but chat on the Internet?" Script asked.

"We spent one glorious night together. We were planning on starting a life with each other," Ron said.

"Did you at any point give that woman money when you spent the night together?" Roscoe asked.

"No. It's not what you all are thinking. I did not pay her to sleep with me. She paid for the hotel, and we spent a beautiful night together. There was no money exchanging hands for sex. We are in love," Ron said proudly.

"About how much money have you given this woman since you began talking to her on the Internet?" Roscoe asked.

"I would say about $15,000. But you cannot put a price on true love,"

Ron said, getting irritated. "This woman made me feel things I have never felt before."

"When was the last time you had an instant message from this woman?" Script asked.

"Eight days ago."

"You didn't hear from her after that?" Roscoe asked.

"No, that's why I knew something was wrong. Keisha has never done anything like that."

Script got up. "She always responds to you."

"Yes, she does. She is very intelligent. She knows African history, politics, medicine, etc. Keisha is a very special young woman. You can talk to her about everything."

"Are you sure this is the woman you are talking about?" Script asked, taking the picture and giving it back to Ron.

"Yes it is, sir. This is my Keisha," Ron said, again with pride.

"Roscoe, I'll be back in a minute. Mr. Wingate, come with me," Script said and went to open the door.

Ron followed Script past a few desks with policemen and women. Some were on the phone while others were talking to each other. Script opened a door and went into a small hallway with a big curtain on one side.

"Mr. Wingate," Script said, pulling back the curtain. "Is this the woman you know as Keisha?"

Ron blinked a few times to get accustomed to the light as he looked at the woman in the room. Keisha was sitting on a bench, her hair all matted, wearing a skirt so short that he saw her red panties. She was making obscene gestures at a mirror and cursing.

"What have you guys done to Keisha?" Ron asked, tears beginning to run from his eyes.

"Mr. Wingate, get a hold of yourself. We did not do anything to the woman. We brought her in for questioning."

"I can tell you right now that Keisha would not hurt a fly. Can I go and see her?" Ron asked.

"No, Mr. Wingate, you cannot meet with Christina."

"Christina? Who is Christina?"

"That's the correct name for the woman you know as Keisha. Christina Robertson is a two-bit whore who works the street on Eleventh Avenue in Manhattan."

"But the woman I talked to on the computer is very intelligent, and she isn't a whore."

Detective Script closed the curtain. "I believe you, Mr. Wingate. Ms. Robertson doesn't own a computer, and she definitely isn't intelligent."

"Are you telling me I gave up my wife and kids for a prostitute?" Ron asked, shaking his head as the detective led him back to the office.

"It's her again," Detective Script said to Roscoe as he walked into the room with Ron in tow. "Mr. Wingate, we believe that we found the person responsible for creating these problems. We will be bringing her in this afternoon."

"Do you mean there was more than one person involved in this?" Ron asked, barely able to sit down.

"I'm afraid so, Mr. Wingate. Christina was only used in some of the cases. This woman had a few women working for her. She trained them and paid them well. She paid them $500 a night. You only gave $15,000 dollars; some of her other clients gave up as much as $50,000. The hustle stopped when one of her clients committed suicide, so you can count yourself lucky. We finally tracked her down and, as a result, her computer was taken away from her. Christina was one of her favorite workers."

"No, don't tell me I gave up my family for a lie. Please go and talk to Christina. Maybe she is just trying to trick you guys," Ron said, tapping his foot.

"Let me take you to get some coffee. You look like you haven't slept in days," Roscoe said as she came around to Ron's chair.

"Why would anyone do this to me? Tell me why? I left my wife and kids for this woman."

"Sorry to hear that, Mr. Wingate, but it will all be over soon. You can sit with the rest of the complainants until we bring her in," Roscoe said as she guided Ron to the small table with a coffee pot and some cups and other utensils on it.

"I'm not the only one?" Ron asked in a state of shock.

"No, Mr. Wingate, you are one of many."

"I'm going to kill her!" a man dressed in a gray business suit shouted as he banged on the mirror.

"I got her first," another black man dressed in blue scrubs with a stethoscope around his neck barked.

"I lost my business and my wife of ten years for her," a middle-aged black man said as he sat on the bench sobbing.

"She's just a kid," Ron said, looking through the mirror at the sixteen-year-old white pudgy-looking girl sitting on the bench. This little white girl had made a fool of all these grown men.

"Her name is Mary and she's a high school dropout," Script said. "Mary has over $250,000 dollars in her checking account. She had been unable to spend it because she didn't want her father to know what she did. When the man committed suicide and we traced it back to Mary, her father took away her computer. Mary is one of many young people that are using the Internet in different ways to accumulate a lot of money." Script looked at the men as he spoke.

"She spends a lot of time on the computer destroying lives," the man with the stethoscope said.

"Mary eats and sleeps on the Internet. You men are lucky. Mary only took money. The last case we had, this man met this woman over the Internet and they made an arrangement to meet at a hotel. The man let the woman tie him up buck-naked in the hotel room. Once she did that, she let about four male friends into the room and they raped the man over and over. So, gentlemen, count yourselves lucky," Detective Script said.

"Can we get our money back?" the middle-aged man asked.

"No, sir. You all gave up your money freely without asking for anything in return. Did each one of you write gift on your checks?"

The men in the room nodded their heads.

"So how much time will she get?" Ron asked.

"The only reason she's here is because her father wants to teach her a lesson. He wants us to hold her here for the day. She didn't do anything wrong. She didn't blackmail you guys or anything like that. The money you guys sent to her was all as a gift. Heck, she doesn't even have to pay taxes on it. I think all her parents might do after this is take her computer away," Script said.

"Take her computer away! I'm being sued because I cut the wrong muscle in this man's leg yesterday in surgery. I want her to suffer," the man with the stethoscope said as he wrung his hands.

"Look at you guys blaming a sixteen-year-old child for your stupidity. She is one out of many. Tomorrow there will be a thousand more complaints. And it's all because of one thing," Script lashed out.

"What's that?" Ron asked.

"The wanting. It runs deep. It can make you rich or make you poor. It all depends on you and the price you're willing to pay for what you think you want. Mary brought out the wanting in you guys and now you guys have to pay the price for it." Script pulled the curtain closed.

~~~

"What is the price for nothing?" Ron asked the quiet, dark room. The room had a funny smell that came from burning electronic parts. A small wisp of smoke was coming from his computer monitor.

ABOUT THE AUTHORS

WILLIAM FREDRICK COOPER

William Fredrick Cooper is the author of *Six Days in January*, a moving novel of self-discovery that invades the heart of a sensitive man damaged by love. *Six Days in January* is scheduled for re-publication in February 2004 by Strebor Books International LLC. An "ordinary guy" from Bronx, New York who was reared on Staten Island, Cooper is the proud father of a beautiful daughter, Maranda. A teen mentor with the Brother 2 Brother Mentorship Program in conjunction with Harlem Hospital as well as a member of Harlem's reknowned Abyssinian Baptist Church, Cooper is a contributing author with "Watering Cherry's Garden" a featured short story in Jossel Flowers Greens' *Twilight Moods, African American Erotica*; "Snowy Moonlit Evenings" for *Journey to Timbooktu*, a collection of poetry and prose as compiled by Memphis Vaughn; and *Corbin's Mantra*, a novella for the forthcoming *Brother 2 Brother Children's Anthology*, to be published in November. Currently working on *Damaged Goods*, his follow-up to *Six Days in January*, Mr. Cooper can be contacted at WFCooper006@aol.com.

EARL SEWELL

EARL SEWELL holds a B.A. Degree in Fiction Writing from Columbia College. He is the author of two novels, *The Good Got To Suffer With the*

Bad and *Taken for Granted*. He is also a contributing author to *After Hours: A Collection of Erotic Writing by Black Men.*

Additionally, Earl is an athlete who is currently training to complete the Ironman, which is a one-day endurance race where participants swim 3 miles, bicycle 112 miles and run 26.2 miles.

To discover more about Mr. Sewell and his work, readers can visit his website at www.earlsewell.com.

V. ANTHONY RIVERS

V. Anthony Rivers has been featured on R.A.W. Sistaz, Sisterdivas.com, Netnoir, and in *Booking Matters* magazine. His work is seen monthly on the e-zine, Nubian Chronicles (www.nubianchronicles.net). V. Anthony Rivers is the author of *Daughter by Spirit* and *Everybody Got Issues*. Both are published by Strebor Books International. He is steadily writing and has short stories and other novels in the works. He hopes to write more novels in the future that bring to light the rich history of our ancestry as well as the stories which feature today's contemporary lifestyles.

V. Anthony Rivers was born in Los Angeles, California but stays very connected to his Texas roots where both sides of his family originate. He currently resides in Van Nuys, California. Visit his website at www.VAnthonyRivers.com or write to him at Romeodream@aol.com.

RIQUE JOHNSON

Rique Johnson is a native Virginian, born and raised in Portsmouth, Virginia. After a quick stint in the U.S. Army, he planted his roots in Springfield, Virginia—located twenty-miles south of Washington, D.C.

His passion for writing started before his teenage years with little love notes to the girls that he liked. From there, he began writing songs and poetry. He's written many things, things that he simply calls thoughts. These sometimes expressed the mood that he was in or they were derived from things that were happening in the world at the time.

He tries to develop his characters so that the readers can identify with parts of their personality or a situation that they are going through. He can be reached at rique@riquejohnson.com or you can visit him on the web at http://www.riquejohnson.com.

MICHAEL PRESLEY

Born in Grenada, West Indies, Michael Presely immigrated to the States (Brooklyn, New York) in 1978. Upon graduation from George W. Wingate High School, he proceeded to get a Bachelor of Arts degree in English Literature at Stony Brook University. He has written two books, *Blackfunk* and *Blackfunk II: No Regrets No Apologies*. He is currently working on his third and fourth novels, *Tears on a Sunday Afternoon* and the final installment of the *Blackfunk* trilogy, *Blackfunk III: Whatever it Takes*. He continues to live and work in Brooklyn, New York. His web site is www.blackfunk-book.com.

⁓

If you have enjoyed *Sistergirls.com*, please make sure you check out *Blackgentlemen.com* by Zane, JD Mason, Shonda Cheekes, and Eileen M. Johnson, and also visit the actual web site at www.blackgentlemen.com.